In LAST CALL, Gavin McLeod is a man who has it all. His corporate climb has positioned him as the next CEO at Holden Enterprises and he is financially stable, allowing him to provide for the grandfather who raised him. His private life is also on fire, as evidenced by the successful seduction of a sexy bartender who gets under his skin and makes him crave more than just sex. Life is perfect until the alluring woman in his arms turns out to be a serious road-block to his future, one that could bring everything he's worked for crashing down around him.

Sunny Black has spent her entire life tending to the needs of others: caring for her younger brother since she was ten, and serving bar patrons night after night. For the first time in years, she puts herself first, taking a trip on the wild side with a customer whose raw sexuality is too strong to deny. The next morning, however, she learns that in addition to rocking her world, the stranger might destroy everything and everyone she's worked so hard to protect.

A game of sexual seduction and corporate chess ensues, but when Gavin and Sunny are unable to negotiate a satisfying resolution, Gavin's boss steps in and puts both their lives at risk.

Last Call

Book #2 in the Heat Wave Series

Alannah Lynne

Dedication

To Charles

Thank you for all your love, patience, and encouraging support on this crazy journey.

I love you!

Acknowledgements

A huge thank you to Penny "Silver" James for an awesome title!! It's perfect on so many levels, and I never would've come up with it myself.

Editing has always been horribly painful for me, but that was before I met Cassie McCown. I looked forward to the daily emails from Cassie, and actually enjoyed the editing process on this book. Thank you! I look forward to the next go-round.

Thanks to my Board of Directors, aka my Mistresses: Amanda McFarland, Cheri Biddix, Liz Henderson, and Michelle Unger. Self-publishing can be a scary, overwhelming place sometimes, and knowing you guys have my back keeps me grounded and away from the Oreo shakes – most days! LOL

Becki Wyer – Wow! What a blessing you are! You're such a strong, supportive member of my street team, and I appreciate everything you do, from proofreading to pimping. I'm still on the lookout for the gold tooth and fuzzy purple hat for you.

Last, but certainly not least. Thank you to my friends and family, immediate and extended, blood and adopted. I tend to get lost in my worlds and spend way too much time in my head sometimes. Thank you for understanding and for loving me anyway.

Chapter One

Gavin McLeod turned into the Blackout Bar and Grill's gravel parking lot, whipped his SUV into the first available parking space, and slammed the shifter into park. The vehicle was still rocking from the abrupt stop when he shoved the door open and stepped out into the crisp evening air.

His chest expanded as he drew the heavy salt air into his lungs, then let the explosive tension trapped in his head and neck escape on a sharp exhale. The hour-long drive from Myrtle Beach to Anticue would have been a relaxing trip, had it not been filled with constant chatter and relentless questions from his three female companions. Finally free of the confining vehicle, he took a moment to let the peaceful calm of Anticue Island seep into every cell of his body.

He hadn't been to the island in... Damn, had it really been fifteen years? The Blackout Bar and Grill was a new addition, and the old fishing pier next door was closed. But other than that, nothing about the island seemed to have changed.

The back doors of the SUV opened, and two-thirds of the troublesome trio climbed out. Their four-inch spiked heels dug into the loose, sandy gravel, pitching them off-kilter, sending them to and fro. Too far away to grab either of them, Gavin held his breath and hoped for the best. Each girl put a hand to the side of the vehicle to gain her balance, then used the car as a handrail as they made their way to the ballast-stone sidewalk.

The other one-third of his problem—which accounted for two-thirds of his headache—remained in the passenger seat. If this were a date, he would open the door and help her from the car like the gentleman his grandfather raised him to be. If it were a platonic, non-forced date with a friend, he still would help her from the car.

But this wasn't a date. And he'd be damned if he'd do *anything* to give the impression he was okay with Max and Callie's plan of manipulating him into pretending it was. In fact, Gavin was so annoyed with Max, he was thinking of demanding an increase in his profit sharing to cover his escort fee.

He stepped in front of the car, slipped his hands into his front pockets, and waited. He would prefer to walk away and leave her sulking, but he couldn't hit the lock button on the key fob until she gave up her petulance and opened the damned door.

As Jen and Tiffany teetered along the uneven stepping-stones leading to the bar's side entrance, he took in the details of the building and surrounding property. Weathered clapboard siding hung like sagging skin on a decrepit skeleton, but bright, lime-green trim gave the place a shot of vibrant color, which made the battered siding seem less tired.

Wrought iron benches, brightly painted Adirondack chairs, and copper yard ornaments created a profusion of color along the sidewalk. Hand-painted price tags hung from each piece, letting visitors know they, too, could have a bit of Anticue in their own backyard.

A smile tugged at the corner of his mouth as his gaze settled on a copper windmill. His grandfather would love the controlled chaos created by the bright colors and whimsical atmosphere of the Blackout. He would especially love that windmill.

The stone sidewalk continued past the side entrance to a front patio and balcony that overlooked the beach. During summer months, the pink, blue, and teal tables would be filled to capacity, but on this early May evening, they sat empty.

His gaze shifted to the deserted fishing pier next door, and his smile faded. He and his grandfather had spent many days tossing hooks there, and heavy sadness filled his chest at seeing it abandoned and left to the mercy of the beach's harsh elements.

Tired of waiting, he peered at Callie through the windshield and cocked an eyebrow, his message loud and clear. *Are you coming or not?* When she stuck her lip out even further and crossed her arms, he gave her a suit-yourself shrug and turned toward the entrance.

From the corner of his eye, he saw her shoulders slump in defeat. She grabbed her purse from the floor of the SUV, pulled the lever to release the door, and shoved against it with a huff. "A gentleman would have opened the door for me."

Gavin smiled and kept walking. Maybe if he turned into a first-rate asshole, he'd finally drop off Callie's radar. God knows, reasoning with her hadn't worked. Neither had the direct approach: I'm. Not. Interested.

All she'd ever seen was his refined business persona. She had no idea the real Gavin, buried beneath the expensive Italian suits, even existed. Maybe knocking some of the polish off his redneck would be the answer to getting her to drop her obsession.

Her friends were perched on wooden chairs at a high pub table, looking around expectantly for a waiter. Out of the ten or twelve people scattered around the bar, none looked too interested in jumping to meet the girls' demands.

The front wall that faced the beach was actually two large doors that could be rolled out of the way to create one large space between the inside and outside deck. At the back of the room sat the L-shaped service bar. One end stopped short of the kitchen entrance, while the other hooked back to the wall. Two older salts sat on barstools at the hooked end, sipping their beers and talking.

One side of the room held a pool table, while a jukebox sat in the middle of the building, wedged against the center support beam. The rest of the area was filled with an assortment of pub and picnic tables. The whimsical outdoor atmosphere carried over to the interior, with brightly painted walls decorated in copper sculptures and stained-glass pieces.

Gavin had wondered why Max would send him to this little bar on an out-of-the-way island, but now he understood the reason for the trip. Max had done this before when he wanted Gavin's opinion on a location. Without giving him any details, he'd send him to "check it out." Gavin would report back with his impression, and, if the two men agreed the place held a unique appeal, they'd mimic its style in one of Holden's resort properties.

This place definitely had a unique appeal.

Had he made the trip alone, he could have a lot of fun roaming around, checking out the artwork, listening to the locals. But he wasn't alone, so he might as well find out what Callie and her friends wanted to drink, hook 'em up, then leave them to get sloshed while he wandered around and soaked up the details.

Bartender Sunny Black had her head down in the beer chiller, her arm buried to the elbow in ice, when she heard, "Can I get a blowjob, sex on the beach, and a screaming orgasm, please?"

She rolled her eyes and continued to shift bottles in the cooler without responding. She really needed a better system for taking inventory.

The problem?

Bent over like this, her ass stuck straight up in the air, which seemed to be an open invitation for assholes to hit on her by ordering the raunchiest drink names they could think of. Hard to believe these guys thought she hadn't heard it all before.

She'd been hoping for a quiet night, so she could close up early. But Mr. Hardy-har-har undoubtedly had a posse—jerks always traveled in packs—and they always stayed until last call, using every available minute to get as drunk and obnoxious as possible. She'd be lucky if she got out of here before midnight.

She shifted the Budweisers to the side and resumed counting. *Seven. Eight. Nine. Ten.*

"Ma'am, did you hear me?"

With her free hand, she pulled the Dum-Dum out of her mouth and licked the sticky from her lips. "Look, Romeo," she said, tilting her head so her voice carried to him, rather than echoing around the cooler, "I'll give you five points for a nice, smooth voice. But you lose ten for being a tad overzealous."

She jammed the sucker back into her mouth and resumed counting. *Eleven. Twelve. Thirteen.*

"What the hell are you talking…" His voice trailed off, and then roaring laughter settled over her like thick, heavy honey drizzled on a piping hot biscuit.

He seemed genuinely amused, and she grew curious enough about the man behind the laugh to risk an encouraging look. She leaned back and lifted her head so she could see over the bar.

Holy cow. Even while slurping on a saliva-inducing butterscotch sucker, her mouth went bone dry.

The guy's features were amazing. The Great Sculptor had pressed her thumbs into the flesh of his cheeks, then pulled an upward stroke, leaving behind a slight indention, while at the same time creating high, rugged cheekbones. His square jaw led to a square chin that projected a strong, confident individual. His eyes were like brilliant sapphires, topped by severe dark brows.

His features were sharp, and if not smiling, he would appear harsh, hostile even. But softened by that grin, she found him utterly—and literally—breathtaking.

"I think you misunderstood my request." His eyes twinkled with amusement.

As a bartender, Sunny met good-looking men on a regular basis. Sometimes they tripped her trigger. Most of the time, they didn't. What she felt now catapulted beyond mild interest and ranked more like an internal explosion capable of launching a rocket.

Her flirting game had been packed away so long she wasn't sure she still had it. And if so, she doubted she could find all the pieces. But this guy... he made her want to sort through the game drawer and find as much as possible.

The biting sting of ice—in which her arm was still buried to the elbow—cut through the lustful haze, and her muscle jerked involuntarily. She glanced down, trying to remember what she was doing prior to having her motherboard fried.

Inventory. Right.

Her cheeks blazed with the embarrassment of her obvious attraction, and she could only imagine the glow they were putting off. She bit down on the sucker, then tossed the empty stick in the trashcan by her feet. "Sorry for being a smart-ass. Let me finish this and"—she smiled, and searched for a flirty tone—"I'll take care of you."

His blue eyes darkened, and his eyelids relaxed. A slow, rakish smile crept across his full lips, causing the tiny cleft in the center of his chin to deepen. "I look forward to that."

Damn. If they weren't talking drinks, this would be the opportunity of a lifetime.

When she finished counting the beers, she patted her arm dry and grabbed three shot glasses off the shelf. She sensed him watching her every move, and her skin heated under his scrutiny. He wasn't excessively tall, maybe six feet, but his presence seemed to dominate her five-foot-four frame.

She wasn't easily intimidated, but the confidence and power he emanated, combined with the raw sexuality she'd glimpsed a moment ago, made her knees weak.

Just once, I want to have sex with a man like that.

God, how she longed for a wild, tumultuous fling that would knock her world off its axis.

Her bracelets jingled and her mouth watered as she shook the canister of whipped cream. What a waste to put it on the drink when she could squirt it on him... then spend an hour or two slowly and deliberately licking it off.

"What's your name?" His voice was huskier than it had been before, and when she met his gaze, the sparks radiating from his blue eyes shot liquid fire straight to her crotch.

"Oh, crap. Was I thinking out loud?"

A smile crawled across his mouth, and her heart stopped. "Nope."

She blew out a breath, then clenched her eyes shut. Even if she hadn't spoken, she was sure she'd broadcasted her thoughts like an idiot. This was why she never flirted. She stunk at it. She opened her eyes and cleared her throat. "Sunny. My name's Sunny."

He looked up to the ceiling and said her name a few times, as if trying it on for size. He cocked his head to the side and looked in her eyes. "That's nice."

The charged attraction between them made her jittery as hell. Because of her job, she got hit on often, but she rarely took the bait. At least, nothing more than a little harmless bantering here and there. She had little to no experience in playing sexual games, and it was beyond obvious this man was way out of her league.

She topped the blowjob off with a shot of whipped cream, and then, careful not to let the tremble in her fingers show, set the drinks on a small serving tray. "Sorry you have to carry that yourself. During the winter things are slow, so we don't have wait staff on hand. Well, other than me."

He grinned and reached into his back pocket for his wallet. "I think I can handle the tray." He slid a credit card across the counter, letting go of it only after her fingers brushed his. "Can I run a tab?"

Prickles of awareness and desire wrapped around her fingers and danced up her arm. She knew he'd asked, "Can I run a tab?" but her body heard, "Can I run my hands all over you?"

Lord, she could only imagine what it would be like to have him stroking her skin. The pulsating current ripping through her system would probably cause a meltdown. "Sure. You can…" *Do anything you like.*

Her desire to close up early had evaporated. She'd be more than happy to stick around for as long as he wanted to stay.

She glanced across the bar to where three well-dressed women, two blondes and a brunette, sat. Everyone else in the bar was a local, so they must be the women he'd ordered the drinks for. Sunny made eye contact with the brunette, who, in turn, shot her a what-the-hell-is-taking-so-long glare.

Sunny grinned and cut her eyes to—she glanced at the card in her hand—Gavin McLeod. "You have your hands full with those three."

Okay, had that sounded like she was on a fishing expedition? She hadn't meant it that way, but it would be nice if he volunteered some information regarding his relationship with them. They couldn't all be sisters, could they?

He blew out a harsh breath and pushed his fingers through his thick, black hair. "You have no idea."

A few rebellious locks broke rank and slipped back over his brow, adding a boyish charm to his otherwise severe profile. The impulse to brush the strands off of his forehead was so strong she had to clench her fists at her sides to resist.

Picking up the drink tray, he said, "I'll be right back for my drink. A double shot of Crown." He turned, then stopped and looked back over his shoulder. "Make it a Budweiser, instead." Sunny didn't understand the humor behind his drink request, but based on the glint in his eye and the lopsided grin, the thought of drinking a beer amused him.

As he strode across the hardwood floor toward the waiting women, Sunny stood on tiptoes to get a better view of the full package. An off-white, form-fitting shirt stretched across his broad shoulders and hugged thick biceps, while black, tailor-made slacks hung from a trim waist and encased a nice, tight ass.

Yowzer. She snagged a piece of ice from the cooler and swept it down the side of her neck and across the sharp ridge of her collarbone.

"Damn, girlie. Didn't take much for that fella to get you all hot and bothered."

Sunny scrunched her eyes shut, hunched her shoulders, and hunkered down her head. She'd been so caught up in Gavin, she hadn't thought about Joe and Ed sitting at the end of the bar. Those two old geezers never missed a thing, and they'd be milking this cow forever.

She laughed at the mental image she had of Gavin, stripped, lying on the sacrificial altar of her bar, doused in whipped cream. If she were going to get grief for her actions, wouldn't it be fun to give them something truly amazing to talk about?

Chapter Two

Callie narrowed her eyes and glared at the bartender as she stood on tiptoes to watch Gavin walk away. Ogling was bad enough. But when she grabbed a piece of ice and ran it along the side of her neck, like she would die of heat stroke if she didn't cool down, Callie rolled her eyes and huffed, "Oh, please."

Granted, Gavin was the hottest thing ever. But, really… what a slut.

The ice snagged the bartender's necklace, causing it to shift and reflect the light. It was a strange piece of jewelry, and Callie squinted, trying for a better look. A chain made of diamonds—cubic zirconia, no doubt—circled her neck, then dipped into her highly exposed cleavage before—"Ohmigod." Callie's hand flew to her throat, and her eyes popped wide open.

"What's wrong?" Jen and Tiffany asked in unison.

Shocked, and possibly traumatized for life, Callie whispered, "Look at the bartender's necklace."

Her friends craned their necks around to peer over their shoulders. Their eyes narrowed, then simultaneously widened. Tiffany said, "Oh. My. God, is right," while Jen said, "That is so cool."

For a second, Callie thought she'd misunderstood Jen. Then she considered the source. She and Jen didn't live in the same moral zip code, and it figured Jen would have that kind of reaction. Callie shook her head. "I should've known you'd like it."

"What?" Jen said, sitting straighter and pulling her shoulders back. "It's just a nipple necklace. They have them at Benedetti's." As if being carried by one of Myrtle Beach's exclusive boutiques made it okay. "I've always wondered how they'd feel." Speaking more to herself than to Callie or Tiffany, she murmured, "I might have to go there tomorrow and get one."

Tiffany looked at Jen with something akin to hero worship. "How does it work?"

Jen, the group's resident expert on everything perverse, said, "It goes around her neck, like a necklace. But instead of falling down the middle of her cleavage and stopping, like most necklaces, it splits into two separate pieces and the ends either attach to piercings or clip around the nipples.

Callie shuddered and wrapped her arms around her chest. "That is so…" *Gross, frightening, slutty… painful.*

"You are such a prude."

Callie's gasp was sharp and loud, like Jen had tossed a bucket of ice in her face. "I-I am not." The denial lacked conviction, and Callie looked to Tiffany for help. "Do you think I'm a prude?"

Tiffany's eyes widened and pink crept over her cheeks. "I'm not the one to ask about that."

True, Tiffany had only had one lover; the guy she dated for three years in college. Since their breakup, she'd sworn off sex, intending to stay celibate until marriage. She was "re-virginizing" herself. Whatever that meant.

Jen leaned across the table and squeezed Callie's arm. "I'm sorry, hun. You're not a prude. You're just… well…" She scrunched up her face, searching for the right word, then sighed and grimaced. "Maybe a little *prudish*."

Callie flipped her gaze to Gavin, who'd stopped to study the playlist on the jukebox. "Do you think Gavin thinks I'm a prude?"

Jen released Callie's arm and sat back in her chair, while Tiffany played with the snap on her handbag. Callie looked from one to the other. "Does that mean yes?"

"Honestly, Cal," Jen said with a huff. "I don't think Gavin spends much time thinking about you, period."

A sharp pain ripped through Callie's chest and her eyes stung. Jen could be a coldhearted bitch at times, and Callie wondered why she maintained the friendship.

"He's just focused on his career right now," Tiffany said in a soft, patronizing tone that made Callie feel like a charity case.

Why was she asking them about Gavin, anyway? They didn't know him, or know what he thought about. Besides, he might not even want her to wear a necklace like that. Lowlife construction workers might get turned on by that kind of thing, but probably not a sophisticated man like Gavin.

He pushed away from the jukebox and closed the distance to their table. As he set the drinks before them, Callie gathered her courage and said, "Gavin? What do you think of the bartender's necklace?"

Tiffany's eyes popped wider than Callie had ever seen them, and Jen sat stone-still. It was out of character for Callie to be this bold, but it was obvious she needed to step up her efforts to snag Gavin's attention.

He set the third drink on the table and turned around. "What neck—" The words died off as his eyes widened slightly and his mouth dropped open.

Jen laughed and held up her shot glass. "Guess that answers that." She threw back the screaming orgasm and returned her glass to the tray… The tray that lay forgotten while Gavin stared at the bartender.

Okay, Jen might be right about the necklace. In which case, she'd go with her to Benedetti's tomorrow. She could adapt for Gavin.

Although, unlike the skanky bartender, who showed off the erotic jewelry for the entire world to see, Callie would keep it hidden under her clothes as her naughty secret...one she would hopefully be able to share with Gavin.

Determined to shed the prudish image she'd accidentally obtained, Callie stroked her fingernail down his forearm and said, "Watch how I take care of this blowjob?" She clasped her hands behind her back, wrapped her lips around the rim of the glass, and closed her eyes.

The position was awkward, and she was terrified she looked like an idiot. But she'd seen girls do this before, and guys always liked it. If the suggestive move helped her win Gavin's attention, she'd do it.

She imagined the two of them alone, her lips wrapped around him, bringing him pleasure. In one fluid motion, she threw her head back, and sent the liquid spilling down her throat.

Anticipation swirled through her as she pulled the glass from her mouth, licked her lips, and opened her eyes. But Gavin wasn't standing there, looking at her with great appreciation, as she'd expected.

In fact, he wasn't standing there at all. He'd left their table and was walking around the perimeter of the bar, appearing genuinely interested in the despicable artwork hanging on the walls.

Tears stung the back of her eyes, and she pressed her lips together to stop the quivering in her chin. She tilted her head back and blinked until the waterworks subsided. Humiliating herself was bad enough. She would not add to that humiliation by having ruined makeup. When she had the tears under control, she slammed the glass onto the table and folded her arms across her chest.

"I think we need more drinks," Jen said.

Tiffany nodded. "I agree." She gave Callie a cheery smile and added, "Let's go back to margaritas."

The three of them had spent the afternoon drinking more pitchers of the frozen drink than they could count. Callie had stopped drinking a couple of hours before Gavin arrived, thinking it would be wise to be sober for the drive so she and Gavin could carry on a nice, meaningful conversation.

Except he hadn't been interested in conversation—nice, meaningful, or otherwise. And she'd tried everything. She talked about Holden's new developments. She asked him questions about his current projects. She'd shown an interest in his family, his college days, his high school days, and everything else she could think of.

All she'd gotten for her effort was a few caveman-type grunts and then nothing but tense silence.

"Margaritas are definitely the way to go," she agreed.

She pulled her cellphone from her handbag and typed a cryptic message to Gavin. If he were going to be rude and walk away from her, she'd be rude in return. When she finished sending the text, she returned her attention to the blond bartender.

Callie needed to start being realistic and logical about Gavin. It was painful to admit, but in the car, he'd been as rigid as a diamond. But as he conversed with the bartender, he visibly relaxed and was completely enthralled with the woman.

Watching him rest the weight of his upper body on his forearms, while leaning across the bar toward the blonde, made Callie ache. He'd never shown that much interest in anything she had to say. But the biggest shock had been watching him laugh. Normally serious and focused on work, Callie had never seen him cut loose like that.

What did the bartender possess that Callie didn't? It certainly wasn't class. Huge silver hooped earrings hung from her ears, and about a hundred bracelets lined her wrist. Then there was the necklace and the low-cut revealing halter-top.

Callie looked down at her conservative silk top, and her heart sunk.

Jen was right. She was a prude.

Without being too obvious, she turned her head and studied Gavin. Maybe it was time to give up. How many years had she been at this without getting any closer? The problem was, she'd dreamt of a life with Gavin for so long, she didn't know how to want anything else.

No, she wasn't a quitter. She just needed to try harder.

While pondering the relationship between Gavin and the women, Sunny wondered if the brunette might be his sister. But after watching that painful attempt at seduction, the answer was obviously no.

Sunny actually felt sorry for the woman, who tried her best to put on a show for Gavin. But as soon as she dropped her mouth over the glass, he walked away.

"*I'll* go over there and watch her suck on that glass." Sunny's brother Robby's mouth twisted wryly. "Or anything else she'd like to suck on."

Robby was a typical twenty-year-old male. Anything in a skirt caught his attention. A short skirt, big boobs, thick, flirty lashes, and long, red fingernails were the same as a hook through the lip reeling him in. "Don't you have glasses to wash?"

Robby crossed his arms over his chest and leaned back against the counter. "Nope." He smiled smugly. "Besides, from what I hear, there's a good show out here that I shouldn't miss."

There wasn't any point in denying the accusation, since everyone had witnessed her dog-in-heat imitation. She turned away from Robby and dug into the cooler for Gavin's Budweiser. The chilled air cooled her heated cheeks and tempted her to keep her head buried there for the rest of the night.

She uncapped the bottle and set it on the counter, then flicked a surreptitious glance across the bar. Gavin had stopped at a copper wall fountain, which happened to be one of her favorite pieces. He brushed his fingers across the topmost magnolia blossom in a gentle sweeping motion, and her body responded as if he'd stroked her.

She always liked it when the customers appreciated her pieces, but Gavin's reaction made her heart flutter a little more than usual.

Certainly more than it should.

He unclipped the phone attached to his belt and read the screen. After shooting the trio of women a look of disbelief, he shook his head, then stalked toward Sunny.

Robby dropped his arms to his side and stiffened. "Jesus, Sunny. He looks like one mean son of a bitch. Flirting with that is like poking a rattlesnake."

Sunny turned and glared at her brother. She'd admit Gavin's scowl was a little frightening. But, on a primal level, she found his intensity and commanding presence as much of a turn-on as the sexy smile he'd given her earlier.

"Wait till he smiles." Good grief, the dreamy singsong lilt of her voice almost made her gag.

Robby looked incredulous. "He smiles?"

Sunny made a shooing motion with her hands, as if trying to chase away a stray dog. "Go away."

Robby grinned, leaned against the counter, and crossed his ankles.

She should've known better than to try to discourage him. In all the years he'd lived with her, he'd never seen her with a man. This was fun for him, a novelty of sorts, and he wasn't about to miss it. Defeated, she blew a piece of hair out of her eye and turned her back on him.

Gavin was almost to the bar when he stopped midstride and unclipped his phone again. He looked at the screen, then swiped a hand over his face and nodded to the beer. "Is that mine?"

He looked more than a little exasperated, so she grabbed a shot glass and held it up. "Yep. But you can always change your mind and go back to the Crown."

He laughed, shook his head, and dropped onto the barstool. "No, thanks. This will be good." Under his breath he muttered, "In fact, it'll be outstanding."

She sensed Robby relaxing behind her and, if she'd been ten, she would have turned around and said, "Told ya so," before blowing a raspberry in his face. Instead, she kept her focus on Gavin and the dimple in his chin.

He lifted the bottle to his mouth, closed his eyes, and tipped his head back for a long, deep drink. Imagining him during sex with his eyes closed, head back, a similar look of ecstasy on his face made her break into a ferocious sweat.

"Damn, that's good."

I can only imagine how good it would be, she thought.

After a long pull that nearly polished the thing off, he set the bottle down with what could only be described as controlled calm. He stared at the bottle as he absently ran his thumb back and forth through the condensation.

Sunny followed the graceful stroke of his well-manicured thumb with rapt fascination. His hands were large, but he had a gentle touch. Watching him stroke the bottle, in the same soft, gentle sweeping motion he'd used on the magnolia blossom, sent her imagination and pulse into overdrive.

How would he stroke her? The confidence he emanated, as well as the intensity surrounding him, made her think having sex with him would be like wrestling a gentle alligator. What a deadly combination.

Coming out of his thoughts, he looked at her and said, "The troublesome triplets would like a pitcher of margaritas." He clenched his jaw. "Strawberry."

Questions bounced around in Sunny's mind like kids on a trampoline. Why was he in Anticue, a little barrier island few people visited? Why did he bring three women… women he didn't particularly seem to like, with him? If Sunny followed her body's urge and went for it with this guy, would he shut her down as he had the brunette?

What did he look like naked?

She was more curious about some of the questions than others, but according to Bartender Handbook rule number one: Never ask personal questions. Rule number two: Never get involved with a customer. In nine years of tending bar, she'd never broken those rules.

So why did Gavin make her not only want to break those rules, but a few state laws, as well?

Chapter Three

While Sunny whipped up the pitcher of margaritas, Gavin took a moment to enjoy her sexy-as-hell necklace. Talk about an instant hard-on. As soon as Callie pointed it out, his cock had swollen to the point he needed to leave the table and wander around in the shadows, waiting for his pants to fit again.

How in the hell had he missed it before?

Her eyes. That's how.

He was so fascinated by her nearly clear, silver eyes he hadn't been able to pull his gaze away from her face. They were old-soul eyes that gave the impression she'd been through a lot. They weren't weary from life's struggles, just wise. And he was completely captivated.

Now that the necklace had been brought to his attention, he found it equally compelling. His gaze followed the diamond chain from her neck to the center of her breasts, where a blue topaz held the lengths of chain together. The chains separated on either side of the topaz and disappeared under the edges of her halter-top.

He drew in a shuddering breath and pondered several important questions. How did the ends attach? Were her nipples pierced? Were her nipples sensitive? How would she respond if he tugged on that chain with his teeth?

He wanted the answers to those questions so badly his bones ached. He snatched up his beer and downed the last of it in one gulp, chastising himself the entire time for being a lecher.

He also waited for the young man standing shotgun behind Sunny to put a fist to his face. But the kid only glared.

"Need another?" Sunny asked.

"Another ten or twelve would be good. But not right now." He surrendered the empty bottle and shook his head. "If I drank all I wanted, I wouldn't be able to walk out of here, let alone drive home."

She smiled, and the room brightened like a thousand-watt spotlight had been turned on. She opened her mouth, then slammed it shut and pressed her lips together. She grabbed three glasses and sat them on the tray. "Where is home?"

He couldn't hold back his smile when she snapped her mouth closed again and shook her head, as if disgusted with herself for asking the question. He found her honest emotional reactions refreshing and felt lighter and happier just being in her presence.

With her blond hair piled on top of her head and the freckles scattered across her nose, she looked like a teenager. But, apparently, a vixen lived under that skin, and she was the one who chose Sunny's wardrobe. She was also the part of Sunny's personality that brought all kinds of down-and-dirty lascivious thoughts to Gavin's mind.

He shifted on the barstool and answered her question. "I live in Myrtle Beach."

"You're not originally from there. You have an eastern North Carolina accent."

Not only pretty, but smart. What a turn-on. "I didn't hear a question in there, but you're right. I've been in Myrtle since college."

She poured the girls' drink into a frosty pitcher, set it and three glasses onto a tray, then turned to the young man still leaning against the counter behind her. When he didn't take the dirty blender from her hands, she shook it at him. "Here, now you have something to wash."

His eyes shimmered with amusement, and Gavin realized that, in addition to Sunny's curly, blond hair, he also had her eyes. The kid laughed and took the container from her, then disappeared through the kitchen door at the end of the bar.

"Kid brother?"

She tried to hide her smile, but gave up the fight and laughed. "Yep. Twenty going on forty."

"Has he always been this protective? Or do I bring out the pit bull in him?"

She laughed and rummaged through a jar of Dum-Dums on the counter. "We take care of each other."

At this rate, the pitcher of margaritas would be lukewarm before he got it to the girls, but he didn't care. He wasn't ready to end his conversation with Sunny yet. He looked around the bar and said, "This is a neat place. Who owns it?"

Her hand froze on the wrapper for a fraction of a second before she slipped it off and slid the sucker into her mouth. As he watched the candy disappear between her pink lips, his body tightened and his mind became a blank slate.

Her eyes shot toward the room behind him, and a mischievous expression crossed her face. She pulled the sucker from her mouth, then licked her lips. "I think you're in trouble."

High heels clicking on the hardwood floor, along with a push of perfume, warned him of Callie's approach. "Gavin?" She slid between his body and the barstool next to him and rested her elbow on his shoulder. "Where's my drink?"

Locking gazes with Sunny, he said, "I'll take that beer now."

She grinned, jabbed the sucker back into her mouth, and reached into the cooler. The stick wiggled in circles as she worked the candy with her tongue, and he almost groaned out loud.

In a move guaranteed to cause him a tremendous amount of grief, probably for the next ten years, he picked up the tray and carefully handed it to Callie.

Her eyes widened and her mouth fell open. "You aren't going to carry it to the table for me?" She rolled her eyes toward Sunny, and her upper lip curled. "Since she's unwilling to do her job and take it for us."

An irrational need to defend Sunny sent a wave of anger from his gut to his chest. "Callie, if you want this, you'll take the tray out of my hands. Otherwise, you're shit out of luck."

If he hadn't seen it with his own eyes, he wouldn't have believed it. She actually huffed and stomped her foot like a two-year-old. When his only response was to cock a you've-got-to-be-kidding-me eyebrow, she took the tray, turned on her heel, then tottered back to the table.

Sunny set the beer in front of him, then scrunched up her nose like she was about to sneeze. "You've probably already picked up on this, but in case you haven't… your girlfriend's not happy."

He watched her wiggle her nose again and realized Callie's perfume was bothering her, too. He'd had to keep the windows cracked during the drive, so he could breathe. But having it bother Sunny made it even more annoying. "She's not my girlfriend."

A delicate blond eyebrow arched, and a sparkle lit her pewter eyes. "Does she know that?"

He laughed and took a sip of beer. "Yeah, but it doesn't keep her from trying." And wasn't that the understatement of the century?

Rumblings from the end of the bar distracted Sunny, and she cringed while cursing under her breath. The two weathered salts, probably in their mid-seventies, sat on the stools at the end of the bar, wearing identical expressions.

Sunny narrowed her eyes and glared—a universal sign all men knew meant *keep your damned mouth shut*. But based on their wicked grins and wily eyes, they weren't the least bit threatened by Sunny's death-glare.

The one on the left, who reminded Gavin of his grandfather, said, "I've been hittin' on you for years, and you've never flirted with me. Why not?"

Color flooded Sunny's cheeks, but she straightened her spine, tossed the empty sucker stick into the trashcan, and propped her hands on her hips. "Your wife would kick both of our asses. Miss Jane may only be five feet tall, but I've seen her ten feet of mad."

Gavin bit the inside of his cheek to keep from laughing. Sunny didn't seem to be much over five feet herself. But he'd bet, with enough provocation, she could reach ten feet of mad, too.

"Remember last year when you forgot her birthday? The way she came in here and yanked you out by your ear..." Sunny shook her head in dramatic fashion. "Uh-uh, I don't ever want to be on her bad side."

The man on the right adjusted his ball cap and stared at his beer while his shoulders shook with laughter.

In contrast, Miss Jane's husband's shoulders slumped and his face sagged.

Sunny mumbled something under her breath that sounded like, "Sensitive old coot," before taking a few steps toward him. She cocked her head to the side, batted her eyelashes, and said, "I don't care how hot you are, Ed. It's not worth being on the wrong side of Miss Jane."

Ed turned to the other man. "Wouldn't ya think after forty years of marriage a man could get a year off for good behavior?"

The other man sipped his beer and nodded. "Sounds reasonable to me."

Ed nodded and looked serious. "I think so, too."

Gavin rested his forearms on the bar and smiled. He liked this place. Without Callie and the bubble-headed bleach blondes, he could have a good time sitting here, drinking beer, listening to the locals give each other shit. And, of course, there was Sunny. He could sit here and watch her all night.

He jerked upright as a ridiculous idea beat at the back of his brain. "How late do you work?"

She wiped a towel across the top of the bar, then dropped it into a bucket of soapy water. "As late as folks stay."

He glanced at his watch. *Eight o'clock.* "How late is that, normally?"

She shrugged. "It varies. On a weeknight, it's usually around eleven. Weekends can be as late as two. It depends on the season and how much fun everyone's having."

He twisted his head and peered over his shoulder. The girls were about halfway through the pitcher. Another ten minutes and they'd be finished. If he left now, he could take them home and be back in two hours.

He shook his head. What a crazy, ridiculous, impulsive, teenage kind of thing to do. "Do you think you'll be here until eleven tonight?"

Sunny's gaze settled on the pool table where two young couples were playing. The guys seemed serious about the game; the girls were picking at their fingernail polish, talking. "I'll be here until eleven fifteen."

His eyebrows drew together. How could she be so certain of the exact time?

Reading his unasked question, she said, "Those kids come in here two nights a week. Every week. They have to be home by eleven, but they live right down the road, so they don't leave until ten forty-five. By the time I get everything wrapped up, it'll be eleven fifteen."

A lot of years had passed since he'd done anything this impulsive, and a sliver of excitement raced down his spine and shot him in the ass. "Can you close out my tab for me?"

His abrupt exit seemed to confuse her, and the smile slipped off her face. "Uh, sure."

He wondered if his departure disappointed her for personal reasons, or because of the loss of business. He hoped for the first and, without thinking, reached across the bar and grabbed her hand.

She glanced down and sucked in a sharp breath.

Afraid he'd frightened her, he let go and eased away from her. "I'm going to take them home and then come back."

Her brows dipped and she stared at the bar, deep in thought. Glancing up, she said, "I thought you lived in Myrtle Beach."

He grinned and winked. "I do."

Driving across the bridge into Anticue, he wasn't sure how he'd feel about being back here again. But after being here this short length of time, he was more relaxed than he'd been in a long time. Doing something crazy for a change made him feel alive, and the compulsion to come back alone was too strong to ignore.

He signed the receipt for his tab and said, "I'll be back in two hours."

"I've got twenty that says he'll be back," said Ed, as he tossed the money onto the bar.

Joe reached into his wallet, then paused. "Back tonight, or another night?"

"Tonight."

Joe threw a twenty on top of Ed's. "You're on. I say he'll be back tomorrow night."

Robby pulled two tens out of Sunny's tip jar and added them to the pile.

Before he could state his bet, Sunny snatched the tens off the pile and jammed them into the back pocket of her jeans. "I knew you were tapping into my tips."

He smiled sheepishly and shrugged. "Only in emergencies."

She rolled her eyes and grabbed a glass. "*This* is not an emergency." She poured herself a Pepsi, then closed her eyes and conjured up a cigarette in her mind. Since quitting a month ago, she'd gone through a million Dum-Dums, and still, the nicotine cravings weren't easing.

Especially when stressed, which was most of the time. Right now, she was light-headed from the tension.

She wasn't sure what to think about Gavin coming back. She knew she'd read his signals right—he was definitely interested—and her inexperience at playing sexual games added to the anxiety squeezing her chest. She felt like an awkward teenager who wanted the captain of the football team to ask her out and an amateur player who could easily get in over her head. Thinking about him coming back, and not knowing what to do with him if he did, made her heart stutter, and a wave of nervous anticipation washed through her.

The cigarette she'd fabricated in her mind evaporated and was replaced by his smoldering stare. Remembering the way he'd admired her necklace made her stomach clench and her nipples harden. The clips attached to them tightened, and a delightfully painful sensation shot from her breasts to her sex and beyond.

She hadn't had sex in years, and she wasn't sure she could handle a man like Gavin. The prospect of finding out made the nervous excitement turn to a rush of nausea.

"I think he'll be back this weekend, but I'm not happy about it." Robby's uncharacteristically serious tone had Sunny's eyes peeling open. He stood in front of her, arms crossed, eyes narrowed.

"Why?" She wasn't going to live her life based on her brother's wants and needs forever, but she respected his opinion. She was curious why Gavin made Robby's light-hearted personality disappear and his hostile side emerge.

"I don't know." He shrugged. "He was definitely into you. But what about those women? Why did he bring them here and then act like a total jerk toward them? And why was he in Anticue in the first place? Surely he didn't drive all the way up here from Myrtle Beach just to have a drink."

Sunny grabbed another Dum-Dum from her stash under the counter. Unwrapping it, she sighed and sank back against the lacquered wood. "I don't know. I had a lot of the same questions, but…" She diverted her gaze and worked the sucker around in her mouth. Something was niggling at the back of her mind; something he'd said had bothered her, but she couldn't remember what it was.

"But what?"

She glanced at Robby, but found herself unable to meet his gaze head on. "I liked him."

From her peripheral vision, she saw Robby's mouth drop open. If he'd made that statement, she'd have laughed it off and told him it was his hormones talking.

The same could be said for her in this instance, but she was usually a good judge of character, and her instincts told her Gavin was okay. However, what she wanted didn't matter.

She pulled the tens out of her pocket and added them to the pile. "I say he won't be back. At all. It sounded like a good idea at the time, but once he gets halfway to Myrtle Beach, he'll come to his senses and change his mind."

Chapter Four

The clock on the dashboard read ten fifteen as Gavin turned off Highway 17 onto the causeway leading to Anticue. "I've lost my damned mind," he muttered with a laugh and a shake of his head.

While driving back from Myrtle Beach with the windows down, the sunroof open, and the stereo cranked full throttle, he decided he liked the temporary insanity. It had been a long time since he'd felt this free. It had been even longer since he'd done something irrational.

Since going to work for Holden Enterprises his senior year of college, he'd operated with one purpose in mind: career advancement. He hadn't taken a vacation in years. Hell, most of the time, he didn't even take time off in the evenings. And he couldn't remember the last time he'd been on a date.

So what about Anticue made him break form?

Maybe it was the fond memories of being here as a kid with his granddad. Or the cheerful, whimsical atmosphere of the bar. Or, as was more likely the case, the sexy bartender and her crazy cast of characters.

Whatever prompted his actions, he liked the feeling. He was damned glad he'd acted on the impulse to take Callie and her friends home, and he was looking forward to enjoying what little bit of the evening was left.

As he pulled into the parking lot, he inventoried the remaining cars: an old beat-up Honda Civic, an equally decrepit Ford Ranger pickup, three newer model trucks, and several cars. All the same as when he'd left, except… His eyes narrowed as he stared at a motorcycle parked near the door.

An uncomfortable chill settled into his chest as he headed toward the entrance. Because of the way Sunny had flirted, he hadn't considered the possibility of her having a boyfriend. Until now.

He pushed his hands through his hair and blew out a harsh breath. If he walked in and found Sunny with biker-guy, he'd shrug it off and get back to his original purpose for being here: assessing the bar. He'd take his time looking around at the pieces on display and get the names of the artists.

Contingency plan in place, he pushed the door open and stepped inside. A whoosh of relief left his lungs when he saw biker-man relaxing in an Adirondack chair with a sweet-looking redhead curled up on his lap. The two old salts were still at the bar; the kids were playing pool.

All eyes turned toward the door, and Ed let out a whoop and grabbed a pile of money off the bar. Joe shook his head and tipped his bottle to Ed in salute, while Sunny stood statue still, eyes wide, jaw sagging.

He settled onto the same barstool he'd used earlier and smiled. "Let me guess… There was a bet on whether or not I'd be back."

She bit her lip and flushed. "Yeah."

"What did you bet?"

She wiped off the bar—something he figured she did when nervous—and said, "I didn't think you'd be back."

"Tonight? Or ever?"

She flicked her gaze to his, then glanced away. "Ever."

"And… in your estimation, was that a good thing?"

Her silver gaze, filled with a ton of uncertainty, met his. "I'm not sure." She reached into the cooler, grabbed a Bud, and popped the top.

Sliding it across the bar, she said, "That one's on the house."

"Thanks." He took a drink and watched Sunny do her wipe-and-swipe thing on the bar.

She seemed more nervous and less confident than earlier, and he realized she probably viewed his return as bold and aggressive, like he was counting on banging her on the bar before the night was over.

God knows, he couldn't imagine a better way for the evening to end than in a wild, sexual frenzy. But his crazy actions had been more about self-discovery than learning Sunny's curves and what made her hot.

Hoping to explain his crazy actions and get her back into a playful, flirtatious mood, he said, "I've always enjoyed coming to Anticue."

She sipped from a straw and tipped her head to the side. "So you *have* been here before?"

He nodded and rested his forearms on the bar. "My granddad and I used to spend a lot of time on the fishing pier next door. From what I could tell earlier, Anticue hasn't changed much in twenty years."

The bright smile reappeared, and her eyes sparkled. "Probably not. Folks are pretty content to keep the status quo. We like our quiet little town." She shrugged. "Myrtle Beach is okay. I used to live there myself. But nothing beats this solitude."

"Are you from Myrtle Beach?" She didn't roll her Rs like a native, but her accent was a strange mix of regions that he couldn't place.

"Not originally. I worked there for several years, learning the bar business, before we moved here."

"We may have already met, then." Although, it wasn't likely since he never went out. And he was sure he would've remembered her, if for no other reason than her eyes.

"I don't think so. I would've remembered you." Flushing from the admission, she turned away and adjusted the liquor bottles on the shelves of the mirrored wall behind her.

"Sunny," Ed called from the end of the bar. "Close us out, girlie."

She glanced at the clock on the wall. "Why? You still have time for two more."

The men flashed toothy, not-so-innocent grins.

The other man said, "If we leave early enough, maybe you'll get lucky."

Ed cut his gaze to the kids at the pool table, and one of them yelled across the bar, "Yeah, we're done."

The biker tipped his beer in acknowledgement and his girlfriend giggled. "We're out, too."

The patrons had apparently planned this, in the event of his return, without Sunny's knowledge. Her mouth hung open and she stood rock still, an expression of utter mortification on her reddening face. "I can't believe this," she sputtered. She looked from the kids to the biker to the older men. "How do you know he's not a serial killer?"

Ed pinned Gavin with a hard stare. "Are you a serial killer?"

Gavin met the man's stare and shook his head. "No, sir." He would have laughed, but he didn't want them to think he took Sunny's safety lightly.

Sunny's gaze swiveled between them. She was still red-faced, but her shock had turned to anger. "Like he'd say so if he was."

Gavin pulled his driver's license out of his wallet, walked to the end of the counter, and slid it over to the men. "Write down my name, address, license number, everything."

He walked back to Sunny, leaned across the bar, and said, "If you're uncomfortable, I'll leave." Lowering his voice, so only she could hear, he went for the whole truth and nothing but. "While the idea of spending the night, or part of the night, with you is incredibly appealing, I didn't come back here with any expectations.

"I like you, and I want to spend time with you. I also like…"—he

grinned and nodded toward the end of the bar—"the old coots. But"—
he leaned back to give her some space—"if I make you uncomfortable,
or you're not interested in spending time with me, I'll leave."

As she worked the situation around in her mind, her eyes turned
hot, then cold, then neutral. He knew the second she made her decision
because her eyes flared to liquid silver and the attraction arcing between
them snapped and crackled, filling the air with an electrical charge. Her
throat bobbed as she swallowed, and a tentative smile played on her
mouth. "I'd like you to stay."

She punched in a couple of buttons on the cash register, exchanged
his license for the men's tabs, and said, "Adios, gentlemen."

As the men gulped down the last of their beers and shuffled off their
barstools, Gavin said, "I really do want to spend more time with them."

Sunny turned to face him and her necklace caught the light. The
sparkling stones twinkled and winked, and everything from his waist
down tightened. Through parched lips, he said, "But I can do that
another time."

Sunny stood at the door, watching Johnny and Liza fasten their
helmets before climbing onto Johnny's bike. His long hair and tats gave
the appearance of a roughneck, but he was a nice guy, and Sunny liked
him and Liza a lot.

Liza's family, however, didn't share the love. They didn't think
Johnny was good enough for their little girl, and they made Liza's life
hell anytime they found out she'd been with him. Even though the
couple was in their early twenties, they found it easier to use the
Blackout as a hideout to keep their relationship a secret. That way, Liza

didn't have to deal with any crap from the parental units, and Johnny didn't get pushed to the brink of committing a felony.

Sunny never understood why parents felt they had the right to steal their children's happiness. She also didn't understand why grown children sacrificed their happiness to please their parents. An issue she was going to have to discuss with Robby, sooner rather than later.

She flicked the lock into place and clicked off the neon sign in the window, then flipped the switches to cut off the overhead lights. Nervous energy had her quivering as she turned to face Gavin.

He sat on the stool, one hand resting on his thigh, the other gripping his beer, his blue eyes trained on her.

Fascinating.

She found him fascinating. When his expression turned fierce and his body snapped taut with tension, he became a very scary dude. Way scarier than Johnny. But that fierceness made her heart race faster, her feminine instincts ignite, and she found her reaction to him frightening.

When he smiled… the scary fell away and beautiful remained. His eyes could flip from hot to cold in a heartbeat, then soft and playful the next. She didn't think she would enjoy being on the receiving end of his cold glare. But his smoldering gaze set her on fire.

While locking the door, she noticed the Lexus SUV in the lot. He had money, apparently a lot of it, but he didn't come across as pompous or pretentious. He seemed like a down-to-earth guy who enjoyed drinking American beer and fishing with his grandpa.

So who was the real man beneath those clothes? And did she want to get to know him on a deep, personal level, or stop at the skin-deep, kissable level?

He cocked his head to the side and smiled. "You're thinking too much."

Her flip-flops slapped the hardwood floor as she put her rubbery legs into action and propelled herself across the bar toward him. "I tend to overthink things."

He narrowed his eyes and his body tensed. "You don't have a boyfriend, or significant other, do you?"

She stopped a few feet in front of him and snapped her mouth shut. Planting her fists on her waist, she said, "What?" She sounded angrier than she intended, but the question offended her.

His expression lightened, and he held his hand up in surrender. "Just making sure. I've learned to never assume anything."

"You think I would flirt with you if I had a boyfriend?"

His eyes twinkled in the ambient lighting from the neon signs, and a smile played at his lips. "You were flirting with me?"

His tone was light and teasing, but the question embarrassed her. She blew out a puff of breath and turned away. Muttering under her breath, she said, "I was trying. Obviously, I need to work on my game."

His laughter came from directly behind her, and she realized he'd followed her behind the counter.

Instinctively, she crossed her arms over her chest before turning to face him. Picking up on her body language, he stopped midstride, then took a few steps back. He dipped his head seductively and looked at her through a fringe of dark lashes. "You didn't need to do much to catch my attention. You needed to do even less to keep it."

Seeking a diversion from the awkwardness jittering inside her, she wrung out her cloth and wiped off the counter. "What do you do?"

Since Bartender Handbook rule number two had gone out the window, she might as well chunk rule number one, too. If she was going to do this, she wanted to know more than his name, and that he was hot. She wanted sexual adventure, but it went against her nature to make it completely anonymous.

"I'm vice president of a multi-location hospitality company."

She glanced up at him. *Okay, whatever that means.*

The corner of his mouth lifted. "It's a fancy title for a paper pusher."

She dropped the rag into the bucket and rubbed her palms on her jeans to dry them off. "That time, I know I didn't speak out loud."

He tossed his head back with a laugh, and the sound vibrated through her chest all the way down to her toes. God, he had a great laugh. "You don't have to say anything. Your face is so expressive it speaks for you."

"So I've been told. It makes me a terrible liar, and I really suck at poker."

He laughed again. "I bet you do." Looking around the bar, he asked, "What can I do to help you wrap things up here?"

"Nothing. Robby washed all the glasses before he left. I'll have him come down before we open tomorrow to sweep the floors and make sure everything is straight."

He took a step closer, then paused, gauging her reaction. When she didn't back away, he took another step. And another. Caught in the grips of his simmering stare, her skin tingled, her panties dampened, and her breasts grew heavy.

The warmth of his body and the spicy scent of his aftershave pulled her to him like a magnet. When she was close enough to see the individual whiskers of his five o'clock shadow, she realized how far forward she'd swayed. She tensed, forcing the forward momentum to halt, then stepped back until she bumped the counter with her butt.

His sapphire eyes turned to midnight as the pupils dilated. His throat worked, and his nostrils flared. He closed the distance between them and rested his palms against the counter at her sides, boxing her in. Even though he wasn't touching her, his body heat mixed with hers, and the temperature in the room rose twenty degrees. Her palms grew sweaty and perspiration popped out on her neck and forehead.

Could anything be more unattractive? She reached under his arm and slid the top of the beer cooler open. As a rush of cool air swept over her, she sighed with relief.

She could tell from his grin and the glint in his eyes that she amused him, but that only lasted for a moment. The humor quickly slipped away, and the sultry heat returned. He dipped his head and drew in a deep breath. "You smell good. Like strawberries." He nuzzled her neck, then nibbled her ear.

The awkward nervousness she'd been feeling gave way to hammering excitement. She'd always wanted a wild ride with a man like him, or what she suspected he might be like. Her body recognized this was her chance, and it responded with a resounding *all systems go.*

As adrenaline and excitement rippled through her body, she started to tremble. She tightened her muscles so the shaking wouldn't be obvious, but he noticed anyway and pushed back to give her space.

He studied her face, then looked down at her breasts. As hard and painful as her nipples were, they had to be visible through the fabric of her halter-top, and she fought the urge to cross her arms to cover herself. He made a soft, appreciative sound before flipping his gaze to her face.

"For a minute I thought I'd frightened you." His voice was low and husky. "But you're not scared, are you?"

She pressed her hand against the side of his face and stroked the sharp ridge of his cheekbone with her thumb. "No. If anything, I'm afraid of my strong reaction to you."

But she sure as hell wasn't going to let a little fear stop her from getting on this ride.

Chapter Five

Slowly, suggestively, Sunny tilted her head to the side, giving Gavin access to her neck.

He didn't move any closer, or press himself against her, but his arms tightened and his body tensed. She heard him swallow; then warm breath and soft lips brushed her neck. His touch sent cold chills racing down her spine, and her internal temperature soared.

He nipped her ear, then kissed a trail down her neck and across her collar bone. His teeth scraped the necklace, sending a vibration rippling along the chain to her nipples. "This thing is hot as hell."

Another nip and a slight tug had her breath coming in short, shallow gasps and her body arching forward.

"Do you have to fight men off every night?" He pulled back and studied her face while waiting for her response. She didn't understand why, but her answer seemed more important to him than if they were just making pre-foreplay small talk.

She was tempted to straight up lie because the truth was so embarrassing. But rather than making up a wild tale, she held his gaze and shook her head. "No. I haven't been with anyone in over three years."

He blinked once. Twice. A third time. "Why the hell not?"

He sounded outraged on her behalf, and she couldn't help but laugh. "Between work and raising Robby, I haven't had time."

His eyebrows pulled tight and the muscle in his jaw twitched. Curiosity shimmered in his eyes, and he didn't seem to be breathing. "Why make time for me?"

Snared in his gaze, she didn't even think about lying this time. "I don't know. Something about you is different." She lifted a shoulder and smiled. "I decided I deserved a one-night fling."

For a split second, his mouth pulled tight; then it relaxed and he smiled. "I'll take that as a compliment." He edged closer and, with his mouth hovering over hers, said, "And a huge responsibility. I'll do everything in my power to make it worth your time. Especially since I only get one shot." He sounded irritated. But then he did something amazing with his tongue on her neck, and she no longer cared what had him annoyed.

Without warning, he stopped with the tongue action, wrapped his hands around her waist, and picked her up. She'd barely had time to gasp before he settled her on top of the counter. His smile was warm, his eyes soft and caring. "You've been taking care of everyone else all evening. Let me take care of you for a while."

He turned around and studied the liquor bottles, then the glasses, and finally the beer cooler. "I have a ton of experience with drinking, but none with mixing. Give me some direction." He turned back around to face her. "What's your favorite drink?"

Even though he probably considered this part of the foreplay, she found the gesture incredibly sweet, and emotion clogged her throat. She'd never had a nice, slow buildup. All of her previous experience fell under basic, boring sex. One minute of kissing. Two minutes of groping. Thirty seconds to shed the clothes. Ten minutes of getting down to business.

He stared into her eyes, as if trying to see inside her head. "You don't strike me as a Cosmo girl."

She laughed. "God, no."

"Tequila? Jack?" He quirked an eyebrow and grinned. "A girl after my own heart... Crown Royal?"

Intending to playfully push him away, she pressed her palms against the hard wall of his chest and gave a slight shove. He didn't budge. But his heartbeat pounding against her open hand and his body heat seeping into her palms caused the playfulness to evaporate into a sharp, painful jolt of need.

Desperate to bring moisture to her sand-dry mouth, she licked her lips and thought of butterscotch suckers. Relaxing her elbows, she allowed her body to fall close to his. In a voice barely above a whisper, she said, "A lot of the younger crowd, like your..." She let the sentence fall, unsure of how to reference the women he'd been with earlier.

"The brunette was my boss's daughter. The other two are her friends. It's a long story. I'll spare you the gory details."

She breathed a sigh of relief at having that piece to the puzzle and confirming he wasn't involved with any of them, and watched the pulse in his neck pound at a strong, steady pace. "The drinks they chose are common. As well as things like buttery nipples or a slow comfortable screw." She swallowed hard. "My personal favorite, though, is a french kiss."

His gaze dropped to her mouth, and, fueled by the fire she saw in his eyes, she flicked her tongue over her top lip, then drug it along her lower. Knowing her action had been strictly for his pleasure, his lids dropped to half-mast, and he smiled appreciatively.

With agonizingly slow movements, he stepped between her knees, took her face in his large palms, and dipped his head. With his mouth inches from hers, he whispered, "You don't mean the kind in a glass, do you?"

She shook her head, then closed her eyes and *felt*. Felt his warm breath against her mouth, his rough palms against her face, and his solid thighs against her softer ones. A viscous wave of need washed through her, and she found it difficult to make her voice work. "I love kisses. french and otherwise. In fact, I love kisses as much as sex."

He drew back, as if horrified. "You've either been with some outstanding kissers, or lousy lovers." He leaned back in. "Which is it?"

Since she could count her lovers on one hand, not including the thumb, she couldn't say for sure. But she refused to admit that. Knowing she hadn't had sex in three years was bad enough. If he knew the full extent of her inexperience, he might wonder what was wrong with her.

She ignored the question and concentrated on his mouth, which was so close she could see the soft lines in his lower lip. Yet, he might as well have been a block away for all the good it did. Trying to close the scant distance between them, she gripped his forearms and tugged. He didn't move, and her desperation twisted into a tight coil in her gut.

"Patience, Sunny." His eyes were full of heat and promise, his voice a husky murmur. "We'll never have another first kiss. Don't rush it."

Unable to form an intelligent thought, let alone speak, Sunny stared into his eyes and willed him to move faster. She held her breath and let her eyelids drift shut as he eased closer and kissed the corner of her eye, then her temple, then her ear.

His hand slipped to the back of her head and held her in place as his lips made a slow excursion along her jawline and ended at the corner of her mouth.

His tongue stroked the crease of her lips, and she opened to him with a sigh. She could tell he was smiling, taking pleasure in teasing her. He didn't make her wait long, though, before he treated her with full mouth-to-oh-what-an-amazing-mouth contact.

Slow, rhythmic thrusts of his tongue kicked her base instincts into gear, and she wiggled closer to the edge of the counter, seeking a different kind of thrusting penetration. His tongue swept across the roof of her mouth in a gentle caress, then slid over her teeth. He nipped at her lip, then worked the sting away with a slow, slick glide.

Good grief, Gavin didn't kiss. He made love with his tongue and mouth. Within seconds, she was trembling and rubber-legged and grateful to be sitting. Otherwise, she'd be a glob of goo, sliding onto the floor. When he broke the kiss for a breath, she said, "If you were trying to convince me kissing isn't as good as sex, you're doing a poor job."

The hand on the back of her head slid to the nape of her neck, while the other trailed over her shoulder and down her arm. He laced their fingers together and pressed his palm to hers. Their energy fields, swirling and combining in their touch, felt as intimate as the kiss. "What are my chances for proving that was *nothing* compared to great sex?"

She gulped, then went with the truth. "You've never had a better chance."

His eyelids dipped and he unleashed a slow, seductive smile. A second later, he put his mouth back to work, blazing a trail down the side of her neck toward her breast.

After three years of denying herself this kind of pleasure, his tender caress broke the dam loose and a flood of desire rushed through her. She scooted so close to the edge of the counter, she was in danger of slipping off. But Gavin was there, keeping her from falling. She wrapped her legs around the backs of his thighs and pulled him flush against her.

With careless, trembling hands, she pushed his shirt up and raked her fingers across the taut muscles of his back. She was starving for his touch and desperate for more contact.

His erection aligned perfectly with where she wanted him, but rather than removing their clothing and satisfying her greedy desire, he stretched the taut band of need tighter.

Whispering in her ear, he said, "We're taking this slowly. If I only have one time with you, I'm making every second count."

"We'll go two times in one night. Shoot, three or four times. Please don't slow down. I need you. I need you touching me, inside me, filling me."

A strangled sound that was half-laugh, half-growl escaped his throat. "You're killing me." He untied her top from behind her neck and let the panels of fabric fall free in the front.

Oh yeah, now we're getting somewhere.

"Fuck, you're beautiful." He slipped his finger under the center of the chain and gave a gentle tug.

When she arched her back and cried out, he froze. "You didn't hurt me," she panted. "I promise. God, that's good. Don't stop. Please, don't stop."

With a touch as gentle and reverent as the one he'd used to stroke the copper magnolia leaf, he ran his finger down the length of chain to her nipple. "You kinky, Sunny?" There was no censure in his voice, only curiosity.

She shook her head and leaned forward, trying to force more contact.

"No? Then why wear the chains?" His tone was low and coaxing in her ear.

At times, she wondered if she had a kinky streak and there was more to wearing the jewelry than making herself feel sexy. But he didn't need to know every freaking thing about her sex life, or her fantasies, so she ignored the question and kissed the side of his neck.

He shivered slightly, then nipped at her ear. Flicking the clip that attached the chain to her nipple, he said, "I'm waiting for an answer."

A cry escaped and her head fell backward. "I don't know." Her words were strangled as she arched toward him in a desperate, pleading move. This time, he dipped his head and took the clip and nipple into his mouth. Afraid she'd pass out of from extreme pleasure, she pushed her fingers through his hair, grasped the ends, and held on.

It didn't take him long to figure out what sent her flying and what registered so-so on the pleasure meter. Sticking with the oh-my-God-that-feels-so-good moves, he quickly had her suspended on the verge of an orgasm, panting and begging for more. Until tonight, she never would have believed it possible to be this out of control without penetration.

He kissed a path to her mouth, and said, "You're going to come for me, aren't you?"

His arrogance turned her on, but at the same time, left her feeling vulnerable, because she no longer had control of her body. He did. Without waiting for an answer, he captured her mouth with his, thrust his tongue, and yanked on the center of the chain.

An electrical charge shot through her breasts, down to her sex, and out to every nerve ending in between. She arched her back and tightened her legs around his waist as the orgasm hit with the speed and intensity of a lightning bolt.

As the haze faded, she became aware of his pulsing length pressed against her. Not only did he need relief, but she needed more. Now. She reached for his belt buckle and began loosening the latch.

His body tensed and he grasped her hands, holding them still. He froze, then his gaze shot to the door.

A breath later, she heard the doorknob rattling and Robby's voice. "Sunny. Are you in there?"

Shit. Shit, shit, shit.

She hadn't thought to tell Robby she'd be late, and he'd probably gotten worried when she hadn't come home at her normal time. The lighting was dim, but he should still be able to see in. Finding Gavin pressed against her like a second skin wouldn't relieve his anxiety.

She fumbled for the ties of her top, but her fingers were shaking and she couldn't grasp the fabric ties. Gavin beat her to it, retying the ends loosely around her neck before taking a step back.

She ran a hand over her hair, then rolled her eyes upward as if she could see. "My hair's a mess, isn't it?"

His lips twitched, even as he bit the bottom one to keep from laughing.

"Sweetheart, there is no way he's going to believe we were just talking." He rubbed his thumb over her bottom lip. "Along with your messy hair, your lips are red and swollen and you have whisker burn on your cheeks." He smiled wickedly. "But we both have our pants on; that's gotta count for something."

Prior to that mind-altering orgasm, she'd have agreed. But not now. She glanced over her shoulder to the door. Robby had his hands cupped around her face, his nose pressed to the glass.

"It doesn't look like he's going away, does it?"

Gavin rocked back on his heels, and shoved his hands into his pockets. Laughing, he shook his head and said, "Not anytime soon."

With a groan, she jumped off the counter and headed for the door.

Gavin watched Sunny pull and push at her hairpins in a futile effort to fix her hair before she reached the door. It would never go back into that sexy little knot without a brush, mirror, and a whole lot of work. The way she had it piled on top of her head earlier was sexy as hell, but damn if he didn't like this tumbled, just-out-of-bed look even more.

Instead of opening the door as he expected, she put her hands on her hips and yelled, "What?"

Robby broke into a huge, shit-eating grin… or maybe a grimace. It was difficult for Gavin to tell from this far away. "Whatcha doin'?"

Gavin could imagine the flustered expression on Sunny's face, and he had to bite the inside of his cheek to keep from laughing out loud. His gaze slid past Sunny and Robby to the dark Anticue fishing pier, and he instantly sobered. The place held a lot of fond memories for him, and even though it was ridiculous to have an attachment to a fishing pier, there it was.

"What the hell do you want?" Sunny asked.

"I, uh…" Robby struggled to find his words. "I was… uh… driving by on my way home from… studying? The lights were out, but with another car in the lot, I thought I should check on you."

"As you can see, I'm fine. Go on home. I'll be right behind you."

Robby looked at the parking lot, then back to her.

"I understand. It's okay." She nodded and made a little shooing motion with her fingers. "Really, go on. I'll be there in a few."

"Okay, if you're sure." He didn't look convinced, but turned and walked away from the door anyway.

Sunny blew out a breath, pushed a clump of hair out of her face, and turned around.

"He seems like a good kid. He obviously loves you very much."

She nodded and smiled. "Yeah. To both."

Figuring Robby's interruption had brought his one night—damn, that stung—to a screeching halt, Gavin went to work on creating another opportunity. He leaned against the counter and crossed his arms. "He lives with you?"

"Yeah, for the past six years."

Whoa, no wonder they were close. Shit, how old had Sunny been when she took on the responsibility of raising her brother? How old had he been? "You told me his age earlier, but I don't remember."

She pulled a pin out, brushed back a strand of hair, then jabbed the pin back into place. "He'll be twenty-one in two months."

He moved in with her when he was fourteen? She didn't look like she could have been much older than that herself, six years ago. Why did she take on such a huge responsibility at a young age? A familiar sadness settled into his gut. "Are your parents deceased?"

"Not exactly." She stopped in front of him, crossed her arms, and bit her lip.

Okay, that body language was loud and clear. The conversation about Robby and her parents was over, as was his night, probably. He spread his legs wide enough to accommodate her, then grabbed the belt loops of her jeans and pulled her to him. "You have that awkward morning after expression."

"Do I?" Her gaze darted past him. "I've never had one of those."

He dropped his mouth to hers and slid his tongue over her lips before dipping inside for another taste of her. It was only a kiss, but the way she melted against him made him feel as if she'd slipped right through his skin and sidled up next to his soul.

He'd enjoyed his fair share of great sex, but this thing with Sunny felt different. More intense. Hell, they hadn't even had sex, yet he felt like she'd moved into his mind and body, moved the furniture all around, put up a few pictures, and claimed the place as hers.

Breathless, and needing to be inside her so badly he ached from his teeth to his toes, he pressed his forehead to hers and said, "Since this opportunity was cut short, do I get another night to prove how good sex can be?"

She shook her head, as if to clear her thoughts, or get her bearings. "What about the rest of tonight?"

"Are you worried about Robby worrying about you?" He leaned back and watched her face so he could judge the honesty of her answer.

She smiled sheepishly and ducked her head.

"That's what I thought. I thrive on challenges, but I'm not making love to you while your mind is preoccupied."

She chewed on her lip and studied the floor.

He tipped her chin up, forcing her to meet his gaze head-on. "I can't tell what you're thinking if you're not looking at me."

"I want to see you again, but it makes me nervous."

"Why?"

"Because… well, then it wouldn't be a one-night fling, would it?"

Annoyance flared so strongly within him he had to consciously force his hand to relax so she wouldn't pick up on the tension. Why did being a one-time fuck to her bother him so badly?

He lived in Myrtle Beach; she lived here. He had his career to think about and didn't need the distraction of figuring out how to split his time between two places. What Sunny offered was a no strings, no attachment affair. The perfect situation.

Funny though, standing here looking into her eyes, the perfect situation no longer sounded perfect.

Maybe it was just an ego thing, since he hadn't gotten the chance to prove to her how good it could be. How good *they* could be.

He dropped a kiss on her nose, then slipped to her mouth. This time, he was less aggressive and more persuasive. He stroked her tongue, the roof of her mouth, and sucked cajolingly on her lip. "Give me a full night. I promise I'll make it worthwhile."

Her lips parted and her eyes turned dreamy. "You win. When?"

Her sexy, ready-for-bed expression nearly made him say the hell with Robby and her state of mind. He could coax her into forgetting about everything except what they were doing. But now he was greedy.

He didn't want a quick lay in the bar. He wanted a bed and an entire night.

"When do you work again?"

"I work every night we're open."

"What's the number here at the bar?" As she recited the number, he plugged it into his cellphone. "I'll give you a call tomorrow and see what night works best for you."

The lusty haze filling her eyes began to dissipate, and he could tell her brain was reigniting. Anxious to get away before she changed her mind, he said, "Grab your stuff and I'll walk you to your car."

She wrinkled her nose and shook her head. "I'll see myself out."

He frowned. "I'm not letting you walk out by yourself."

"It's okay," she said, her tone forceful, as it had been when telling Robby to go on home. "I walk out by myself all the time."

Protectiveness rushed to the surface and filled him with concern. "That's not safe. You should have Robby, or someone, with you."

She waved a hand in the air, brushing off the comment. "This is Anticue, the safest place on earth." She herded him toward the door. "I'll be fine." As they reached the door, she shocked the hell out of him by standing on tiptoes to kiss him long and deep.

When he found his voice again, he said, "I'll call you tomorrow."

Chapter Six

*M*orning sunlight danced on the hood of Gavin's SUV as he made his way through the iron gate and under the towering sego palms leading to Max Holden's estate. Gavin had pulled into this driveway every weekday morning for nearly twelve years, but he'd never grown comfortable with the massive show of wealth or air of pretentiousness surrounding the home.

Why did two people need twelve thousand square feet of extravagance? Even when Callie came home from college, or from one of her European vacations, it left four thousand square feet per person. It made sense if you didn't like the people you lived with and never wanted to see them, but that wasn't what Gavin wanted for himself.

Unfortunately, as the one on deck to take Max's place as CEO of Holden Enterprises, ostentation on his part was expected. Max believed living in an enormous show house, belonging to the top social clubs and country clubs, and being seen with the "right people" encouraged trust in investors and reassured them they'd made a wise investment.

Gavin had been carefully selected and groomed for the CEO office, but he didn't know if he was cut out to be Max's successor. Gavin possessed the intellectual ability to run Holden Enterprises, but he couldn't change who he was at the core: a country boy, more comfortable in jeans and work boots than the thousand dollar Armani suits he wore to work every day.

He parked in the circular driveway, climbed from his SUV, and found himself whistling as he buttoned his suit coat and circled the side of the house. This was the same routine he followed every morning, but today felt different.

He felt different.

He should be exhausted, considering he didn't get to bed until after two a.m. and then spent the next four hours tossing and turning, assaulted by erotic images of a certain, sexy bartender. However, rather than being tired, he felt more alive than he had in years. Sunny sparked something inside him—something far more substantial than the fire in his pants.

He let himself in through the home's side door that led into the kitchen. Morning didn't officially start for him until his first cup of coffee, and Angelina, the Holdens' housekeeper, made the best coffee in the world. "Good morning, Angie."

"Good morning, Mr. Gavin." Her thick Spanish accent made the greeting sound like a song, and her ever-present smile was radiant as she turned and handed him a steaming mug.

Gavin laughed and hugged the small woman, careful not to spill a drop of the cherished coffee. "Bless you." He took a sip, then nodded in the general direction of Max's home office. "Is he in his office?"

"He is." She spun around and flipped off a burner on the industrial-sized stove, then checked the oven. "Would you please tell him breakfast will be on the patio in ten minutes?"

"Sure will." Gavin left the kitchen—the only room in this mausoleum in which he felt comfortable—and made his way to Max's office. His shoes *clip, clip, clipped* on the marble floor as he crossed the expansive foyer and traveled the long hallway leading to Max's office.

The humongous room housed Max's cherry desk and chair, two guest chairs, a leather sofa, two leather chairs, and a coffee table. The leather sofa, chairs, and table created a seating area in front of the left wall that served as a small library. On the opposite wall, floor-to-ceiling windows flanked a set of french doors that opened to the patio and pool.

Gavin shook Max's outstretched hand before sinking into one of the guest chairs facing Max's desk. "Morning, Max. Breakfast will be ready in ten."

"Good." Max relaxed into his chair and gave Gavin a warm, fatherly smile. "I presume you and Callie had an enjoyable evening."

Thanks to Sunny, Gavin's evening had been incredible. It remained to be seen how Callie viewed things.

She hadn't minded the abrupt departure from the Blackout. If anything, she was relieved to leave the "disgusting place" behind. But she was plenty pissed-off when she realized Gavin's intentions were to drop her off, then get the hell out. Over the next several hours, he received a dozen texts and voicemails, all letting him know the fun he was missing out on.

The last slurred message came in around four a.m., so he assumed she passed out shortly after. He figured if she saw the light of day any time soon, she'd seriously regret it.

However, those weren't details a father needed to hear. And the details of his return trip to Anticue weren't relevant, so he settled on a vague response. "I had a great time. I can't answer for Callie and her friends."

Max glanced at Gavin with obvious confusion. "Friends? I thought the two of you were going to the beach for a nice, quiet evening alone."

Gavin shrugged. No one had been more surprised by the change of plans than him. Yesterday, while Max gave Gavin details about the Blackout, Callie conveniently strolled in. Call him paranoid, but he was convinced she lurked outside the door, waiting for just the right moment to breeze into Max's office and insinuate herself into Gavin's life.

He learned long ago that Callie got what Callie wanted, at least if her father had anything to say about it. And unfortunately for Gavin, she had her sights set on him. He didn't share her enthusiasm and had zero interest in a spoiled daddy's girl whose biggest concern was making sure her shoes and handbag matched.

He wanted someone who could carry on an intelligent conversation. Someone with depth of character, who cared about things of importance. Someone who knew how to have fun and with whom he shared a strong physical attraction.

Silver eyes and a brilliant smile flashed in his mind's eye and the corner of his mouth inched into a smile. His attraction to Sunny skipped the sparks of attraction and rocketed to near-detonation. Hell, he couldn't remember anyone *ever* affecting him as strongly as Sunny.

Reeling his wayward libido under control, he redirected his attention to Max. "Jen and Tiffany were here when I arrived to pick Callie up."

He'd been both relieved and irritated. Relieved he wouldn't have to be alone with Callie, irritated because those three would make a saint swear.

He glanced out the window overlooking the pool and guesthouse. "I imagine they'll sleep late this morning."

Max's gaze followed Gavin's, and his shoulders slumped. "I thought after spending the past six months in Europe, she'd be more serious. I hoped she'd have the partying behind her and be more settled." He shook his head. "I don't know what to do with her."

Start by cutting up her credit cards and making her find a job.

As if remembering he wasn't simply talking to an employee and confidant, but also his daughter's pick as a potential husband, Max brightened and straightened his shoulders. "I'm sure she'll come around soon. Besides, we want her to have this wild streak out of her system before she settles down." He winked conspiratorially. "Right?"

Gavin propped the ankle of one leg onto the knee of the other and chuckled at Max's attempt to paint Callie in a positive light. Callie made her intentions toward Gavin clear, and Max wholeheartedly supported her chase. Despite Gavin's attempts to politely and tactfully let both of them know he wasn't interested, Max continued to believe Gavin would someday come around.

Wanting to, once again, reiterate his position, Gavin said, "I know what you're trying to do, but I've told you. I don't have any romantic feelings toward Callie."

Thinking about her attempted seductions the night before started a shudder he had to fight to suppress. When he'd walked the girls to the guesthouse, Jen and Tiffany disappeared like smoke. Before he could get out the door, Callie had her body pressed against his, one hand wrapped around his neck, and the inch-long fingernails of the other scraping down his chest.

The effect had been the same as nails on a chalkboard.

Not only did he not think of Callie the way a man would a lover, but when he'd looked into her dark brown eyes, sparkling silver ones had shimmered in their place.

"You say that now"—Max's words snapped Gavin back to the present—"but someday you might feel differently. You're a good man, Gavin. Stable and solid, with a good future ahead of you. I want my daughter with someone who'll treat her well and give her a good life."

He appreciated Max's confidence and the compliment, but he wouldn't ever change his mind. He'd been treated like a member of the family for most of his adult life, and the only feelings he had for Callie were brotherly. But he couldn't seem to make anyone else understand that. "She's only twenty-four, Max. Give her time and let her find someone who'll not only treat her well, but will love her."

While Max nodded thoughtfully and watched the guesthouse, Gavin switched gears to a more important matter. "That bar in Anticue is quite a place."

The frown lines in Max's forehead lifted in direct proportion to the corners of his mouth. "I thought you might find it interesting."

"I liked the eclectic flair." Damn, he'd forgotten to get the names of the artists from Sunny.

"Yeah, well, I'm afraid that eclectic mess will need to go."

Confusion, along with a dash of alarm, bounced around Gavin's brain. "Excuse me?"

Max half-smiled, half-snarled, an expression Gavin had seen a million times. It was Max's pit bull face, which meant Max wanted something that someone stood in his way of getting. Which, in Max's book, meant war. "You know the resort/condominium complex I've wanted to build in Anticue?" He paused for Gavin's nod. "I finally have a group of individuals who can make it happen."

Gavin leaned back in his chair and tried to appear relaxed, even as prickles of unease danced across his skin. Most coastal areas of the North and South Carolina coast had been overly developed, but a few barrier islands, like Anticue, remained virtually untouched. The locals liked it that way and had measures in place to keep the area protected. "What about zoning? They have ordinances restricting things like this. That's why the area wasn't developed long ago."

Max's smiled broadened, losing some of its nastiness and gaining in the confidence department. "Having a group of hand-picked… investors has been the key to getting this project off the ground."

Ah, in other words, money in the pockets of the right people would ensure the zoning ordinances were modified to accommodate Max's needs.

"That little bar, however, is a fly in the ointment." Max's words were like gunshots echoing around the room. "The owner is elusive and obstinate and won't return phone calls." Max's unwavering determination was evident in his expression and demeanor. "We need that property in order to move forward. You need to make it happen."

Gavin averted his gaze and stared out the window. He understood why the owner had an attachment to the place. Hell, after thirty minutes, he developed a warm fuzzy attitude toward it. Well, mostly for the bartender. But the teak bar and old woodwork trimming the windows made the place warm and friendly. The artistic displays added flair, and the people reminded him of the TV show "Cheers." Everyone knew each other, and it was fun to watch their playful ribbing.

"Why didn't you tell me any of this yesterday?"

"I was going to. But after you expressed an interest in taking Callie—"

"I didn't express an interest in taking Callie. She wanted to go. You told me to take her. End of story." His comment came out harsher than intended, but this deal had him irritated and edgy. He didn't want to mess with the Blackout. He thought he was checking it out because it was popular and could be duplicated in a Holden resort. Not demolished.

Gavin swallowed the unease swelling in his throat. If they excavated the building, where would Sunny work? What would happen to her and Robby?

Maybe she'd move back to Myrtle Beach.

That thought tempered a little of his trepidation and settled the upheaval in his stomach. If she lived here, maybe he could see her on a regular basis.

But she didn't like Myrtle Beach. She made that clear when she talked about living here before moving to Anticue.

He drew a hand down his jaw and pulled in a deep breath. "Who owns it?"

Max steepled his fingers and propped his chin on them. "A.L. Black. I don't know any more than that since none of our calls have been returned. I've tried, unsuccessfully, to use my local contacts, since you don't like dealing with the…"—Max waved a hand around in the air, searching for a word Gavin knew would mean *underhanded*—"unpleasant details."

Gavin dropped his foot to the floor and grabbed a pen and paper from the corner of Max's desk. He wrote the owner's name, then asked, "What's the owner's address?"

"311 Atlantic Avenue."

His gaze shot to Max's. "That's the address for the bar."

Max nodded.

"I suppose this is a priority."

"Top priority," Max said. "I need you to make this happen. Fast."

"Okay," Gavin said, standing. "I guess I'll go to Anticue today." Not a bad way to spend the day. Not only would it give him the opportunity to see Sunny sooner than anticipated, but he'd like to check the island out in the daylight to see how much had changed. Or, as was more likely the case, had not changed.

The same wave of sadness he'd experienced at seeing the abandoned pier crept over him again. After the resort went in, the landscape and atmosphere of the island would change drastically. Nothing about Anticue would ever be the same.

Halfway to the door, Gavin paused and turned around. "Max, do you ever regret altering the landscape like we do?" Max looked perplexed, so Gavin continued. "Anticue is a nice, sleepy little beach community. They barely have a town, and the beaches are pristine. Do you ever regret what happens after a Holden resort is built?"

Max seemed completely bewildered. "Why should I care? We build luxury condominiums with first-rate amenities. Everything the condo owners and their guests could possibly want is provided onsite. The beach is the beach, regardless of its condition, and they don't need a large town nearby."

He should've known Max wouldn't understand. Gavin had asked from the viewpoint of the residents, the ones who liked things the way they were and enjoyed the solitude. Max was single-minded in his pursuit of the next development, regardless of the environmental or personal impact. He nodded to acknowledge Max's answer and sighed. "I'll have my cell if you need me."

As he exited through the large, oak panel doors of the study, he heard Max say, "I'm counting on you, son."

From Gavin's first day on the job, Max had treated him like a son. It was evident from the beginning, for reasons still unknown, that Max would groom Gavin to be his successor.

But for months now, Gavin had been unsettled about his future. This new development caused the unease to snarl and expand, and once again, he questioned if he was the right person for Max's job. He didn't think he had the stomach to make the same decisions Max made, or to continue the company in the same direction.

As he approached the massive front doors, Gavin couldn't shake the sensation that he wasn't just leaving Max's house, but crossing over one of life's significant thresholds.

Chapter Seven

"Oh, God." Callie squinted against the debilitating morning rays and pushed her sunglasses tight against her face, but the polarized lenses didn't stop the blinding light from piercing her bloodshot eyeballs. With every footfall drilling a hole into the side of her head, she traversed the brick walkway leading from the guesthouse to the patio, where her father sat reading his *Wall Street Journal* and eating his breakfast.

At her approach, he lowered the paper and gave her the same warm smile that had greeted her every morning of her life. "I was beginning to think you wouldn't make it this morning."

As she dipped her head to kiss his cheek, the sudden shift in altitude sent a wave of nausea from her stomach to her throat and produced a sledgehammer-worthy whack in her temple. She swallowed hard and gently took her seat, allowing everything in the cranial region to settle back into place. "I'd never miss our breakfast."

He smiled at her, the adoring father he was, and set the paper aside. "That means the world to me. How are you this morning?"

"I'm good."

Wise eyes studied her, and his mouth twitched slightly. "Have you ever gotten away with lying to me?"

She tried to laugh, but the agonizing throb in her temple stopped her short. She took a sip of her orange juice and gently shook her head.

"No, I don't think I have."

"Want to tell me what's wrong?" After a brief pause, he added, "Besides the hangover."

She cringed and shook out her napkin. "Do I look that bad?"

She'd hoped her large frame, Hollywood-style sunglasses would keep him from seeing her red and glassy eyes ringed with the deep dark circles, but apparently the disguise wasn't enough.

He shook his head and smiled. "You know I think you're always beautiful. Just had a feeling, is all."

She picked up her fork and flipped a piece of cantaloupe around in her bowl. "I don't know what to do about Gavin. It seems hopeless to think he's ever going to care about me. At least the way I do for him."

"Why do you say that? I thought last night was a positive step. I was a bit surprised, though, to hear you took friends along."

She stabbed the cantaloupe and brought it to her mouth. As it neared her lips and she caught its sweet scent, her stomach sent out a warning growl: *Don't you dare.* Following her stomach's command, she left the fruit untouched and lowered the fork to her plate. "I thought it might make the evening less awkward."

She played with the corner of the napkin and debated how honest she should be. Deciding she had nothing to lose and everything to gain, she said, "Sometimes Gavin makes me nervous. Not that I think he would ever hurt me. At least not physically. But he's so... intense."

"His intensity is what makes him such an asset to Holden Enterprises. He's single-minded in his focus." Max smiled. "Sometimes that can be intimidating."

He was right, as usual. Most people found her father intimidating. Some even called him dangerous because of his strong personality and tendency to be overbearing.

"There's more." His words were a statement, not a question.

She tried to meet his gaze, but couldn't. "Sometimes, I wonder if he even likes me."

"Don't be ridiculous. Everyone likes you. You're a beautiful young woman. Any man would be crazy not to fall in love with you."

"You're a little biased, don't you think?"

"Absolutely. But that doesn't change the facts."

She wished she shared her father's confidence. "On the way to Anti-cue, I tried to engage him in conversation, but it only made him angry."

Her daddy smiled knowingly. "Gavin's not a big conversationalist."

"He spent a lot of time talking to the bartender." She slumped in her chair. "He was really into her."

Her father's gaze drifted to the pool and he... smiled?

"Why are you smiling? It was awful."

He jerked his attention back to her and frowned. "I'm sorry you were uncomfortable." Taking hold of her hand, he said, "Sometimes, Gavin's going to need to do things you might find unpleasant. Probably, the less you know about his work, the better off you'll be."

The hangover must be making her brain fuzzy because she couldn't have heard, or at least understood, her father correctly. "You mean... he was supposed to flirt with the bartender?"

His smiled returned and his eyes gleamed. "He didn't know it, but that was my plan."

She pulled her fingers free of his grasp and leaned back in her chair. "Then why did you insist I go?" How could he be so insensitive to her feelings? And what kind of crazy assignment required Gavin to flirt with a skanky bartender?

Her father's brow rose. "You're the one that insisted you go. If you remember, I suggested it wasn't a good idea. But you argued. If I were too insistent that Gavin go alone, he would've gotten suspicious."

"Suspicious of what?"

"He would wonder why I didn't want you to go."

Needing to concentrate so she could follow this crazy conversation, she scrunched her eyes shut to block the overpowering light. "So... you want Gavin to..."

"Become friendly with the bartender."

Dread settled over her like a cold, wet blanket. "How friendly?"

"As friendly as necessary."

Reading her despair, he reached across the table and patted her hand. "Eat your breakfast, sweetheart, and don't worry about Gavin." His jaw took on a determined set, and his eyes turned to steel. "Don't worry about that bartender, either. She'll be a non-issue in no time."

He dropped his napkin to the table and pushed his chair back. "Now, if you'll excuse me, I have a few phone calls to make."

Knowing Gavin would be forced to spend time with the bartender made the leftover contents of her stomach bubble and churn like a test-tube science experiment gone wrong. Drastic, heavy-duty diversion tactics would be necessary to get her mind off his assignment, and she could think of only one thing powerful enough to do the trick.

"I'm going shopping with Jen and Tiffany today. Is it okay if I take the black MasterCard?"

"Of course." He dropped a kiss onto the top of her head and patted her shoulder. "Don't forget to get something for Lorraine's retirement dinner tomorrow night."

"Oh, shoot. I forgot about the party." Lorraine had been her father's secretary since before Callie was born. Her father was throwing a huge party to thank Lorraine for her years of service. Translation: to thank her for all the years she'd tolerated him. Everyone in the organization had been invited, and Callie was sure Gavin would be there. Which meant she needed something extra special to wear. "Do you know Gavin's favorite color?"

Max chuckled and shook his head. "No, Callie, that's not something I've ever asked."

Last night, getting a new, wildly sexy, and revealing wardrobe seemed like a great idea. The party offered her the perfect opportunity to try out the new look. But today, in the harsh daylight, she wondered if she had the nerve to go through with it.

On the hour-long drive to Anticue, Gavin formulated a plan and made a mental "to-do" list. First stop: the Blackout to see if the owner happened to be around this early in the day.

Wonder what time Sunny goes to work?

He blew out a breath, and forced his thoughts back to his job. Why would A.L. Black be so elusive?

Wonder if he knows where Sunny lives.

What would motivate Mr. Black to—

Maybe I could see Sunny before she goes to work?

Jesus Christ. Forgetting about Sunny was like forgetting to breathe. Absolutely impossible. Her cheerful attitude and the way she traded barbs with the locals made him smile, inside and out. Her loyalty to and personal sacrifice for her brother was a testament to her caring nature. And her sex appeal rocketed off the damned charts. Everything, from her unique eye color to the tantalizing necklace, intrigued him. Water pooled in his mouth as he remembered the smell of her strawberry shampoo and the taste of her soft skin. Holy hell, she was a firestorm erupting in his arms, and he couldn't wait to feel that heat again.

He told himself he brought an overnight bag as a precaution, in case he got tied up trying to locate the owner. But it was time to call bullshit. His plans of staying overnight in Anticue had nothing to do with work, but everything to do with Sunny.

She made him feel like a horny teenager, barely able to control himself. He'd tossed and turned all night, contemplating the variety of ways to bring her pleasure. In the process, he made himself crazy with need. The quick hand job in the shower this morning hadn't done a thing to ease his ache. If anything, it ratcheted his lust even higher.

As he turned onto Atlantic Avenue, he glanced at the clock on the dash. He doubted the bar would be open at eleven o'clock on Friday morning, but since it was the only address he had, that's where he'd start.

How would Sunny take the news of the Blackout selling? And closing?

Idiot, how would you take the news of being out of a job?

For a startling second, the thought brought him a sense of relief. Talk about crazy. He'd worked too hard, too long, to get to this point in his career. How could he possibly feel relief at not having a job? Besides, it would be a little difficult to continue supporting two households without an income.

As he pulled into the Blackout parking lot, he noticed the beat-up Honda Civic and Ford Ranger—both on the downward spiral of life—that were there last night. One of those cars must be Sunny's, and the prospect of seeing her again kicked his heartbeat into double time.

The inside of the Blackout was dark and appeared to be deserted, but he tugged on the door handle anyway. Locked. He cupped his hands and peered inside, like Robby did last evening. *Oh, shit.* He would have been able to see everything. The only saving grace was that Sunny's back had been to the door.

He retraced his steps, then kept going until he rounded the back of the building. On the far side, he found a set of steps leading to what appeared to be an upstairs apartment.

The door at the top flew open and Robby burst through the doorway. He was halfway down the stairs before he noticed Gavin standing at the bottom. He jerked to a stop, eyes narrowed and full of suspicion. "What are you doing here?"

"Uhhh…" Gee, that sounded intelligent. But Gavin was caught so off-guard, he couldn't come up with anything better.

The kid's expression said he wasn't any happier about Gavin's presence today than he was last night. Trying to appear as friendly and nonthreatening as possible, Gavin took off his sunglasses and tucked them into his pocket, then let his hands fall loosely at his sides. With the fine hairs on the back of his neck standing at attention, and his internal guidance system sending off warning flares, he couldn't form a proper response.

Taking his silence as an unwillingness to answer, Robby said, "Yeah, I guess that was a dumb question." He dropped down to the next step and jerked his head toward the door at the top. "I assume she's expecting you." He continued downward, and as he brushed past Gavin, muttered, "And she bitches at me for me being on the make all the time."

Gavin was still standing flat-footed and dumbfounded when Robby fired up the Ford and spun tires out of the parking lot. His gaze slid to the door at the top of the stairs, and a feeling of dread sank into his bones.

He propped a hand on the railing and thought things through. It was possible Sunny and Robby leased the upstairs apartment from the owner. It would be to Mr. Black's benefit to have someone living on the property, someone who would be right there to take care of things. It would also make things easier for Sunny and Robby and cut down on their travel expenses of getting to and from work.

But the owner had listed this address as his…

Shit…

Gavin pinched the bridge of his nose and tried not to finish the thought. *Or* her *address.*

He had a terrible feeling things were about to get awkward. There wasn't any point in delaying the inevitable, so he drew in a deep breath, then headed up the stairs.

Chapter Eight

*G*avin knocked on the door, which was left slightly ajar in Robby's hasty exit. It swung open, and he found Sunny standing on a stool, reaching into an upper cabinet, an oversized T-shirt barely covering the curve of her ass.

"What did you forget?" she asked, twisting toward the door. Her T-shirt shifted and—because his eyes were glued to her ass—he caught a glimpse of her pink thong. His gaze slid higher, and through the thin, cotton fabric, he could tell she wasn't wearing *the* necklace. Nothing but beautiful Sunny under that shirt.

Time stood still. He hadn't left last night… and hadn't been to work this morning. The need to touch and taste her was as strong as it had been in the bar twelve hours earlier, and the desperate drive to have her consumed him.

He lifted his gaze to her face. Her eyes were smudged with last night's makeup, a sucker stick hung from her mouth, and her blond hair tumbled around her face and shoulders in a just-out-of-bed tangle.

His fingers twitched and burned with the need to touch her, and he cursed the southbound flow of blood that left him lightheaded and aching from teeth to toes.

Sunny squeezed her eyes shut and shook her head, as if clearing cobwebs. When she opened them and found him still standing in the doorway, her nose crinkled and her forehead creased with confusion. At least she didn't seem to be alarmed at finding him on her doorstep, only puzzled.

When she lifted her hand to take the sucker from her mouth, he caught sight of a tattoo circling her wrist. She was wearing bracelets last night, so he hadn't noticed it. He sure noticed it now.

Holy hell. One more item to add to the ever-growing list of things he found so fascinating about this woman.

She smiled awkwardly and raised an eyebrow. "When you said you'd call, I thought you meant on the phone. And"—she laughed nervously—"I sort of thought you meant at the bar."

"Surprise." Talk about understatements.

Her gaze dipped to his shoes, then casually made the climb to his face. Going by her heavy-lidded, glassy-eyed look and the way she worked the sucker with her tongue, he guessed she was as affected by the magnetic pull as him.

"Can I come in?" he asked, pushing the door wide open so he could see the entire kitchen. The walls were a cheery yellow, the cabinets a bright white. A hand-painted border decorated the top of the walls, and painted grapevines surrounded the doorway leading into the living room. A small, round table and two chairs sat in the middle of the room; a window seat filled the space below a large picture window overlooking the beach.

"Sure." She moved a step lower on the stool and sat on the edge of the counter. The T-shirt rode high on her thighs, and her bare feet swung freely. Her gaze turned assessing as she asked, "How did you know where to find me?" She stiffened and her eyes widened. "Did you follow me last night?"

Her tumbled hair, short shirt, and smooth legs distracted him to the point of almost forgetting his reason for being here. He blew out a breath, then shut the door behind him. "No, I didn't. Although I should have, because it would've kept me from worrying." He tucked his hands into his pockets and rocked back on his heels. "I'm looking for A.L. Black."

She narrowed her eyes and squinted at him like he was a bug that needed to be squashed. "Why?"

He took a step closer. "I work for Holden Enterprises. We..." *No, not we.* "Max Holden is interested in buying this property. All of his phone calls have gone unreturned, so he sent me to find the owner."

In the blink of an eye, her demeanor shifted from guarded to combative. Her pupils narrowed to pinpoints. Her lips compressed around the sucker stick, and the rapid rise and fall of her chest had him a little concerned she might hyperventilate.

So, that's what ten feet of mad looks like.

In a completely inappropriate response to her anger, his heart rate picked up and sweat broke out on his forehead. He didn't like that he'd upset Sunny, but seeing that fiery passion—even if it was in the form of anger—cranked his damned libido into maximum overdrive.

"The property isn't for sale."

He wanted to loosen his tie to get oxygen to his burning lungs, but that would send a clear signal he was hot and bothered. And if he'd learned anything over the years, it was to never give his thoughts or feelings away. "Mr. Holden is willing to pay a generous sum. More than enough for..." He hesitated, wanting like hell to refer to A.L. as Mr. Black. But he knew, deep in his gut, he was staring straight into *Ms.* Black's gunmetal gray eyes. "The amount would be more than enough to purchase another building and move the bar elsewhere."

With slow, measured precision, Sunny stepped off the stool and stalked toward him, stopping only when they were toe to toe. Because she was so much shorter than him, she had to crane her neck back to look him in the eye, but the size difference didn't slow her down or intimidate her at all.

She threw her shoulders back and glared with unyielding determination. "You can tell Mr. Holden this property isn't, nor will it ever be, for sale. Regardless of his generous amount." The last was spat out in a way that suggested rather than offering a large sum of money, Holden Enterprises was offering her a flaming pile of dog shit.

Gavin drew in a deep breath and glanced around the cheerful kitchen. He'd looked forward to seeing Sunny's house, spending time with her, and getting to know her. This wasn't the way he envisioned it happening.

But he was here, and he needed to continue this conversation. He glanced at the inviting yellow-and-white checked pillow on the window seat. Moving toward it, he asked, "Can I sit for a minute?"

Sunny eyed her surprise visitor and debated the wisdom of allowing him to stay. Being angry didn't lessen the staggering awareness flowing between them, or the extreme pull she felt from it. Rather than being turned off, she found herself imagining how fabulously intense make-up sex would be.

As she considered the possibility, a whisper of a memory floated through her mind... *Who owns this place?*

She knew something he said last night bothered her, but she got so caught up in the magic of his mouth and hands, she forgot to go back and figure out what it was. The memory was crystal clear now.

"You used me." She jabbed a finger at his chest. "You asked me who owned the bar, but you already knew. Was your plan to get me all sexed up, then spring this on me? Did you think if you got me crazy, out of my mind, I'd be agreeable?"

Shock flashed over his face first, then anger, then a blank mask that erased all emotion. "I didn't know you were the owner until I walked into this kitchen. Last night, I thought I was sent to take notes so we could *replicate* the bar in one of our resorts. That's why I asked for the owner. I also meant to get the names of the artists, but I got a little sidetracked." His face might have been a calm mask, but his words were heavy with emotion.

His surprise at realizing she was the owner seemed sincere, but she was wary of it being an act, another attempt to get close.

Unfortunately, if that was his goal, it seemed to be working. Standing this close, his spicy masculine scent filled the air around her and seeped into her lungs. His blue eyes, looking at her with a mixture of anger and desire, heated her from the inside out. And the primal drumbeat of need still throbbed.

"No."

He cocked an eyebrow. "No?"

"No, you can't sit down."

He stilled to the point of barely breathing, and she had a brief moment of lucidity. This was where she showed him to the door and told him to never return. But the lust pumping through her veins won the battle over logic, and she heard herself say, "Not until you reach into the top cabinet and find the coffee." She shrugged and took a step back so he could move around her. "I'm a little bitchy until I've had my morning brew."

His eyes flickered with amusement and the corner of his mouth kicked into a lopsided grin. "Then by all means, let's find your coffee."

While he rummaged through the cabinet, Sunny stood off to the side, sucked on her Dum-Dum, and admired the rear view. Through the loose-fitting dress shirt, she watched his back and shoulder muscles ripple and crawl as he moved boxes and jars around. His tailored slacks fit his tight butt just right, then hung loosely on his long, muscular legs.

She worked so hard suppressing the urge to grab a handful of his spectacular ass she made herself dizzy. Or maybe it was a lack of caffeine, her highly aroused state, and Gavin sucking all the air out of the room.

After sorting and rearranging the contents of the cabinets, he turned to her with a grave expression. "I have bad news. There isn't any coffee."

She sighed and wilted into one of the kitchen chairs. "I knew you were going to say that, but the news is still devastating."

He laughed and rested a hand onto the counter. "I'd be happy to get some. Just tell me where to go."

She waved the offer off and pushed to her feet. "I'll go get it." Allowing someone else to fix her problems wasn't part of her genetic makeup.

She paused and glanced at Gavin, considering what to say or do. He came to buy her place. She said no. And yet, here he stood.

What did that mean? Was he also considering picking up where they left off last night? Easy enough, since she was barely dressed—a detail he'd definitely noticed.

"Do you mind if I go with you?" he asked.

"Why?"

He stepped forward and brushed a stray curl from her face, then gave it a tug before tucking it behind her ear. "My plan was to spend the day in Anticue. Can I start by spending part of it with you?"

How could she possibly refuse when she felt that tug in a million other places besides her scalp? So what if he was here to buy her business. She wasn't selling and nothing would change her mind, so what would be the harm in spending some time with him?

She stared at his lips and remembered the way he made her come with that wicked mouth. She closed her eyes and gulped. She really wanted to know what else he could do with that mouth. And those hands. And his...

She flipped her eyes open and met his stare. "Nothing, and I mean *nothing,* happens until I've had my coffee."

His throat bobbed as he swallowed hard, and heat blazed from his blue eyes. "I'll be waiting outside."

Gavin stepped onto the small stoop at the top of the stairs, loosened his tie, and rolled up his sleeves. The temperature must be close to eighty, which was above average for this time of year, but frigid compared to the blast-furnace heat he'd experienced in Sunny's kitchen.

The second he saw her in nothing but a T-shirt and skimpy panties, his blood had turned into a lava flow. The longer he stayed with her in the small space, the worse it got. And when she stared at his mouth like he was breakfast, he thought he would erupt. Christ, she was the sexiest woman he'd ever met, and it took every ounce of self-control he possessed to keep his hands, tongue, and dick to himself.

It was obvious that, along with her physical beauty, she possessed a sharp wit and tender heart. She was a feisty, successful businesswoman. And, after seeing her personal space, he suspected she was one of the artists who created the pieces he admired last night. The whole package triggered a primal, Neanderthalian response deep in his soul that he didn't understand.

He pressed his hands to the railing and leaned over far enough to see the beach. The property was oceanfront, but the building sat back a hundred yards from high dunes, which provided a small measure of protection from the surf and storm surge.

How had a young, single woman come to own and run this place on her own?

"You ready?"

He straightened and turned to find Sunny behind him, wearing a pink tank top, Daisy Dukes, and flip-flops. Sunglasses rested in a mass of curls piled on top of her head, and another sucker stick hung from her mouth… grape, based on the smell.

He didn't know how far they had to go, but watching her slide that sucker in and out of her mouth would undoubtedly make it the longest trip of his life.

When they reached the parking lot, Sunny headed to the far side where the Civic sat. He paused by his SUV and opened his mouth, ready to offer to drive. But when he caught a glimpse of Sunny out of the corner of his eye—hand on waist, weight shifted to one leg, massive amount of attitude—he snapped his mouth shut.

"My car may be old, but it's clean. You don't have to worry about getting your expensive suit dirty." She dropped her arm, straightened her shoulders, and kicked her chin out. "Or, you can stay here."

Gavin paused, waiting to see if she would say more. Comments like this offered valuable insight into a person's mindset and might provide useful information for re-approaching her about the sale of her property.

It also gave him insight into Sunny, the woman. And at the moment, that was most important.

Sensitivity to perceived socioeconomic differences usually developed one of two ways: a childhood of lack, or a previous life of luxury now lost. He thought of Callie and her friends. No way had Sunny grown up like them, so he was going with the first scenario.

He found the idea of her struggling, or even wanting something she couldn't have, unacceptable. His beast rose to the surface, declaring he'd take care of her. She'd never want for anything again.

Jesus, he needed to get a grip.

He cleared his throat and lifted a shoulder. "I was going to drive because it's the gentlemanly thing to do." Hoping to lighten the mood and see her smile, he added, "This coffee thing seems pretty serious. I didn't want you going into withdrawals while behind the wheel."

"Oh." Her shoulders relaxed and her chin dropped. "Sorry." Her gaze shifted from his vehicle to hers and back to his again. She worked her mouth around the sucker a few times, then said, "I think I'm already pretty close, so…" She dropped her keys into her bag and headed his way. Stopping next to him, she flashed a sheepish smile and said, "We might want to hurry."

He threw his head back and laughed. Everything about this woman was a delight, and he was happy just being in her presence. Propelled by an uncontrollable need to touch, he slung an arm around her shoulder and pulled her to him for an impromptu hug.

The press of her body against his was like slamming into a brick wall. His nuts tightened. His cock turned to granite. And his heart jumped up and grabbed him by the throat, threatening to choke the life out of him.

Jesus Christ. It was only a playful hug, but his body registered the contact as full penetration. He dropped his arm from her shoulder, stepped away, and dug into his too-tight pocket for the keys.

He was in a fuck-load of trouble. Mixing business and pleasure was a dangerous game, but it seemed unavoidable. He had no willpower where she was concerned, and if she didn't mind a little mixing, he sure as hell wouldn't.

Chapter Nine

Gavin got behind the wheel, buckled up, and cranked the ignition. The engine turned over and Metallica blasted from the speakers. "Oh, shit." He hit the power button on the radio, and the car fell into silence. "Sorry."

She stared at him, open-mouthed and wide-eyed, for a second, then burst into laughter. "Why do you look embarrassed? I play my music loud all the time."

"Yeah, well… When I'm alone it's different. I hadn't expected anyone to be with me when I got back in the car." Until last night, he'd forgotten how awesome it could be to drive down the road with the wind whipping through the car, music blaring, not a care in the world. A simple pleasure he'd recreated on the ride back to Anticue this morning.

He couldn't see through her sunglasses, but he felt her gaze on him, studying him. "You don't strike me as a Metallica person," she said.

"What would you have expected?"

"Classical."

"Classical?" He nearly choked on the word. Disgusted, he shook his head and slipped on his sunglasses. Backing out of his spot, he asked, "Which way to the coffee?"

The sucker made a popping sound as she pulled it from her mouth, drawing his attention. His gaze followed the path of her tongue as she licked the sticky residue from her lips, and his tongue pushed against the back of his teeth, wanting a shot at finishing the cleanup for her.

"Turn left out of the parking lot. We're going to the convenience store by the bridge."

He noticed the old store when he turned off the bridge, but *convenience* wasn't the descriptive word he would have used. *Decrepit. Rundown.* Maybe *condemned.*

Pulling onto Atlantic Avenue, he said, "I've worked this every way imaginable, and I can't figure out how you get Sunny from A.L.?"

From the corner of his eye, he saw her glance his way and smile. "Did you hurt anything with all the thinking?"

The thinking hadn't been painful. Seeing Sunny nearly naked and not touching her had been excruciating. "Nope." He looked at her over the top of his sunglasses. "Everything works just fine."

Her lips parted as she pulled in a breath, and he hoped like hell her thoughts were running along the same lines as his. She licked her lips before returning her gaze to the road in front of them. "My name's Aimee Lee, but my dad nicknamed me Sunny."

"It certainly seems to fit your personality."

"That's what he said." She laughed. "He also thought it was funny to mix a first name like Sunny with the last name Black."

"You must have gotten your sense of humor from him. Last night, I thought Blackout was just a clever name for a bar. When I pulled into the parking lot this morning, I made the connection between the bar name and the owner's name."

Sunny relaxed against the headrest. "Robby came up with it. I'll never forget the night he came running into the house, so eager to share his brilliance he was about to pop. I had to admit it was catchy and agreed to use it."

"How long have you owned the bar?"

"The bar's been open two years. It took us almost a full year to get the repairs and renovations made to the building before we could open."

Gavin eased into the Anticue Quickstop parking lot, and Sunny tore out of the vehicle before he cut the engine. As he lagged behind, making his way to the front door, he took in the peeling paint, rusted awnings, and non-functional gas pumps.

Max's complex would lure large chain stores and strip malls to the area, forcing small mom-and-pop businesses like this one to close. Sunny would have money from the sale of her property to start over, but owners of businesses like this would be left out in the cold.

And what about the residents who liked Anticue the way it was?

Not for the first time, a load of guilt settled on Gavin's shoulders as he considered the negative impact of doing his job well.

He pushed the store's squeaky screen door open and found Ed, one of the two older men from the Blackout, sitting behind the counter, watching Sunny pour a large cup of coffee from an industrial-sized coffee pot. The older gentleman turned an assessing gray gaze toward Gavin. After studying him for a beat, he looked back to Sunny. "I figured you must be getting low."

Sunny stopped pouring and turned to Ed, total disbelief written all over her face. "Why didn't you say something?"

"Well, I didn't think about it till yesterday, when I saw your big bag of Dum-Dums sitting here, waiting to be picked up." He paused, and a mischievous expression creased his weatherworn face. "Last night you were too busy flirting with Mr. Hot Shot for me to have a chance to mention it."

Mr. Hot Shot?

Sunny pressed her lips together, then slowly and carefully set the pot back on the burner. Gavin had the impression she was being overly cautious, afraid of slamming it down, otherwise. With full-to-the-brim coffee cup in hand, she stalked to the counter. She rested one elbow on the aged wood, then leaned over so she was nose to nose with Ed. "What about after Mr. Hot Shot left?"

"Well, by that time I'd forgotten."

Sunny drew back and shook her head. "No, you were pouting and decided to let me suffer."

"That too."

Gavin pulled a hand down his face, suppressing his laughter.

"You're spoiled. I should've never gotten you and Joe those personalized barstool covers for Christmas." She crossed her arms and tapped her toe. "What are you going to do in a few weeks when the summer crowds start coming in, and I'm not able to give you two my undivided attention anymore?"

A short, older woman ambled from a room at the back of the store. "Hey, Sunny. I thought I heard you out here. What's Ed done now?"

Sunny wrapped the other woman in a warm, affectionate embrace. "The old fart let me run out of coffee. He knew I was getting low, but he didn't warn me."

The woman sent Ed a chiding look, then turned her attention to Gavin. "You must be the young man from the bar last night."

Having grown up in a small town not far from here, Gavin knew there was no sense in being evasive. By nine o'clock this morning, every Anticue resident knew he'd been in the Blackout. They also knew he'd stayed after closing. That's where the knowledge ended, but, no doubt, each of them had chosen to create their own ending to the story. Miss Jane was difficult to read, giving no clue what outcome she'd chosen to go with. He nodded and said, "Yes, ma'am. You must be Miss Jane."

Her eyes narrowed slightly and her brow dipped. "How do you know that?"

Gavin glanced at Ed and let a slow, devilish smile crawl across his face. The old man snapped flagpole rigid and paled to a color that matched the dirty white walls. "I heard all about you last night," Gavin said, turning back to Miss Jane. "You've been married forty years, right?"

Suspicion clouded her eyes, but her mouth lifted slightly. "Almost forty-one."

Gavin knew the old man was reliving every word of the conversation in the bar last night, the part about taking a year off for good behavior clanging loud and clear. Gavin winked at Sunny, who'd also gone statue still, then turned to fully face Ed and Miss Jane.

He'd been teasing Ed in retaliation for the Mr. Hot Shot comment, but being married forty years was nothing to joke about. He grew serious, and said, "That's a long time and something to be proud of. Congratulations."

Miss Jane's demeanor once again shifted. "You think you and Sunny could make it forty years?"

Sunny gasped. "Miss Jane." Her voice was a high-pitched screech. "I can't believe you said that."

Miss Jane was a smart lady, and not someone to underestimate. Normally in situations like this, he would turn on the charm, be friendly, and get to know everyone associated with Sunny, trying to learn as much as possible about her. Even though it hadn't been intentional, his old MO had come through, and Miss Jane hadn't missed a beat in turning his charm against him.

Sunny threw Gavin an apologetic glance, then turned to the older woman. "We've only just met. He came here for business and…" Her lips tightened and her forehead creased. "His business is finished, so he'll be leaving soon."

"What kind of business?" the older couple asked simultaneously.

Since the project was still under wraps, he needed to be careful about divulging information. The public relations people were paid a lot of money to put their magical spin on things like this. Presenting the resort as good and positive and deflecting the possible negative impacts wasn't his forte, especially when he wasn't sold on the project himself. He hedged for a moment, then flat-out lied. "I work for a distributor. I came to talk to Sunny about using our products." The lie tasted like shit in his mouth, and he couldn't meet Sunny's gaze.

Without commenting further, Sunny ran to the back of the store and grabbed three containers of coffee. Dropping them onto the counter, next to the huge bag of Dum-Dums, she said, "This should last me a few weeks." She gave Ed a look that was a mixture of sweet and spicy. "If it appears I might be running low, I'd appreciate a reminder."

Clearly unconcerned by her passive-aggressiveness, the older man chuckled and shrugged. "We'll see." After tallying and bagging the items, he pulled a receipt from the register, wrote Sunny's name on the top, and dropped it into a box. "It's on your tab."

Sunny dropped the spice and poured a super-sized helping of sugar onto Ed, going so far as to bat her eyelashes dramatically. "You know, you could bring the coffee and suckers to me at the bar every couple of weeks. That way I'd never run out."

"I might could do that." He glanced to Gavin, then gave Sunny a toothy grin. "Depending on how you treat me, I'll see what I can do."

Sunny settled into the passenger seat of Gavin's SUV and drew in a deep breath. However, rather than calming her jumbled nerves, the smell of new car, warm leather, and hot Gavin stirred her inner turmoil into an increased state of agitation.

When Ed showed up tonight, she would throttle him. First, for letting her run out of coffee. Secondly, for embarrassing her—again—over Mr. Hot Shot.

"Back home?" Gavin asked, climbing behind the wheel.

"Yep." She studied his profile as he put his sunglasses on, then steered out of the lot. "Why did you lie about your business?"

The muscle in his jaw worked as he clenched his teeth together. After a long time of thinking about the simple question, he blew out a breath and said, "I didn't want to upset them. It wouldn't be prudent to spill the beans before we're ready to break ground."

"That was smart, because if your project depends on me selling, you won't be breaking ground." Okay, that sounded bitchier than she'd intended, but the coffee hadn't kicked in yet and she wanted to make sure he understood. She. Wasn't. Selling.

Ever.

He didn't respond, and they rode the rest of the way to the Blackout in silence. Gavin pulled into the same spot and put the car in park, but left the motor idling as he stared at the building in front of them. "You would make enough from the sale of this building to open another bar anywhere you wanted."

Well, shit. He hadn't understood. She grabbed her bag and climbed out of the car. Before slamming the door shut, she said, "Thanks for the ride."

The car's engine died and Gavin was hot on her heels as she rounded the back of the building and climbed the stairs. "Sunny, just listen to what I have to say. I'll even let you name your price."

Ha! Wonder what he'd say if she told him ten million dollars. She must have completely lost her mind, though, because she didn't think she'd sell for even that ridiculous amount.

She stopped and turned to face off with him. "This is more than a bar, Gavin. This is our home. There are some things money can't buy. Roots. A solid foundation. Friends." She bit her lip to stop the tirade and took a deep breath. "Robby and I poured our hearts and souls into this place. It's not for sale. And I refuse to continue this discussion any further."

Adrenaline pumped through her veins as she pushed through the kitchen door, then fought the urge to slam it in his face. Figuring he still wasn't ready to give up, she tore a chunk out of the brown paper bag, grabbed a Sharpie, and in huge, clearly legible letters wrote: NOT FOR SALE!

He'd followed her into the kitchen and was standing by the door, hands stuffed into his front pockets, watching her. She held the note up to his face and said, "Read it out loud."

Gavin looked at the note, then pinched the bridge of his nose and pressed his lips together. She got the distinct impression he was trying not to laugh.

When he didn't answer, she rattled the paper under his nose. He shook his head and, holding back most of his laughter, said, "Not for sale."

"Good. One more time. With feeling."

This time, laughter filled his words as he said, "Not for sale."

"Okay." She pressed the paper to his chest and waited for him to take hold before letting go. "We clear now?"

He didn't reply, but as she turned her back on him to unpack the bag, she heard the paper methodically crinkling, like he was folding it. Good, maybe he'd keep it to take back to his boss as her final offer.

She needed a cigarette in the worst way. Rather than caving—only because she didn't have any—she grabbed a butterscotch Dum-Dum and popped it in her mouth.

"What's with the suckers?"

"I used Dum-Dum's to quit smoking. Now I can't quit the damn suckers." She jammed the coffee into the cabinet and refilled the dangerously low sucker jar. Running out of coffee had been bad. Running out of Dum-Dums would spell disaster. Moving around him to throw the empty bag into the trashcan, she said, "I swear, I put something in my mouth one time, and I'm addicted. I think I have oral fixation issues."

The humor dissolved from his eyes and his body tensed. "That's a dangerous thing to say to a man."

She hadn't meant the comment to be leading or provocative, but as the tension crackled around them and his eyes grew smoky, all kinds of images rushed to mind. "I guess that did sound kind of bad, didn't it?"

"I didn't say it was bad. I said it was dangerous." His voice was a low, suggestive purr, and his gaze dropped to her mouth. "Maybe that's why you like kissing so much."

She was still pissed, but that incessant pulsing need for him hammered away at the anger and turned it into something else. Something hot, intense, and consuming.

She stepped toward him, but then stopped. He denied knowing she was the owner last night, but what if he was lying? As the magnetic pull between them grew stronger, she wondered if it mattered. Explosive attraction like this couldn't be faked. And it didn't come around every day. Why not enjoy it while she had the chance?

"I've said I'm not selling, but you're still here. Why?" The breathy wisp to her voice made her sound desperate. But hell, she supposed when it came to him she was.

His jaw popped as if he was chewing the question over... or fighting an internal battle. His eyes said he was sticking around for personal reasons, and she boldly glanced down at his slacks, hoping to find confirmation of his interest.

Oh, yeah. A big checkmark on the interest.

"That's a damned good question," he said before turning to look out the window.

She waited for further clarification, but none came.

Uncomfortable with the awkward silence, she said, "Do you want to go for a walk on the beach, or...?" She looked at his strong profile, the flexing muscles in his shoulders and back, and the pulse pounding in his neck. She'd never been this bold, but he made her want to step out of her comfort zone and ask for things she never had the courage to request in the past. With sweating palms and a heart pounding so loudly she could hear its steady whoosh in her ears, she stepped next to him and blurted out, "We could pick up where we left off last night."

Gavin's eyes squeezed shut and his face scrunched up like he was in physical pain.

Okay... So not the reaction she'd hoped for. "I'm sorry," she said, crossing her arms over her stomach and taking a step backward. "I shouldn't have been so forward. I just thought—"

In the blink of an eye, Gavin had her in a tight grip by the elbows, an intense, scary-as-hell look on his face. "You make me crazy. I don't think I can say no to you, even though I should. I was sent here to do a job, and sleeping with you isn't going to make that job easier. But you zap all of my willpower, and the illogical suddenly seems to make perfect sense."

He wrapped his arms around her and pulled her so tightly against him she could barely breathe. Resting his chin on top of her head, he said, "I want to make love to you so badly my entire body feels like it's going up in flames. But when I get out of your bed, I'm still going to try to talk you into selling. Can you handle that?"

That was an easy answer. "Yes. You can talk until you're blue in the face, but I won't change my mind. So, really, there's no problem. Your *business* is over."

He closed his eyes and released a long breath. "It's not that easy. You don't know Max Holden. He won't stop until he's gotten this property."

Sunny smiled. "He doesn't know Sunny Black."

Gavin laughed. "You've got a point."

"So..." She pulled back slightly and glanced away. "Does that mean...?"

Gavin held her chin and turned her head, forcing her to look at him. His dark blue gaze, filled with heat and desire, settled on her mouth. A breath passed between them before he dipped his head and kissed her softly. Drawing back just enough to speak, he asked, "Sex on the beach?"

Chapter Ten

*N*ot wanting to give him time to change his mind, Sunny grabbed Gavin's hand and sprinted toward the bedroom. "I don't want to chance Robby walking in on us. Normally, he isn't home until late afternoon. But since he has a test today, I don't know how long he'll be."

As she reached her bedroom doorway a neon sign flashed in her mind: CONDOMS.

She stopped and pivoted on her heel so abruptly Gavin didn't have time to stop and they collided. Before she toppled over backward, Gavin wrapped an arm around her waist and steadied her. "Change your mind?"

"Oh, hell no." The press of his body against hers added to her desperation, and nothing would stop her from having Gavin this time. She slipped out of his arms and backtracked to Robby's room. "Be right back."

Even though she'd never searched his room for condoms, she was confident... well, hopeful, he had a stash. Protection was something she'd preached relentlessly, and she had to believe he'd be prepared in the event he got lucky. Who would have believed she'd be looking for one in the event *she* got lucky.

She rummaged through his bedside table and found an unopened box. Well, crap, so much for sneaking one. Or two. She thought it over for a second, then grabbed the entire box and ran back to her bedroom. Hopefully, she could replace the box before he realized it was missing.

Gavin was standing next to her bed, waiting for her to return. At the sight of her holding the box in the air like a running back that just scored the winning touchdown, Gavin broke into laughter that echoed off the walls of her small room.

She knew he wasn't laughing *at* her, but she still felt the need to defend her aggressiveness. "I don't seduce men I meet in the bar. Ever."

His laughter faded into a soft, warm smile, and he nodded once. "I believe you."

As she drew closer, she slowed her pace and considered how different her bedroom looked with Gavin filling a chunk of the space. The large chest-of-drawers she'd always considered too big for the small room seemed to shrink to the size of an end table. Since the double bed didn't have a headboard, or a footboard, she always thought it looked smaller than an average bed, but today, it looked like a cot.

She'd never put much thought into the room's furnishings, viewing it like the other furniture in her house—function over appearance. Now, she wished her room had more life and pizzazz and definitely something to make it more romantic.

But with Gavin looking at her through the thick fringe of his lashes, heat and desire evident in his hooded expression, she supposed it didn't really matter what the room and furnishings looked like.

"I've never met anyone who's affected me the way you do." Her nerves were getting the better of her, making her ramble. And her heart was planting itself on her sleeve, in wide-open view. "What little bit I slept last night, I dreamt of you. The rest of the time, I tossed and turned, thinking about you." She shrugged. "I guess you're too hot to be forgotten."

He grinned and dropped his head, appearing embarrassed by the compliment. When he lifted his gaze from the floor, his eyes were heavy lidded and filled with a hunger that made her tremble.

He wrapped an arm around her waist and pulled her to him. "Feel that?" It was impossible to miss the prominent erection pressing into her stomach, but he rocked his hips into her for emphasis.

He brushed a wisp of hair from her face and dropped his forehead to hers. "That's what you do to me. I'm like an out-of-control teenager. In the shower this morning, I imagined you were there with me." He nipped at her ear, then nibbled a path down her neck. "It was your hands on me... stroking me."

His words and the mental image of him pleasuring himself snapped the last thread of her control. Enough talking about what they did to each other mentally, it was time to get busy physically. She pushed him backward until his legs hit the bed. Playing along, he toppled over and landed spread eagle across the mattress. His long, muscular body stretched taut, and his gaze grew hotter as he watched and waited for her to make the next move.

All this prime hunk of man... where to start... where to start...

She dropped the box of condoms on the bed, then crawled next to him. She felt like a cat, filled with the urge to rub up against him, while kneading his flesh with her short nails. She straddled his thighs and aligned her sex with the hard ridge of his erection.

He closed his eyes and sank his teeth into his lower lip as a groan vibrated up from his chest. A sharp, hard thrust of his hips had her whispering, "Oh, God," as she let her head fall back and rode the sensations rolling through her body.

More. She wanted more. But she also wanted to take things slowly and make this last. She ran her palms up his sides, feeling the ridges of muscle and rib as she made the journey. When she reached his neck, she stretched out on top of him and drew in a deep breath. "You smell good."

She rested her palms on his pecs, lifted her weight from his chest, and ground her sex against his, riding him as if they were already joined. "And you feel amazing."

An unintelligible grunt passed his lips, and she smiled. Rendering a man incapable of speech was heady stuff. Standard missionary position had never given her this kind of sexual confidence or prowess, and she liked the accompanying surge of power.

She slid his tie through her fingers, enjoying the soft, sensual feel of the silk. Carefully, she loosened the knot, then wrapped the fabric around her fist and pulled it free of his shirt. "Hmmm... this might come in handy later."

His eyes flared in anticipation, and he slipped his hands under the hem of her tank top. "Stop that," she said, smacking at his hands as she sat up and slid back out of reach. "I can't concentrate with you touching me."

He grinned and let his arms fall to the bed. "Yes, ma'am." His gaze settled on her breasts. "You aren't wearing your necklace." The raw edge to his voice and the intermittent, seemingly involuntary thrust of his hips further bolstered her courage.

"No," she said, fumbling with the buttons of his shirt. "I only wear it at night."

His throat bobbed with a hard swallow. "Why haven't you pierced your nipples?"

She drew in on herself and shuddered. "Just the thought of it makes me light-headed. I'm a huge wimp. No way could I handle that."

"You have a tattoo," he said, glancing at her wrist.

"There's a big difference between a tattoo and piercing. Especially a nipple piercing." She bit her lip and grinned. "Plus, I had a tattoo artist friend who overlooked the competent and coherent thing. Otherwise, I wouldn't have had the guts for the tattoo either." She stopped struggling with the buttons with a huff. "I give up. You need to undo these or I'm going to get frustrated and rip your shirt off."

While he undid the buttons, she thought about her necklaces. He obviously liked them, and she liked the way they felt. Deciding to put one on while he finished unbuttoning his shirt, she shifted her weight, preparing to slide off him.

He grabbed her thighs and held her in place. "Where are you going?"

"To put on a necklace."

He shook his head and brushed a wild tendril of hair from her face. "Later. I don't want you going anywhere right now." He crooked his finger, and as strong and independent as she was, it never occurred to her to refuse the command. He wrapped his large hand around the back of her head and pulled her mouth to his. It took a matter of seconds for her to learn that being on top didn't give her *all* the power. Gavin still controlled the kisses.

When she'd been reduced to a quivering pile of mush, he slipped his hands under the hem of her top and pushed it up to her neck. Clips flew out of her hair, and a tangled mass of curls fell around her face and over her shoulders as he pulled the top off and tossed it to the side. As he rubbed the ends of her hair between his fingers, his face held such a soft, tender expression it knocked the breath from her lungs and made her heart cramp.

Warning buzzers rang in her brain. Anytime the heart felt something, things got complicated and dangerous. That would be especially true in this case, because she didn't *really* know if Gavin was friend or foe.

But she didn't want to think about that now. She didn't want to think about anything; she only wanted to feel. "Will you *please* get rid of your shirt? I need to feel your skin against mine."

"Yes, ma'am."

She cocked her head to the side and eyed him suspiciously. "What's up with all the ma'aming?"

"You seem to enjoy being in charge, so we're doing this your way." He winked and the corner of his mouth lifted. "This time."

Sunny had only been on top once, and the whole experience had lasted two minutes, maybe less. Her high school boyfriend hadn't been the King of Stamina, or originality. Since him… more of the same, but with different names.

Being a professional dominatrix would never be in her future, but controlling Gavin turned her on in a major way. The wicked thought was followed by the urge to hide her face so he couldn't read her mind. Even though the inclination to look away was strong, she forced herself to meet his gaze and in a stern voice commanded, "Take that shirt off. Now."

His eyes fired and his nostrils flared. "Can't wait for my turn to be in charge…"

A thousand butterflies took flight in her stomach, and a tremble wracked her body. Keeping herself in the present moment, she scooted further down on his legs and began loosening his belt buckle.

Her efforts were derailed when he slowly and deliberately slipped his shirt buttons free, then sat up just enough to slide the shirt off his shoulders. *Damn.* His incredible abs and the sprinkling of dark hair covering his chest snagged her attention, and she quickly abandoned the belt in favor of a new toy.

Fascinated by the texture of his skin and the hard muscle beneath, she smoothed her palms over the ridges of his stomach, then moved on to the soft and gently curling chest hair.

He lay back to unfasten his pants, but when she tweaked his nipple, he hissed and his fingers froze on the button of his slacks. He flipped his gaze to hers and said, "You get rid of your shorts, I'll get rid of my pants, and we'll get where we want to go a whole hell of a lot faster."

Ten seconds later, he was in boxer briefs, lying on the bed with his arms by his sides, patiently awaiting her next command. If not for the rapid pounding of his heart and the harsh rise and fall of his chest, she would have taken his stillness for disinterest. But he wasn't unaffected, and she realized he was actually expending a lot of energy to remain still and impassive.

She'd taken her panties off with her shorts and wondered why he hadn't removed his underwear with his slacks. But as she sat next to him, completely naked, she appreciated the building anticipation and tension. With trembling fingers, she slowly pulled the waistband down.

His cock sprang free and a single drop of moisture glistened at the tip, beckoning her to lick it away. Her mouth watered, and she slicked her tongue over her lower lip.

As she lowered her head, his eyes turned to midnight, and he gave a short, hard shake of his head. "No. You put your mouth on me, I'll shoot off in less than thirty seconds. I'm too far gone."

Staying in dominatrix mode, she worked up a stern face and said, "I thought I was in charge."

"You are." He wrapped his hand around her calf and slowly massaged his way northward. "But if you want to keep me in the game, you'll keep your mouth above the waist." He grinned. "Above the neck would probably be best." With a quick, playful slap on the ass, he added, "For now, anyway."

She definitely wanted to keep him in the game. "Okay, we'll do things your way this time. But later…"

Would they have a later? And why was she speaking in terms of *later* and *this time* when this was supposed to be a one-time thing?

Unwilling to spoil the moment, she grabbed the box of condoms and ripped it open. She took one out, looked at it, then handed it to him. "I want to watch you put this on."

She never would have believed watching a man touch himself would be such a turn-on. But by the time he'd lost the boxer briefs and finished rolling the condom into place, she was nearly frantic. Hovering over him, she slowly lowered herself until the tip of him met her soaking wet sex. The plan had been to taunt and tease and prolong the anticipation until he reached a fever pitch that matched hers. But her control disintegrated, and she couldn't wait another second.

She cried out from an overload of sensations as she dropped onto him in one fluid motion. He was larger—and she was tighter—than she'd anticipated. She froze, allowing her body to adjust to his size and giving her neurons a chance to catch up with the feelings attacking her body from the inside out.

"Okay?" His voice was soft, almost a whisper, as he studied her face.

"Oh, yeah." She rose until he'd almost slipped free, then slowly slid down again.

He allowed her to control the depth and pace, but no longer remained impassive. He massaged her breasts with large, capable—*Good God*—talented fingers and hands. As she increased the pace of her rise and fall, he increased the pressure on her nipples, first rolling, then pinching them between his thumbs and fingers. The sensation was similar, only better, to that of her necklaces, and a firestorm sparked in her belly.

She leaned forward and rested her palms on his chest. The change in position created a delicious friction against her clit, and in a matter of seconds, she was spiraling out of control.

He closed his eyes, ground his teeth together, and drew in deep, harsh breaths. When he opened his eyes again, they were the color of summer storm clouds. "This isn't going to last much longer. You feel too damned good."

He dropped a hand to her clit while the other lavished her breast with attention. Within seconds, the simmering heat in her abdomen erupted into an inferno, and she screamed as an explosion of energy blasted through every cell of her body. Right there with her, he rammed into her one last time, then rode the waves of his orgasm.

Struggling to breathe in short, jerky gasps, she collapsed onto his chest as the microbursts continued. Strong, protective arms wrapped tightly around her, and soft, gentle kisses fell on her head. It seemed like hours passed before her breathing and heart rate returned to normal and her bone density returned.

Nodding to the closed door on the right side of the room, he asked, "Is that the bathroom?"

"Yeah." She summoned the strength to roll off him and landed on the mattress with a thud. "Towels and washcloths are in the wicker rack on the wall. Help yourself to whatever you need."

A moment later, he returned with a washcloth and towel. "Spread 'em, sweetheart." His eyes gleamed with humor, but his tone was kind and his actions gentle.

As he carefully wiped her clean, then patted her dry, a lump of emotion formed in her chest and rose to her throat. No one had ever taken care of her after sex. Hell, no one had ever taken care of her in any situation, and his thoughtfulness touched her deeply.

She swatted the gushy feelings away like a pesky mosquito. Dammit, she couldn't make more of this than it was. It was sex. Plain and simple. Nothing more.

While her head understood the rules of engagement, her heart didn't seem to grasp the danger. She and her heart would need to have a serious talk about this later.

Chapter Eleven

Gavin wrapped the washcloth in the towel and laid them in the sink before returning to Sunny's bed. Wanting to extend what he considered a perfect moment for as long as possible, he wrapped his arms around her and pulled her close.

Snuggled with Sunny, listening to the waves rolling on shore, was the most tranquil environment he could imagine. But his thoughts were unsettled and whirled like the ceiling fan overhead. He *should* crawl out of the bed, explain what a terrible mistake this had been—even though he didn't believe it—and haul ass back to Myrtle Beach.

Instead, he rested his cheek on top of her head and drew in a deep breath. The smell of her strawberry shampoo reminded him of her suckers, and a smile tugged at his mouth. How could a woman be so sexy and adorably cute at the same time?

He laced his fingers through hers and massaged her palm with the pad of his thumb. Her breath fanned across his chest as she softly sighed. The pleasure he took from doing something for her, even something as simple as massaging her hand, was enormous.

And ridiculous.

And scary as shit.

He *thought* he was in trouble before. Now, he *knew* it. Every moment spent with her was like quicksand, pulling him in deeper and deeper. And yet, here he lay, allowing himself to be swallowed whole.

He rubbed the calluses on her hands—proof of the hard work she put into renovating the building. And the equally hard work required to maintain the building, as well as run the bar on a daily basis.

Without knowing her history, he couldn't say for sure, but he suspected they were more alike than their current circumstances indicated. As a boy, he spent a lot of hot, hard, seemingly endless days working on his grandfather's farm. Crazy as it sounded, sometimes he missed the physical labor and the satisfaction that came from building something from nothing. He regularly worked out in his home gym and enjoyed the exertion, but that wasn't the same as using his body to fulfill a purpose.

He studied the tattoo wrapped around her wrist. "My Latin is rusty. What does your tat say?"

She lifted her head from his shoulder and smiled. "Never give up."

His bark of laughter combined with a sharp exhale of disbelief. "Are you kidding me?"

"Nope. It's a constant reminder that's served me well over the years." She rested her head back on his shoulder and finger-combed his chest hair. "You can tell your boss he'll never win, and I've got the tattoo to prove it."

He sighed and scooted up so he could lean against the wall. He hated to lose this moment of post-coital bliss, but he might as well use the opening she gave him. "Tell me about this bar. Why are you so firm in your resolve to keep it?"

She scooted up next to him and pulled the sheet with her. "Can we have this conversation dressed and with food? I haven't eaten since early last evening, and I'm starving."

"That's probably a good idea." He smiled and took another moment to admire the splendor of a mostly naked Sunny. "I'm not sure how much talking we'd get done sitting in bed. Naked."

Her gaze traveled down his chest to his lap, then back to his neck. Despite what she'd said, her thoughts were revealed in the way her eyelids dipped as she sank her teeth into her lower lip. As much as he liked the idea, more sex wasn't going to fix the problem. It would only complicate things further, so he crawled out from under the sheet and pulled on his pants.

"Can you hang out for a few minutes while I take a shower?" she asked.

"Sure." He leaned over to kiss her forehead and once again found himself lost in her eyes. In the bright sunlight, they changed from silver to a pale, pale blue. The longer he stared, the more fascinated he became. When the expression buried in them went from why-the-hell-are-you-staring-at-me to crawl-back-into-bed-with-me, he took a deep breath and stepped back.

He could easily stay in bed with Sunny for days. But that wouldn't settle anything, and she was hungry. "If you're okay with me rummaging through your kitchen, I'll fix you lunch while you shower."

Her face lit up with a smile that turned him inside out. "Why would I mind?" She crawled out of bed and swung her way to the bathroom. "What girl doesn't dream of having a man cook for her?"

When Gavin was finally able to pull his gaze away from her naked ass—because she shut the bathroom door and blocked his view—he scrubbed a hand over his face, then headed to the kitchen. He couldn't change millions of years of genetic coding, but he was thoroughly disgusted with the primal beast roaring to the surface... taking great pleasure in fixing his woman something to eat. No, he wasn't out bludgeoning something to death with a club, but he was still preparing her a life-sustaining meal, and that was highly gratifying.

The Neanderthalian part of his brain may be no larger than a speck of dust, but it recognized, the moment Sunny called him Romeo and blasted him for his inappropriate drink requests, his life had jumped off the track.

The larger part of his brain, the one he used on a daily basis for logic and reasoning, was beginning to have its doubts that he'd ever find the old track again.

Sunny showered and dressed, then went in search of something more appropriate for Gavin to wear to the beach. Taking their food outside seemed to be the best option. She wanted to strip and lick and suck him like one of her Dum-Dums and didn't trust herself to behave if they stayed within the confines of her apartment.

He and Robby were about the same height, but whereas Robby was still boyishly thin, Gavin seriously outweighed him in muscle. After rummaging through all of Robby's drawers, she settled on a large T-shirt and a pair of running shorts she thought might work. She had no idea what size shoes Gavin wore, but hey, he was at the beach. He could go barefoot.

She carried the shorts and T-shirt to the kitchen, where she found Gavin looking completely at home. This was getting out of hand and no longer felt like a one-time fling. Especially since she'd been trying to figure out ways to keep him around. "Are you okay with having a picnic on the beach?"

He gave her the beautiful smile that transformed his face from harsh to handsome. "Sure." He cut a sandwich in half, then stacked it on a plate with two others. "Do you have any sandwich bags?"

"Yeah, but I'll finish this up." She held the clothes out to him. "I thought these might be more comfortable than your dress clothes."

He swallowed hard as he looked at the clothes, and for a second, she didn't think he would take them. His eyes softened and his mouth curled in a smile. Reaching for the clothes, he said, "You make it tough on a guy. How am I supposed to go back to work after this?"

Yeah, well, if he didn't want to go back to work today, that was okay with her. He wouldn't hassle her about selling her property. And she'd have more time to explore his body.

While Gavin changed, Sunny packed the sandwiches into her seldom-used picnic basket. They looked and smelled great, but sandwiches alone didn't a picnic make. She tossed in a bag of chips, then dug around in the fridge until she found a bunch of grapes.

With her head stuck in the refrigerator, she yelled, "What would you like to drink? Your choices are Pepsi and water. Or we can go down to the bar and get something."

She heard him coming through the living room and glanced up in time to see the T-shirt fall over his head, then slowly crawl down his chest and stomach. Gavin in a suit was sexy. Gavin barefoot, wearing running shorts and a T-shirt that hugged his broad chest and shoulders was freaking fantastic. She chewed on her bottom lip and once again debated the merits of food versus sex.

He leaned in close and whispered, "If you keep looking at me like that, we'll never get out of here." He reached around her for a bottle of water, then backed away. "Where's a blanket?"

She gulped and nodded toward the hallway. "In the closet." Shaking her head to get herself back in the game, she grabbed a Pepsi, a couple bottles of water, and a handful of Dum-Dums.

Gavin returned with the quilted blanket flipped over his shoulder, picked up the basket, then opened the door. "Lead the way."

The path across the dunes took them past the old Anticue pier, with its rusted roof, peeling paint, and missing shutters. "I've heard rumors that a group of investors were going to buy this, make the necessary repairs, and reopen it." She shrugged. "Far as I know, though, no one's gone through with the purchase."

Gavin sighed and wrapped his arm around her shoulder.

"What's with the sigh? It would be great to have that old building refurbished and reopened."

Gavin nodded and the muscle in his jaw jerked. "Yeah, it would. But that's not the investor's plan."

"How do you…? Oh. Your boss is the one who's buying it." Rather than a question, the words came out as a nasty-sounding accusation. "Why does he want to buy all this property, anyway?"

"He wants to build a resort."

Relief blasted through her and exited in a nearly hysterical laugh. "Then he's wasting his time. And yours. We have ordinances to prevent things like that from being built. This is a non-issue." Happier by the second, she pointed to a spot between two vacant summer homes. "Is that okay?"

He opened his mouth, as if he had more to say on the subject, but then snapped it closed and shrugged. "Sure."

He set the basket down before wandering along the water's edge while she spread the blanket on the soft sand. Kicking at the wet sand, with his hands tucked into his pockets, he looked like a sad little boy who'd lost his best friend, and the urge to comfort him was overwhelming.

Stupid. Stupid. Stupid. Not the appropriate reaction to someone who was nothing more than a fling. Whatever was bothering him, he'd have to deal with on his own. Resolve in place, she unpacked the basket and waited for him to make his way back to her.

Without saying a word, he sat across from her, then pulled a grape from the bunch. Looking at her through the dark fringe of his lashes, he brushed the grape against her lower lip and said, "Open up."

The grape was cool, his fingers warm, as she drew them into her mouth. His breathing quickened, and her heart raced as she stroked her tongue over his thumb and forefinger before flicking the fruit free of his grasp.

He drew in a shuddering breath and slowly withdrew his fingers. "Do you know how incredibly sexy you are?"

She chewed the grape and contemplated his question. "I like to *feel* sexy. That's why I wear the necklaces. But I don't think of myself as *being* sexy."

"Well, you are." He handed her a sandwich. "You better feed yourself. Anymore of that and your lunch will go by the wayside… like breakfast."

She drew in a deep breath and savored the fragrant aroma of chicken and peppers wafting from the sandwich bag. "This smells wonderful. What is it?"

He'd been watching her reaction and, seemingly pleased with the response, grabbed another sandwich for himself. He leaned back on his elbow and kicked his legs out in front. "Chicken salad. Sort of."

"Sort of?" She pulled off the top piece of bread and studied the sandwich. He'd shredded leftover chicken, added salad dressing, diced green and red peppers and onion. Impressive. She replaced the top slice and took a bite.

Her eyes drifted shut as she savored the flavors mingling on her tongue. "This is really good." She opened her eyes and took another bite. "Would you mind telling me exactly how you made it? This would be a great, easy-to-make addition to our menu."

He slid a glance her way and winked. "We can probably work something out." After eating in silence for a few minutes, he asked, "Where are you from, originally?"

She took a drink of her Pepsi and considered this getting-to-know-you business. Sex was one thing. Getting to know each other on a personal level seemed dangerous to her emotional wellbeing.

She started things with him as a one-night fling, which turned into a one-night-and-one-morning, scorching-hot fling. At this point, she could still walk away and be fine. Mostly. But what if, in the process of learning more about him, she accidentally fell for him? As strong as her attraction to him was, she could easily see that happening.

She decided to be cautious. She'd share a little, but not reveal too much. "I'm from Randall, West Virginia." No one knew where Randall was. And, based on his blank expression, he didn't either. "It's a little town halfway between Charleston and Pittsburgh." She pulled off a bite of sandwich and popped it into her mouth. "What about you?"

"I was born in Virginia, but grew up outside of New Bern." Shadows dulled his eyes as his gaze shifted to the ocean's horizon. Before she could ask about the sadness she sensed in him, he said, "Why did you leave West Virginia?"

"I wanted to live someplace warm." Where even if they had no heat in the house, or she was forced to sleep in the car, she wouldn't have to worry about freezing to death. "When I first left home, I went to Myrtle Beach. I didn't want to go any further south because it was too far away from Robby." She watched a wave roll onshore and thought back. Life had never been a cakewalk, but leaving Robby almost killed her.

"What about your parents?"

"Mom subscribed to Ed's theory of time off for good behavior. In her case, she only waited ten years, not forty. And rather than taking a year off, she took a lifetime. Dad wasn't a bad father, and he did the best he could. But after Mom left, everything pretty much went to shit."

She rolled a loose grape around on the blanket. "Dad worked in the coal mines, usually pulling double shifts for the overtime wages. But there never seemed to be enough money. We were always being forced to move from place to place. Each worse than the one before.

"I hung around for a year after graduation, trying to work and help Dad pay the bills. And help raise Robby." She pulled off a piece of her sandwich, but had lost the desire to eat. "There aren't any good paying jobs in the area, so I had to do something. For Robby and me. I left Robby with Dad and prayed he'd be okay until I could get back to get him."

She could still see the tears streaming down his face the day she told him she had to leave. "I packed my car and left for Myrtle Beach, promising to come back for him as soon as I could. I waited tables, learned the bar business, and put away as much money as possible. Summer months were great, and I made a killing in tips and wages. Winter months were lean, but I still managed to sock away enough that I was comfortable going back for Robby a year and a half later." She pushed her fingers through her hair. "God, it was so hard being away from him for that long. Always wondering if he was okay."

She stopped talking and cleared her throat. Shit, so much for not being too revealing.

Gavin had stopped eating and was watching her closely. The intensity of his stare, and the pity behind it, made her uncomfortable. "I'm not telling you any of this because I want your sympathy. In fact, pity is not accepted. Period." She'd had enough of it from her teachers and classmates to last ten lifetimes. "I'm telling you this so you'll understand what that building means to us. It isn't just a bar. It's our home. Other than Robby, it's the most important thing in my life."

His angular features sharpened and his brow dipped low in a frown. "It's not pity, Sunny. It's awe." His expression softened. "Robby's lucky to have you. I don't know many people who…" He stared off into the distance and chewed on the inside of his cheek. "Only a special person would sacrifice themselves the way you have for Robby." He frowned again and grew agitated. "I hope he appreciates all you've done for him."

She shrugged off the compliment. "I love Robby; it wasn't a sacrifice."

He ate a few chips, then took a drink of water. "How did you end up in Anticue?"

"Myrtle Beach was okay, but we wanted to live someplace smaller. Someplace like Randall. We stayed in Myrtle Beach until Robby graduated high school. By that time, we'd saved enough for a down payment on the property. We traveled back and forth, both of us working our *real* jobs as much as possible, then coming here and working on the building during our time off."

She searched Gavin's face for understanding. "Do you understand why I'll never sell that building? It's the first house, or anything for that matter, that Robby and I have had that was ours. We worked and scraped and saved and busted our asses, not only to open the bar, but to have a decent place to live." She stiffened her spine and squared her shoulders with renewed determination. "No one is going to take it away from us." She locked eyes with him to drive her point home. "No one."

Chapter Twelve

Gavin scrubbed a hand down his face, then pulled a long drink from the water bottle, wishing like hell it was a bottle of Crown. He thought he was in a tough spot in Sunny's kitchen this morning.

Fuck that. *Now* his ass was jammed between a rock and a hard place.

Many people grew bitter and disenchanted with life after struggling the way Sunny had. But through it all, she maintained her bright, cheerful spirit, laughing and smiling with ease. He admired her grit and determination and especially her unwavering loyalty and love for her brother. As she picked at her sandwich, he studied her tattoo. Life forced her to adopt a never-give-up attitude, and she was right, it served her well.

Unfortunately, Max lived by the same rule.

Gavin reached across the blanket and stroked her leg. "Max has already invested too much to let your... stubborn"—he smiled—"yet admirable determination stop him."

"What do you mean 'invested too much?'" Her steely gaze cut him to the core. "No one has invested anything in this property but me and Robby."

He nodded to the old pier. "He's already purchased all the property surrounding yours." *And a few county officials.* He brushed a lock of hair off her shoulder and stroked her cheek with the back of his hand.

"You're forgetting about the island's ordinances."

Gavin stuffed his sandwich bag into the cooler, then watched the waves. "I don't think that's going to be an issue."

"Why not?"

He didn't know why, but he hesitated to tell her about the bought-and-paid-for commissioners. Maybe it was because he didn't have proof of those transactions. Or maybe, because Anticue was a small place, he feared she knew some of them. Given Sunny's feisty personality, she was likely to go knocking down doors to confront them. Not a bad idea at a later time, but a terrible idea at the moment.

When he didn't answer, she lifted her chin and tossed her shoulders back. "I don't even know why we're still discussing this. I own this property, and no one can make me sell."

True enough, in theory. Not in practice. "Max will make your life hell until you give in."

Anger vibrated from her, but her voice was low and calm. "I've lived through hell before. I never planned to repeat the experience. But I survived the first time. I can do it again."

He didn't like that her life had been difficult, and thinking about Max making it rough again made him crazy. Anger and frustration pushed at his temples until he thought his head would explode.

A lot of his frustration came from knowing exactly how Sunny felt. He was ten when his parents disappeared. He remembered the overwhelming feelings of helplessness and loneliness, at least, prior to his granddad selflessly moving him to the farm and promising to always keep Gavin safe.

His granddad had sacrificed everything for him, like Sunny did for Robby. While the small farm his grandfather owned didn't bring in a lot of money, they had each other and a comfortable home. As an adult, Gavin busted his ass to make sure his grandfather was able to keep the farm. He would have fought like hell if someone tried to take it away from them.

Guilt punched him in the gut with the reminder he didn't visit his grandfather nearly as much as he should. Hell, he didn't even call like he should. But Granddad never complained. He just accepted Gavin's excuses with total understanding.

And really, that's all they were. Excuses. At first, he was busy working his way through college. Then he was busy climbing the ladder at Holden Enterprises. He was so wrapped up in himself he lost touch with the person who mattered the most.

He had a nagging suspicion if he looked real close, he'd also find he lost touch with himself, as well as the values instilled in him as a child. But it wasn't the time to start dissecting his life. He had more pressing things to worry about.

It seemed they'd both lost their appetite, and he was getting restless. He thought through problems and found solutions better when moving; he needed to walk. "What's down that way?" he asked, pointing toward the far end of the island.

"More of what's right here. A few houses and beach." Her body language was still stiff and guarded, but her voice was calm and impassive.

Gavin stood and offered her his hand. "Show me."

While they walked in silence, he took the time to appreciate the natural beauty and peaceful solitude of Anticue. It was beautiful now, but when the resort was built, the beach would be crawling with people and the dunes would be damaged, despite warnings to stay off of them.

From the corner of his eye, he watched Sunny work a Dum-Dum around and around and around. He figured she was rolling this situation around in her mind at the same frantic pace she was wearing out the candy. He imagined her fortifying her mental walls, figuring out all the angles to make sure her home and business were untouchable.

The same thing he'd be doing if the situation were reversed.

After walking for what seemed like a week, they turned and headed back toward her place. "When did you move to North Carolina?" It was the first time either of them had spoken since they started walking, and her question startled him.

Satisfying an annoying craving for constant contact with her, he took her hand and laced their fingers together. "I was ten."

She swiveled her head so she could see him and waited for more information. Apparently, she wasn't satisfied with the simple answer and was willing to stare him down until she got more.

He wasn't used to sharing anything about himself, especially not this part of his life, and a lump formed in his chest, blocking the words. "My parents…" His voice cracked like a prepubescent teen, and he had to clear his throat and start over. "My parents disappeared in a boating accident when I was ten. After that, my grandfather moved me to his farm."

"You don't look like a guy raised on a farm."

Her words weren't derogatory, but his brain registered them as such. Half afraid to ask but curious enough to risk it, he said, "Okay, I'll bite. What do I look like?"

She didn't immediately answer, and the longer she studied him, the more his gut twisted with unease. He never worried what others thought, and it surprised him to realize how much her answer meant.

"The farmers I know don't wear designer suits and shoes."

As he considered her words, he tried to understand the agitation he felt over this ridiculous subject.

She tugged on his fingers and smiled. "It's not a bad thing. You just don't look like a farmer."

True enough, he supposed, but her answer still irked him. They stopped and grabbed the picnic gear, then headed back to Sunny's. As they approached the house, Gavin saw Robby's Ford Ranger in the parking lot.

"Well, shit," Sunny said, as her shoulders slumped forward.

Gavin raised an eyebrow. "Excuse me?" Maybe she was thinking like him and planned on sex for dessert. But with Robby home, that was probably off the menu.

She pointed to the parking lot. "Robby's home." She gasped, then tensed. "Oh shit! Robby's home."

Jesus, he knew her brother didn't like him, but he didn't think it should cause her this much distress.

Panic settled over her features. "I left the box of condoms on the bed, and your clothes are in my bedroom."

Gavin bit his lip to keep from smiling. "How old are you?"

She cringed. "I know it's ridiculous to feel like a teenager who's gotten caught making out with her boyfriend while her parents were gone. But I've never had a man over, or had to deal with this situation before."

Several things about that statement stood out and caused a stir of emotion in his gut. She said last night she hadn't been with anyone in three years, and this supported that claim. But it also sounded like she never had a serious boyfriend who spent time with her and Robby. His male pride liked knowing she didn't have a rash of lovers over the years, and it also wanted to be the first to make himself at home in her living room.

And wasn't that fucked up given their current situation.

"I didn't mean that the way it sounded," he said. "I'm curious. How old are you?"

"Oh." She dipped her head to hide her face as a blush settled over her cheeks. "I'm twenty-nine. Robby'll be twenty-one in two weeks and can finally help me serve alcohol. It's not that big of a deal because he's the dishwasher, and he helps in the kitchen if they get backed up. But it'll be nice to have a little relief behind the bar."

She shrugged. "But then he'll leave for the university in the fall, and I'll be back to flying solo. I'm nervous about doing it on my own." She turned to him, eyes wide, as if realizing she'd revealed a great secret. "I never want him to know that."

Gavin nodded in understanding. "Where's he going?"

"He's supposed to go to East Carolina University, in Greenville. He wants to do something with art, and they have a great art program."

"Did he make these?" Gavin asked as he stopped at the copper windmill and pushed on one of the paddles, sending the propeller into motion.

Sunny smiled and ran her fingers along the edge of a dogwood leaf on another piece. "No. Well, he helps me sometimes. I make these in my spare time."

He cut his eyes to her. "When could you possibly have spare time?"

"Now that we've gotten all the renovations taken care of, I have a lot of time during the day to work on them."

Gavin's mind jumped to the future, when Robby was gone and Sunny lived alone. He could think of a million ways to fill her... time.

As they rounded the back of the house, Gavin asked, "Why do you say, 'he's supposed to go?'"

"Because I think he's hesitant to leave me. He's done two years at the community college, getting all of his general classes out of the way. But now that it's time for him to leave, I think he's afraid of abandoning me. That's why I'd never tell him how nervous I am about doing this on my own." She stopped at the bottom of the stairs and glanced up at the apartment door. "Even though the thought of him leaving makes my chest feel like it's filled with wet sand, I need to get up the courage to talk to him about it and let him know I'll be fine."

"I can't believe a lack of courage has ever kept you from doing any-thing. You're a remarkable woman, Sunny." Before she could respond, he wrapped his hand around the back of her neck and dipped his head. With his lips against hers he added, "A sexy, beautiful, amazingly remarkable woman."

Chapter Thirteen

Sunny pushed the kitchen door open, slowly stepped inside, then glanced around the corner.

Gavin bit his lip to keep from laughing when he realized she was holding her breath and practically tiptoeing across the kitchen. She oh-so-carefully set the blanket on the counter, then soundlessly dipped into her jar for a grape Dum-Dum. When she turned around and saw the big, stupid grin spread over his face, she frowned and whispered, "What?"

His grin grew wider.

Meaningless relationships had burned Gavin out on dating long ago. On the rare occasion he did go out, it was usually with someone he met through work. Aggressive, assertive, out-to-prove-something-to-the-world women with huge chips firmly settled on their shoulders.

He bet Sunny was stronger than all of them put together. Yet here she was, shifting from foot to foot, afraid her younger brother would find out she had sex. "You're absolutely adorable. Especially when you're nervous."

She squared her shoulders and lifted her chin. "I'm not nervous."

He set the picnic basket on the kitchen table, then stepped in front of her. When he rested his hands on either side of her, boxing her in, she sucked in a breath and stiffened. Leaning over, he whispered in her ear, "Yes, you are. You're afraid you've been caught doing the nasty in the middle of the day."

From the corner of his eye, he watched the sucker stick jerk as she worked the candy around in her mouth. Her cheeks drew in as she gave a long pull on the Dum-Dum, and his body tensed in response. If she sucked on him like those damned suckers, the fun would be over before it even began.

"I'm almost thirty years old. I can do whatever I want, whenever I want, with whomever I—" She jerked back and cocked her head, listening. Gavin made out the sound of footsteps on the stairs at the same time Sunny pressed her hands against his chest and pushed him away from her.

He stepped away, laughing. "You want to tell me that again?"

The door opened and Robby stepped into the kitchen. His gaze landed on Gavin, then traveled to Sunny. He crossed his arms over his chest, trying to assume a tough-guy stance. "I thought you'd been kidnapped."

"We were on the beach," Sunny said, nervously glancing from Robby to Gavin and back again. She waved her hand between them. "Robby, this is Gavin McLeod. Gavin, this is Robby. My brother."

While they shook hands, Robby sized Gavin up. Again. He did some of this last night, and again on the steps, but Gavin understood Robby's need to do it over and over until he was comfortable with the situation. Gavin was in their personal space, and he needed to let Robby do his protective-brother thing.

After a moment, Robby said, "I noticed the pile of clothes on the chair in Sunny's room. I'm glad to see you're not naked."

Gavin glanced at Sunny's pale face. He could read her thoughts. If Robby discovered the clothes in her room, he saw the condoms. She might have been able to fudge around the truth before, but not now.

Gavin smiled and winked at Sunny as he took a step closer to her.

He didn't know what would happen between the two of them, but he wanted her to know he was *with her* in this.

The big question remained: Would he be *with her* in the fight against Max?

Pushing the unpleasant thought aside, he said, "She thought these would be more appropriate beach attire." He glanced back to Robby. "I hope you don't mind."

Robby relaxed his stance and dropped his hands to his side, the moment of examination and challenge over. Apparently, Gavin passed the test. This time. "No problem." Robby leaned against the doorframe and switched his attention to Sunny. "I've got some things to do downstairs. I'll be in the bar if you need me."

Sunny blew out the breath she probably hadn't even been aware of holding, and frowned. "What are you working on?"

"I need to figure out what's causing the kitchen sink to leak."

"Is there anything I can do to help?"

Robby and Sunny turned to Gavin with identical, incredulous expressions that broadcast their thoughts loud and clear. *How could you possibly help?*

On top of the discussion with Sunny about not looking like a guy raised on a farm, their attitudes chapped his ass. "Don't let appearances fool you. I'm more useful than I look."

Sunny narrowed her eyes. "I need to talk to Gavin for a second." She cast a glance at Robby. "Alone."

"Sure." He stopped with his hand on the door handle and swiveled his head toward Sunny. "Make sure you keep both feet on the floor. And he's not to be in your bedroom without me in here."

Sunny crossed her arms and glared at the closing door.

Gavin laughed. "Let me guess where he's heard that before."

"What are you doing?" she asked, pinning him with an intense stare.

He thought she would relax in direct proportion to Robby easing off, but something had gone off kilter. She was tenser now, and he was confused. "I was teasing you."

"I mean, why are you being nice and offering to help Robby? Do you think you can get close to him, talk him into selling, then use him to convince me?"

The air left Gavin's lungs in a whoosh, and he stumbled backward as if she'd physically punched him. "What? No, I would never…"

The thought died a painful death as another, truer thought rushed in. *Bullshit. That's exactly what you'd do.*

That realization stung more than Sunny's words because, yeah, in any other situation, that would have been his MO.

He scrubbed a hand down his face and turned to the window. Watching the waves roll onshore, he felt like a tiny seashell, tossed and turned and swept away in the current of the vast ocean. "No," he said, barely loud enough for her to hear. "That's not what I was doing. I honestly just wanted to help. It's obvious he doesn't like me, or at least, isn't happy with me being here. I thought it might help if he got to know me better."

"Why?"

He looked over his shoulder at her. "Why what?"

"What difference does it make if he likes you? Your business is finished. I assumed you'd be leaving."

Jesus, she swung a verbal switchblade with alarming accuracy. He didn't think it was intentional; she simply spoke the truth as she saw it. But intentional or not, her stabs hurt like a bitch.

He sat on the seat under the kitchen window, rested his forearms on his knees, and looked up at her through his lashes. "I'm not sure what I'm doing. I enjoy being with you, and I guess I'm not in a hurry to leave. This is a complicated situation, and I'm only making it more complex, but… there you go. The honest truth."

Slumped against the counter, arms crossed over her chest, she opened her mouth, then closed it. Anger, frustration, and what appeared to be sadness crossed her face before her expression settled on wary. "Is this like the saying, 'keep your friends close, and your enemies closer?'"

"What?" He waited, hoping she was kidding. But neither her expression nor demeanor changed, and he realized she was serious. "We're not enemies, Sunny."

"Yeah, we kind of are. You still want my land. I'm not selling. We're definitely not teammates."

He stood and went to her. Sweeping a lock of hair away from her face, he said, "We have…" He averted his gaze and took a deep breath. "*Had* different goals. I'm not sure what I'm doing at this point. But that doesn't mean we're enemies." He couldn't think of anyone he considered an enemy, but if he did have any, he knew with absolute certainty he'd never rolled around naked with them.

He turned away from her and paced the kitchen floor. "There has to be a way to work this out. I just have to figure out what it is."

The first step would be calling Max to report in, but he didn't know what to say. Gavin couldn't grab hold of a thought long enough to figure out what needed to be done, let alone devise a plan. He was flailing without direction, but that needed to change ASAP. Max would be expecting a report, and Gavin needed to give him one.

Christ. That conversation was going to be as much fun as running his nuts through a grinder.

Hours and hours of shopping left Callie famished.

And with a nervous twitch in her right eye.

For the most part, she stuck with her plan to plunge necklines and raise hemlines. She even bought what she considered to be a few obscenely short skirts—although the idea of wearing any of them in public caused cold sweats and severe dizziness.

The low-cut, ruby red Valentino she got for tomorrow night's retirement party was a whole lot racier than anything she normally wore, but she was excited about it and couldn't wait to see Gavin's reaction. If his jaw didn't come unhinged and a small amount of drool didn't escape the corner of his mouth, she'd be terribly disappointed.

Her big failure of the day was at Benedetti's.

She'd been on board with getting one of those ridiculous nipple necklaces... until she went into the dressing room with Jen and saw how the clips attached by twisting around her nipples. *Owww.* She'd grown feathers and had the urge to peck at the ground and lost all desire to buy something resembling a medieval torture device.

Jen, of course, did not chicken out.

"It doesn't hurt at all," Jen said, with glassy eyes and a dreamy smile. "In fact, it feels really good." She left the dressing room, went back to the display case, and picked out three different styles.

Despite Callie's begging and attempts at bribery—and she spared nothing on either count—Jen insisted on wearing one to lunch. If they'd gone back to Callie's, it wouldn't have been a big deal. But they weren't at Callie's.

The three of them were at the Seaside Pines Country Club, where their parents were long-time members. Callie would expire on the spot if they saw someone they knew. Just thinking of seeing a familiar face made her stomach turn, and she wasn't even wearing the damned thing.

"Why are you so nervous?" Jen asked as they waited for the host to return to his station.

Callie, who'd been holding her breath while checking out the dining room to make sure the coast was clear, jumped. "I'm not." Okay, that was ridiculous; obviously she was. "It's that necklace," she hissed. "What if we run into someone we know?"

"What if we do? Look…" Jen pulled the edges of her jacket aside to reveal her sweater and, in Jen's opinion, the lack of evidence. "Even if I wasn't wearing a jacket, you wouldn't be able to tell it's there."

Callie slapped Jen's hands away, then smoothed the lapels back into place.

"That's why I say you're a prude," Jen whispered harshly. "You're not even wearing it, and you're freaked out."

"Good afternoon, ladies. I'm sorry you had to wait." At the sound of the deep-voiced greeting, Callie jumped again.

Her heart tripped, just a little, when she saw *him*—the dining room host with the dark chocolate eyes and legendary, high-wattage smile. And he was smiling directly at her.

She'd only met Jason once, a few weeks earlier while dining with her parents, but she overheard women in restrooms, on tennis courts, and at social gatherings talking about that smile. Women of all ages and marital status swooned when he flashed it. Held spellbound by it now, she understood the fuss.

Never one to miss a chance at flirting with a hot guy, Jen smiled coquettishly and said, "We need a table for three." She widened her blue eyes and batted her eyelashes. "Unless you can join us. In that case, we need a table for four."

Jason's laugh was easy and natural and… *unbelievable*… his smile grew even brighter. "I wish I could." His gaze shifted between the three of them before settling back on Callie. "Unfortunately, I've just started working and won't get off for another eight hours. That would be a long wait."

"I'd wait six months," Tiffany muttered under her breath.

Callie was too caught up in his mouth to say anything intelligible, but Jen's extensive experience kept her from missing a beat. "Maybe we'll come back for drinks this evening."

He laughed politely but didn't comment. Grabbing three of the daily menus, he said, "Follow me."

Anywhere.

The thought came from nowhere and sent a wave of guilt through Callie. How could she be breathless over Jason when she was head-over-heels for Gavin? Shouldn't she be blind to all other men?

Jason stopped at a table overlooking the fifth green of the world-class golf course. "Is this table suitable?" The question was directed toward all three of them, but his dark chocolate eyes were on Callie.

That was what she wanted from Gavin. She wanted his full attention directed at her like she was the only one standing in front of him. For him to ask her a question—even if it was something as simple as a table choice—and for her answer to matter.

The way he interacted with the bartender.

The mental jabbering made her head spin, so she slapped a lid on it by wondering if Jason would be working tomorrow night. How would he react to the little red dress? How might Gavin respond to some competition? Maybe a good dose of jealousy would get Gavin moving in the right direction... Toward her.

She smiled at Jason and tried to be flirtatious without being as obvious as Jen. "This is great. Thanks."

While Jason pulled out chairs to seat them, Callie glanced around the mostly empty dining room, then into the side room reserved for groups. Her gaze landed on a familiar face... with features nearly identical to hers. On a gasp, she said, "Ohmigod."

Jason, Jen, and Tiffany all swung their attention to Callie. Concern filled Jason's eyes as he let go of the chair and reached for her. "Are you okay?"

"I'm sorry. Yes, I'm fine. It's just… well…" Her fingers went to her throat as she turned to Jen and made big, our-mothers-are-in-that-room eyes. Smiling nervously, she said, "I was supposed to get something for my mother while I was shopping, and I forgot. When I saw her standing over there"—she narrowed her eyes at Jen—"with Jen and Tiffany's mothers, I remembered." She straightened and pinned an all-is-well smile onto her face. "No biggie. I overreacted. Sorry."

Jason laughed and let go of her forearm. She was in such shock over seeing not only their mothers, but the entire women's investment group in which their mothers belonged, she didn't even realize he had hold of her. But now that he'd let go, she missed the heat of his palm and the tender concern in the touch.

Somewhere, in the recesses of her mind, she realized that was an inappropriate reaction. She shouldn't have liked his touch. She shouldn't have had any reaction at all. But she did, and at some point, she supposed, she'd have to consider what that meant.

Right now, however, she needed to speak with her mother. "We'll need to wait to be seated," she said to Jason. "If we don't speak, we'll never hear the end of it."

Tiffany and Jen were already headed toward the private room, leaving Callie alone with Jason. He laughed and pushed the chairs back into place. "I understand. I made sure I spoke to my mother as soon as she arrived."

"Your mother is part of that group?" Why did that shock her?

Probably because she assumed anyone who worked here didn't come from a family wealthy enough to be a member of the country club. Let alone have a mother with enough expendable income to belong to an investment group that required a twenty thousand dollar membership fee.

If he was offended by her surprised response, he didn't let on. His smile didn't falter, and his eyes showed no signs of cooling. "She's one of the founding members."

"Oh, wow." If that was the case... "Why do you...?" Realizing how rude her question was, she let the sentence fall off.

"Why do I work here?" he asked.

She cleared her throat and tried to meet his gaze, but failed miserably. "I'm sorry. That was rude."

"It's okay. It surprises most people. Especially those who know I have a large enough trust fund that I don't have to work a day in my life. But I can't hang around and do nothing but play golf and tennis. I have a degree in finance, but the idea of sitting in an office all day makes me itch." He shrugged and smiled confidently. "I like working here. I get to see old friends and their parents. I get to meet new people." His gaze softened, and she had the impression he considered meeting her a good thing. "Someday, I'll do something different. For now, I like this."

Callie was stunned. She and Jason were more alike than she believed. Yet they were very different. She had no problem hanging around all day, doing nothing. The idea of getting a job, especially in the service industry, made her shudder.

Agitated by the conversation and, she realized, with herself, she said, "I guess I should go."

He nodded and smiled. "Hopefully I'll see you again. Soon."

She started to walk away, then turned back. "Are you working tomorrow night?"

He smiled, and something shifted in his eyes. "I am."

A flitter of anticipation rushed through her system and settled low in her belly. She pressed a hand to her stomach to soothe the unease, but the pressure caused the excitement to fragment and spread to a thousand locations throughout her body. Uncomfortable with the response and anxious to leave before she embarrassed herself, she muttered, "I'll see you tomorrow night," then rushed to the safety of her mother.

While Robby worked on the leaky sink and Sunny worked on a new copper sculpture in her workshop, Gavin sat on the stoop of her porch like a stray dog. He should be gone by now, but for some reason he kept hanging around.

He'd been sitting on the stoop, phone in hand, Max's number brought up on autodial for ten minutes. All he needed to do was hit the "send" button, but he couldn't bring himself to do so.

Mostly because he still didn't have a freaking clue what to say to Max.

He'd never been faced with a situation like this, and he was at a total loss as to how to proceed. Max knew Gavin so well, it would take less than twenty seconds of conversation for him to figure out Gavin was as big an obstacle as Sunny.

If this were any other woman, he'd use Robby's leaving for college and her fear of running the place by herself against her. He'd exploit her insecurities. He'd point out how helpful the proceeds from the sale would be in paying for Robby's college tuition, along with his other expenses. It wasn't something she mentioned, but it had to be a concern.

He would remind her of those fears and keep reminding her of them, until they grew and expanded into giant, scary monsters she didn't think she could slay. At that point, she would agree it was in her best interest to sell and be out from under the bar.

But the thought of doing any of those things to Sunny made him physically ill. The fact that he would have done it to anyone disgusted him and left him so full of self-loathing he felt like he needed to scrub his insides with bleach.

She may feel like Robby was an integral part of getting the bar up and running, but aside from the physical labor, how much help could an eighteen-year-old have been. Whether she admitted it or not, the lion's share of work and stress had been on Sunny, and she was more than capable of running the business alone.

Gavin wouldn't—couldn't—crush her spirit by planting any doubts in her mind about her ability to keep things going after Robby left for college.

He glanced at the phone in his hand and cringed. He still didn't know how to handle this, but he couldn't put the inevitable off any longer. He took a deep breath, hit the send button, and waited for Max to answer.

Chapter Fourteen

By the time Callie put away her purchases and returned to the living room of the guesthouse, Tiffany and Jen had the blender whirling. Three o'clock was margaritas-by-the-pool time, and after the harrowing afternoon she had at the club, she needed several. However, before she changed into her swimsuit and dove into a tall, frozen glass, she needed to go to her father's office.

Gavin didn't come by the house every evening, but since he was sent to Anticue on that special project, she thought he might stop by today. If he was expected, she wanted to be in her best swimsuit, sitting in the right chair when he arrived.

The problem was, she couldn't remember which chair was the *right* one.

She tapped on the french doors and peeked through the glass. As expected, she found her father sitting at his desk, motioning her to come inside.

"Good afternoon, princess. How was shopping?"

"Wonderful." She kissed him on the cheek before taking up residence in Gavin's chair. "I found a gorgeous Valentino to wear tomorrow night. It's not like the dresses I usually wear, so I'm really excited about it." And petrified.

Max beamed. "I'm glad you found something you like."

Without being obvious, she glanced out the door and scoped out the chairs lining the far side of the pool. Sitting in the pink one, she'd be in Gavin's direct line of sight. She would wear her purple two-piece.

That settled, she turned her thoughts back to the conversation. "I hope Gavin likes it."

Or Jason.

The thought was so strong she almost expected to see someone standing behind her, whispering in her ear. She hadn't been able to stop thinking about him since leaving the club, and she found it disconcerting. He wasn't only handsome; he was also nice. But the thing she liked the most was the way he looked at her. *Really* looked at her.

The desk phone rang, jarring her from her thoughts. Max looked at caller ID and smiled as he hit the speakerphone button. "Hey, Gavin. Give me some good news."

Gavin muttered something that sounded an awful lot like cursing, then said, "Sorry, Max. No can do."

Her daddy's eyes narrowed and his lips thinned. "Why not?"

"The owner adamantly refuses to sell. She won't even discuss the possibility."

She?

Max leaned back in his chair and glared at the phone like it was a noxious piece of debris. "So change her mind."

Gavin cursed again. After a pause that seemed to drag on for hours, he said, "She's pretty strong-willed and determined." He laughed. "She even has a tattoo on her wrist that reads 'never give up.'"

Callie didn't like the way Gavin's voice went soft and mushy, and an icky sickness began to build. She grabbed a piece of paper and pen from Max's desk and wrote, *Ask him if he's talking about the bartender.*

Max flipped his gaze to Callie and nodded before turning to stare out the window. A blank expression—what she always called his thinking face—settled over his features. The house could fall down around him when he was in this mode, and he wouldn't notice. "What's your next move?" His voice was as tight as the set of his jaw.

Gavin didn't answer, and she knew he was wearing his thinking face, too. When Gavin didn't want to answer a question, he'd pause and think it over, carefully choosing his words. Finally, he said, "I'm not sure."

The uncharacteristic lack of confidence in his voice sent a lead weight rolling around in her stomach. Gavin was supposed to convince the owner, who Callie now realized was also the bartender, to sell her property. Max wanted Gavin to do *whatever* was necessary, and she wanted Gavin to come home. Trying to grapple with the mounting hurt and frustration, she wrote, *Is he coming here this evening?*

Her father nodded in acknowledgment of the note and said, "I guess we need to discuss this further and figure out our next move. How soon can you be here?"

Another long pause. "I won't be able to make it tonight."

Max's expression remained impassive. "Why not?"

"I'm still in Anticue."

Callie swallowed the rising nausea and panic. Her father's plan was working. Gavin was with the bartender. And not with her as in working out negotiations, but with her in the way Callie wanted to be.

She wanted to yell and scream and cry and punch something. But she was an adult, so she'd settle for getting drunk. Her father had gone from annoyed to smiling... until he glanced across the desk at Callie. His face fell and he snatched up the receiver.

"I guess if you can't make it back tonight, we can spend some time talking about this tomorrow night." He paused, listened to Gavin, then said, "Lorraine's retirement party."

Her father seemed momentarily caught off-guard, then said, "You can't disappoint Lorraine by not showing."

She couldn't hear Gavin's response, but Max's eyes narrowed and his jaw popped. "Watch yourself, Gavin."

Callie knew her father and Gavin argued at times, but she never witnessed it. Hearing her father's tense chastisement sent nervous jitters down her spine.

After another long pause, her daddy said, "I don't know how much vacation time you have. What the hell does that have to do with anything?" Another pause. "You can't be serious." Another pause. "Fine. We'll discuss all of this at the retirement party." Without giving Gavin a chance to respond, her father slammed the receiver into its cradle.

Callie was stunned. She'd never seen her daddy upset with Gavin, and it unnerved her. "Is everything all right?"

Max took a deep breath and smiled. "Of course. Now, go on out and enjoy the pool with your friends. Don't worry about a thing."

She tried to smile as she slipped through the french doors, but it was kind of hard to do with her bottom lip quivering. She led a sheltered life, and that's probably why this seemed like such a big deal. But she had a really bad feeling about this situation.

She saw the way Gavin looked at that bartender and the way the bartender responded to Gavin. No matter how hard she tried, Callie couldn't make herself believe this would turn out okay for her.

Growling in frustration, Gavin disconnected the call and slammed the phone down on the stoop. He jammed his elbows onto his knees and dropped his head into his upraised hands.

He didn't know why he was so annoyed. The conversation had

actually gone better than he expected. The only thing Max went ape-shit over was Gavin missing the retirement party—like Lorraine gave a shit if he was there or not. She'd probably rather not be there herself.

Knowing she'd go crazy with nothing to do, Gavin planned to visit her next week, anyway. Now, he'd have a good excuse. He'd also send her a dozen roses, along with a note of apology.

However, Gavin was smart enough to read between the lines and figure out the real problem with him not going to the party wasn't Lorraine, but Callie. The time was coming for a sit down with Max, or with Max and Callie, to spell things out for them… slowly…. and plainly.

He. Wasn't. Interested. Not today. Not next week. Never.

He thought about the note in his pocket and laughed. Maybe he should write a note, stick it under their noses, and make them recite it out loud. With feeling.

"What are you laughing about?"

He lifted his head and found Sunny at the bottom of the stairs, watching him. "I'm thinking about writing a note to get my point across. Like someone did to me."

She grinned as she walked up the stairs, then sat on the step below him. "Was that your boss?"

"Yeah."

She tilted her head to the side and studied him. "He's not happy."

"He's never happy." Gavin picked at a piece of peeling paint on the steps. "It actually went better than I expected."

Hope lit her eyes. "He accepted my refusal without a fuss?"

"Hell, no." The laugh that burst from his chest was harsh and held no trace of humor. "He's mostly pissed off about me standing up the little princess tomorrow night. The whole sale thing will hit him later tonight or tomorrow morning. Then he'll call back."

For the second time since ending his conversation with Max, something tugged at the back of Gavin's mind. He couldn't put his finger on what, or where, in the conversation he felt something was off, but something surprised him.

Sunny's eyes crinkled as she grinned. "The little princess? Would that be the brunette?"

"The one and only."

Sunny relaxed back against the railing. "Do you mind explaining that situation to me?"

"It's pretty simple. Callie's had a crush on me since I went to work for Holden. I was twenty-two; she was fourteen. I imagine it was her first crush, and it's one she's insisted on retaining."

"So you guys never dated?"

Gavin felt his lip curl and his face scrunch up like he was about to hurl. It wasn't that Callie revolted him, but the idea of dating someone who felt like a sister made him… well, want to hurl.

Sunny laughed and slapped him on the knee. "Okay. I get it. That's a definite no." She picked at a string hanging from the bottom of her cut-off shorts. "So what about this property? What happens when he gets mad?"

"A shit storm to rival Hurricane Hugo." Gavin pushed his fingers through his hair. "I'll meet with him on Monday to find out what he's thinking and planning. Then I'll figure out what we need to do to keep the storm from reaching the shore." He smiled. "I did tell him I was going to use some of my accumulated vacation. That should buy us a little time."

"You keep saying 'we' and 'us.'"

"Do I?"

"Yes." Her eyes searched his face. "What does that mean?"

He shrugged. "I don't know."

"What do you know?"

Gavin looked at Sunny and grinned. He was pretty good at avoiding questions, but she was way better at the question-answer game than him. It probably came from years of experience raising a teenage boy. She knew how to keep hammering away until she got answers.

"I know I'm walking around in unfamiliar territory. I know why this property means so much to you and Robby. Personally, I like Anticue the way it is. I have a lot of fond memories of this island, and I'd hate to see it changed by the addition of a resort."

She watched him for a minute, probably gauging his sincerity, then stood. Rather than walking away as he expected, she stepped in front of him, straddled his legs, and sat on his lap.

Oh yeah, this was good. Real good. And pretty damned dangerous. He was already in deeper than was wise, and this crotch-to-crotch action wasn't helping.

"Will you help us keep our property safe?" She wrapped her legs around his waist, her arms around his neck, and scooted as close as she could get.

His body responded to her close proximity, a fact she couldn't miss, given the tight fit of their bodies. He considered telling her he would walk barefoot through hell if that's what she wanted. But common sense prevailed, and he said, "I'll do everything I can to make this work out okay for you."

Her eyes softened, then melted. She rested her forehead against his, and in a heartbreakingly gentle tone, said, "I'm trusting you."

He swallowed the lump clogging his throat and tried to find the right words. Problem was, he didn't have a fucking clue what those words were.

The freckles dotting her nose grew a shade darker after their time in the sun, and her cheeks carried a pink tint. His voice abandoned him, like his words. So rather than say anything, he brushed the hair out of her face and kissed the tip of her nose.

Switching to an easier subject, he asked, "Do you mind if I stay here tonight?"

She looked at him through her lashes and chewed her bottom lip. Her eyes liquefied, and he wondered if she was imagining all the things they could do if they had an entire night together. Then her forehead wrinkled, and her demeanor shifted, and he figured this was where she started to worry about Robby and his thoughts on Gavin staying all night.

Hoping to persuade her in his favor, he said, "I want to go to New Bern tomorrow to see my grandfather. Since I'm this close, if I stayed here, I could get up first thing in the morning and be there in time for breakfast."

It was a lame excuse, especially since he'd driven an hour to take Callie home, only to then turn around and drive another hour back to Anticue. But he'd use any excuse to spend time with Sunny. "If you're worried about Robby, I'll sleep on the couch. And if you're really uncomfortable with me being here, I'll go home."

Sunny smiled mischievously. "I'm almost thirty years old. I can do whatever I want, whenever I want..."—she lowered her mouth to his— "...with whomever I want." With a sheepish expression, she added, "Maybe Robby can stay with a friend."

"We could camp on the beach." He lowered his voice and nuzzled her neck. "Do you like making love on the beach?"

She shivered. "I don't know."

The beast growled. He really, really, *really* fucking liked being the first person Sunny experienced these things with. "I guess we'll find out tonight."

Her breathing accelerated. "Talk about something to look forward to. This will be the longest work night of my life."

Chapter Fifteen

*C*allie wasn't normally a mean drunk. Usually, she was the mushy-gushy one, hugging her friends, telling them how much she loved them. Tonight, however, the more she drank, the meaner... well, the *madder* she got.

Mad at Gavin. Mad at the sleazy bartender. Mad at the whole damned world.

Wasn't there a famous movie scene where a character stood on the rooftops and yelled at the world about being mad as hell before taking charge of their life?

She glanced to the peak of her parents' rooftop... about a million miles up in the air. Maybe she should quietly take charge. No yelling, just a simple proclamation. "I'm going to Anticue."

Jen dropped her chin and gave her a don't-be-stupid stare.

Tiffany, always a step behind, said, "Why would you want to do that?"

"Because Gavin is there. I think."

"Oh, hon," Tiffany said, grabbing the next pitcher from the cooler. She topped off Callie's glass. "You don't want to go there."

"Yes, I do." A new wave of mad washed over her. "I do want to *go there*. I want to confront him while he's with that bartender."

"Callie, he's not doing anything wrong." Jen sounded perturbed, like Callie was dense and Jen was tired of repeatedly having this conversation. "He's not made any commitments to you. He's never even acted interested in you. In fact, I'd say he's gone out of his way to let you know he's *not* interested."

Pain slashed through Callie's anger, then mixed with it to create a volatile combination. "You are such a bitch."

Jen took a sip from her drink and shrugged. "Maybe. But you need to face the truth. It's painful to watch you follow after Gavin like a puppy dog. You need to forget about him. Find someone who's interested in you. Like Jason."

Callie sniffed. "I don't want Jason."

Do I?

She thought for a beat. No, definitely not.

Probably not.

No, she wanted Gavin. She'd always wanted Gavin.

Jen flicked her gaze from Callie to Tiffany. "I think you're over-looking something important. None of us are capable of driving anywhere."

True. Callie deflated like she'd been popped with a pin.

Who did she know that could drive them? She checked the time on her cellphone. *Nine-thirty.*

Her heart thumped heavily as an idea struck.

A crazy… outrageous… terribly wrong idea.

But drunkenness was on her side, so she grabbed her phone, pulled up the number for the country club, and hit call. "Hi. This is Callie Holden. Is Jason still working?"

Tiffany gasped and, in a harsh whisper, asked, "What are you do-ing?"

"Finding a ride."

Jen shook her head. "Callie, the way to get a guy is not by having him help you spy on another guy."

134

Eyes wide and panicky, Tiffany nodded and quickly said, "Tell Jason we're going to spy on *my* boyfriend."

"Very good, Tiff. I'm impressed." Jen sipped her margarita. "That might actually work."

"I'm not trying to—"

A click on the line indicated Jason picked up the call. "This is Jason."

Callie smiled broadly, hoping it would come through on his end of the line. "Hi, Jason, this is Callie Holden. How are you?"

"I'm great. And you?" Although he sounded surprised to hear her voice, he also sounded pleased.

Taking that as a positive sign, she forged ahead with her plan. "I'm good. But... Well... We have a little dilemma and need some help."

"Okay." His reply was filled with hesitation, but she refused to let her courage be squashed.

"Jen, Tiffany, and I need to go to Anticue. You know, the little island near the North/South Carolina border? The problem is, we've had a few margaritas, and... well..." She hoped he'd fill in the blanks and offer to drive them without her actually asking.

After a long pause, he asked, "Why do you need to go to Anticue?"

She wasn't interested in Jason. Really. But for some reason, she found herself saying, "Tiffany thinks her boyfriend is cheating on her. We want to see if we can catch him in the act."

She kept her eyes locked on the ground, unable to meet Tiffany and Jen's stares. He didn't answer, as if thinking it over, and a terrible thought hit Callie square in the chest. "Do you have plans?" *Oh, crap.* "Do you have a girlfriend?"

She closed her eyes and absorbed the sound of his laughter echoing through the phone. "No, on the second, and the plans I have can be changed. But I don't get off work for another hour. By the time I get changed and pick you up, it'll be at least eleven. Will that be too late?"

Waiting might give Callie time to change her mind. But that's okay. If she decided going to Anticue was a bad idea, Jason could hang out with them here. "No, that'll be great," she said. "We're at my house. Do you know where I live?"

"I sure do. My parents live in the same neighborhood."

"No way! Why haven't we met before?"

"They moved into that house after I left home."

"Oh, so you don't live with them now?" Did she sound disappointed to find he wasn't her neighbor?

"I left when I turned eighteen. I love them, but I needed to be on my own."

"Hmmm…" Callie looked at the pool, at the guesthouse where she lived, at her parents' house. She spent six months out of each year traveling, so she never considered getting her own place. But, at twenty-four, maybe she should.

Feeling a lot less mad, and way less ambitious about this taking-charge-of-her-life business, she said, "Thanks, Jason. I'll see you when you get here."

She disconnected the call and took a long drink from her glass.

"Well?" Tiffany asked.

"He'll be here at eleven."

Jen jerked upright from her relaxed slump, her enthusiasm nearly launching her out of the chair. "We need good spy clothes."

Tiffany grinned and bobbed her head. "Those black leather pants and that black Vera Wang sweater would be awesome on you, Callie."

Callie perked up. "With the black onyx-and-silver bracelet Daddy gave me last year for my birthday."

Tiffany and Jen were out of their chairs in an instant. "What can we wear?"

She loved having two best friends who wore the exact same size as her. It was like they each had three closets to choose from, creating a never-ending supply of new clothes. Especially since they all had the same favorite hobby: shopping.

Energized by the idea of dressing like Batgirl and charging off to save the world—or at least her little piece of the world—Callie grabbed her glass and jumped out of the chair. "I have two pairs of leather pants and a leather mini." She giggled. "I think I should wear the mini and let you guys have the pants."

A roar of laughter from the end of the bar brought Sunny's head out of the beer cooler. Gavin, Ed, and Joe had been talking and laughing for the past three hours. They were like old friends who'd known each all their lives but hadn't been together in years. Gavin, seeing her glance up, winked, then returned his attention to his counterparts.

"He sure does make friends easy," Robby said, drying a shot glass to set on the shelf.

Sunny dried her hands and jotted down the inventory numbers for each brand of beer. "Yeah, he does."

Not only had Gavin made friends with Ed and Joe, he also befriended the kids during several intense games of pool. He held his own and even won a few, which earned him instant respect from the normally reserved group.

It bothered her to keep wondering if he had ulterior motives for getting to know everyone. He denied the accusation when she confronted him on his offer to help Robby, but she couldn't stop the idea from sneaking up on her every now and again.

He was one hell of a kisser and a great lover. But should she trust him?

"What's his deal, Sunny?" Robby asked, standing behind her, peering over her shoulder. He didn't know the real reason behind Gavin's appearance, but he obviously had suspicions. Last night, he questioned why Gavin brought three women he didn't like to a bar in Anticue to drink two beers.

She knew the answers to those questions now, but Robby didn't. He probably formulated all kinds of crazy reasons, although none could be crazier than the truth.

She made another note on her notepad and grabbed a sucker. Closing time was in half an hour and she'd hoped to escape without having this conversation. Apparently, that wasn't going to happen.

"If I ignored you, you'd be pissed."

She turned and glared at him. His cranky attitude was another item on her must-talk-to-Robby-about list. "I'm not ignoring you."

"Really. Could've fooled me."

Even though they were siblings and not a parent and child, she didn't like it when he got mouthy like this. He wouldn't talk to anyone else like that. At least, she hoped he wouldn't. And just because they were related, it didn't give him the right to treat her badly.

But she also recognized he needed to create discomfort between them so it would be easier to leave home and go out on his own. She once overheard a psychologist soothing a friend on the subject, explaining that since humans didn't toss their young out of the nest, conflict was necessary in order for the child to make the separation happen.

Knowing that little bit of psychobabble didn't help when Robby was being a jerk. But she had to admit, the way they were going at each other lately, they'd both celebrate in the street the day he left for college.

Grinding her teeth, she said, "Follow me to the kitchen." She rounded the corner, out of sight of everyone in the bar, and said, "Last night, Gavin thought he was sent here to get ideas from us. Ideas he could use in the resorts he builds."

"And now?"

"It turns out his boss wanted him to find out who owned the bar. They want us to sell the property so they can tear it down, along with the old fishing pier and a few houses on either side of us, to build a resort."

"You can't be fucking serious."

Sunny's eyebrows shot to her hairline and her chin dropped to her chest.

Robby scrunched his eyes together, and his shoulders slumped. "I'm sorry. That wasn't directed toward you." He grabbed her and squeezed her in a big bear hug. The kind he used to give her all the time… up until about six months ago when he stopped hugging her at all. As the last vapor of air left her lungs, he let go and stepped back. "You told him no. Right?"

"Of course."

Robby paced around the kitchen, staring at the floor. He spun around and glared at her, his posture rigid, his voice tight. "He's using you. He's getting close to you so he can change your mind." His thoughtful pacing turned to stomping. "Why are you letting him hang around? Why are you spending time with him?"

Sunny blew out a shaky breath and chomped on her Dum-Dum. They were valid questions; ones she'd asked herself a hundred times. The easy answer: he was amazing in bed and gave her the chance to live out a few fantasies. The hard answer: she liked him.

She winced. There was a third, more legit reason, but she hesitated to share it with Robby.

Gavin made it sound as if his boss would resort to foul play, if necessary, to get what he wanted. Even though she didn't really believe it, it would be an explanation as to why he was sticking around. She didn't want to tell Robby that, because he would worry about her. But in case Gavin's concern held some validity, she wanted Robby to be aware of the slight risk, so he could be more cautious. "Apparently, his boss, Max Holden, can be pretty unrelenting in his pursuits. Gavin is acting as a buffer, of sorts, between us and his boss."

Robby stopped and scowled out the door, no doubt drilling a hole in Gavin's head. "Why?" He turned toward her. "Why would he do that for us?"

"He used to come to Anticue with his grandfather when he was young. I think he has a sentimental attachment to the area and doesn't want it changed by a big development."

She took hold of Robby's hand. "Bottom line, Robby. At this point, we don't have any choice but to trust Gavin. If he's hanging around here, at least we know what he's up to."

"He better not hurt you." Robby's tone was a combination of his two sides: a man who wanted to be her protector, and a helpless little boy who worried about his sister.

"I'm a big girl. I can take care of myself." It might have been the lack of conviction in her voice, or maybe her wariness showed in her eyes, but Robby didn't seem convinced.

She wasn't lying. She could take care of herself. But she also couldn't shake the fear that she was playing with fire. And not in reference to Max Holden. She already liked Gavin more than she should, and the possibility of getting hurt was very real.

Apparently, though, she was willing to take the risk.

"Is he staying here tonight?" He sounded as disgusted as if he were asking, "Is the boil on my ass a permanent condition?"

She found herself hesitant to answer but then remembered her emphatic statement to Gavin. *I'm almost thirty years old...* Dammit, if she wanted to have wild, crazy sex on the beach, so be it. "Yes. He's staying here tonight."

Robby rubbed the back of his neck. "I think I'll stay at Chad's." He swung out of the kitchen door, then looked back over his shoulder. "Things are winding down. Is it okay if I go ahead and take off?"

"Sure. I can handle it from here."

He shifted his gaze to Gavin, then looked back to her with serious, wary eyes. "I hope so."

She blew out a breath and rubbed her forehead. She hoped so, too.

Chapter Sixteen

Gavin watched Sunny snag a Dum-Dum from the jar, then go to work cleaning the counter. "You told him why I'm here?"

"Yep." She didn't look up but continued to scrub a spot only she could see.

He figured that's why Robby slammed out—after firing ocular silver-bullets at him. He considered going after Robby, to explain the situation from his standpoint. But as angry as he appeared, Gavin decided it wouldn't do any good.

He took a sip of his beer and watched Sunny scrub the polish off the counter. "What can I do to help?"

"Nothing." Rather than sparkling with their normal brightness, Sunny's eyes were flat and dull as she turned away from him. The guilty pangs that came with seeing Robby upset intensified. He didn't like being the one that brought darkness to their lives, and he wished—again—he knew how to fix it.

He sighed and reached for a Dum-Dum. "I don't like him being nasty to you, especially when I'm the source of the conflict."

She shrugged it off. "Nasty is his middle name right now." She muttered something about "stupid conflict" and "necessary evil" while rearranging the liquor bottles on the shelf. Gavin didn't understand, but the muttering seemed to make her feel better, so he let her have at it.

"Sunny, we're gone," the biker and his girlfriend yelled from the door.

Sunny waved and blew them air kisses. "Y'all be careful going home. See you Wednesday?"

The girl ducked her head as if embarrassed, and the guy hugged her. "Maybe one of these days we'll get married," he said. "Then we won't have to do this anymore." He laughed and kissed his dumbstruck girlfriend on the head before leading her out the door.

"I guess they've never discussed marriage."

Sunny blinked and snapped her mouth shut. "I don't know. They haven't been dating for long, and it's a bad situation. But they're both great, and they seem like a perfect couple."

"You don't always need a long time to know someone's right for you." *Well, shit.* Where had that ridiculous pansy-ass statement come from? Gavin glanced at the bottle in his hand. He'd only had three beers, so he couldn't blame the alcohol.

Going for a quick subject change, Gavin nodded toward the door and got to his feet. "Want me to lock up for you?"

Sunny glanced around, only just realizing everyone else had left. "Uh… Sure."

He flipped the lock on the door, then plunged the *open* sign into darkness. As he turned back toward the bar, a flash caught his attention. Looking through the windows of the rolling door, he studied the dunes. The only thing he saw was a spectacular full moon. A perfect night for camping on the beach.

He picked up the blanket from the corner he'd stashed it in earlier, then laid it on the pool table closest to the door. "How long will it take you to wrap things up here?" he asked, stepping behind Sunny. "I have special plans for you."

She was facing the mirrored wall, and he watched the dullness in her eyes turn to glittering anticipation. "Just a few minutes." She picked up the container of Redi Whip then hesitated. Smiling, she set it back down and caught his gaze in the reflection of the mirror. She popped the sucker from her mouth and said, "Robby is staying at a friend's tonight. We don't have to go to the beach."

He pressed his body against hers and stroked his fingers down her arms. "Yeah, we do. I promised you sex on the beach." Holding her gaze in the mirror, he nuzzled her neck. "You know you're killing me with those damned suckers, right?" A smile played at her mouth, and she shook her head. "I can't watch you suck on one without imagining what it would be like to be the lucky bastard."

Her breath hitched, and she twisted in his arms. "Oh yeah?" She trailed her fingers down his chest, past the drawstring on his borrowed shorts, and cupped the hard proof of his confession. "Mmmm… Do you know what my favorite flavor is?"

He gulped. "No."

"Peppermint." She looked up at him with a sad, pouty expression. "But they don't make suckers in that flavor." She reached behind her and grabbed a bottle of peppermint schnapps off the shelf. "Maybe I could make my own."

He struggled to make his lungs work as he followed her train of thought. He'd never experienced this personally—hey, a first for him—but he heard other guys talk. The peppermint, combined with the cool air in the room, added to the already intense sensations of the woman's mouth.

But hell, he was cranked so tight it wouldn't take but three seconds of Sunny's mouth on him and he'd be a goner.

Her fingers shook as she pulled at the drawstring of his shorts and loosened the waistband. She flipped her gaze to his and hesitated, as if gauging his reaction to make sure it was okay for her to continue.

Only a fool would tell this woman no… to anything.

He took her face in his palms and lowered his mouth to hers for a hot, searing kiss. Keeping their mouths connected, he murmured, "I'm okay with *anything* you want to do… or try."

"Ugh, I hate the beach," Callie whined as she followed Jason across the soft sand in front of the Blackout. Tiffany and Jen were behind her, equally unhappy about picking their way across sand and seashells in three-inch heels. Next time they turned into spies, they'd remember functionality was as important as being cute.

Callie didn't know why she agreed to take a hike down the beach in the first place. She already knew Gavin was in the bar. She saw his SUV in the parking lot when they cruised past a moment earlier.

When Jen suggested they could turn around, park a few houses away, and take a look into the bar from the beach, Callie hesitantly agreed. Now, she questioned why she'd done such a stupid thing.

It could be a perverse need for more torture. Or maybe, a part of her still hoped against hope that things weren't as they appeared. The lights in the building had gone out as they approached, so they knew the bar was closed. But Gavin, or the bartender, hadn't exited, so they must still be inside.

Since the customers were gone, she hoped they were finalizing the deal so Gavin could wrap things up and head back to Myrtle Beach.

Jason helped each of them climb to the top of the sand dune directly in front of the bar. "Okay," he said. "What now?"

Callie had stuck the small binoculars she used on European sightseeing trips into her purse. Swallowing the fear and nausea rising in her throat, she pulled them from her bag. Sticking with the story of checking up on Tiffany's boyfriend, Callie glanced at her and said, "I'll look first and tell you what I see."

Tiff bit her lip and frowned. "Are you sure?"

No, not at all. But she nodded and said, "Yeah, give me a second to get these adjusted." Her breathing was choppy and her hands shook, making it difficult to see as she pressed the lenses to her eyes. She turned the knob to adjust the vision, and... *Oh, God.* The view through the front windows was blurry, but it was good enough to see Gavin sealing the deal all right. Not with pen and paper, but with an intense kiss.

His hands cupped the bartender's face, and their mouths fused together. While Callie tried to catch her breath, Gavin trailed his kisses from the blonde's mouth, across her cheek, and then down her neck.

In a perfectly orchestrated movement, he and the bartender exchanged places so he was the one with his backside pressed to the counter. The bartender slipped her hands under the hem of his shirt, pushed it up over his chest, then stripped it off.

It was like watching a horror movie. Callie wanted to turn away from the gruesomeness, but the images held her captive.

The blonde took a drink from a bottle, then kissed her way across his collarbone, down to his nipple. Gavin said something; then his head fell back, a look of pure rapture on his face.

He liked having his nipples kissed. She'd have to remember—

She froze mid-thought. No, she needed to forget everything about Gavin. Knowing he'd been with other women was one thing; watching him with someone else left her cold and numb. Even if Gavin came crawling to her tomorrow, she could never get past this.

"What do you see?" Tiffany asked.

The painful knot in Callie's throat kept her from speaking, so she simply shook her head. They must have interpreted that to mean she didn't see anything, because no one asked more questions. They just patiently waited for her to provide information. Which she was incapable of doing.

The bartender took another drink from the bottle, then dropped to her knees. The bar prevented Callie from seeing anything below Gavin's chest, but really… did she need to see more?

When the trembling got so bad she feared accidentally blinding herself with the binoculars, she handed them over to Jen.

Jason wrapped an arm around her shoulder and turned her into him for a hug. He stroked her hair and her back and whispered, "He's not Tiffany's boyfriend, is he?"

She shook her head no, but couldn't get the words out. The ache in her chest was a raw, open wound she doubted would ever heal. Desperate for relief from the pain, Callie gripped the back of Jason's shirt and held on with all her might.

"I see Gavin, but I don't see the bartender. Where'd she… Ohhh… shit, she's—"

"Uh, Jen," Jason said softly, continuing to rub slow, sweeping circles on Callie's back. "I don't think we need a play-by-play."

"Oh, right." Jen glanced to Callie. "Sorry."

"How long have you been seeing each other?" Jason's voice was as soft and soothing as his touch.

"We're not."

His hand stilled for a moment, then resumed the slow caress. "I don't understand."

"God, this is so humiliating." She swiped the tears off her cheek. "I've been in love with him forever. But if he didn't work for my father, he wouldn't even know I exist."

When Jason drew back, her humiliation grew in proportion to the distance he put between them. He took her chin between his thumb and forefinger and turned her face so their gazes met. "I don't know who this guy is, but he's a fool."

"He's a happy fool," Jen muttered. At Jason's sharp look, she snapped her mouth shut. "Sorry." She looked through the binoculars again and said, "I think we got the answers we came here for. Can we get off this disgusting beach now?"

"That's a good idea," Jason said, clasping Callie's hand.

"I hope she's not going to serve out of that bottle again," Jen said, sidestepping her way off the dunes. She gasped and grabbed hold of Callie's arm. "That's it. You need to report her to the health department for this." Her mouth worked into a tight scowl and her eyes narrowed. "That'd serve them right."

Callie drew in a sad, shuddering breath. "I don't want to do that, Jen. I just want to forget all of this. I want to try to forget Gavin ever existed."

Jason smiled. Not his normally brilliant, ultra-bright smile, which Callie didn't think she could handle tonight anyway, but a small, genuinely consoling one. Without saying anything else, he squeezed her hand and led her off the dune.

Callie heard Jen giving Tiffany the gut-splitting details, but for once in her life, she was sensitive to Callie's feelings and kept her voice down.

The closer they got to the car, the more insensate Callie grew. From the day she laid eyes on Gavin, she believed she'd marry him. She had a few boyfriends over the years, but nothing serious. Her heart had always belonged to Gavin. Deep down, she believed with every fiber of her being Gavin would eventually feel the same for her.

Reality had just bitch-slapped her into admitting that dream would never come true. It was also time to admit she *was* a prude, because she didn't want Gavin anywhere near her. In the instant she'd seen him kissing the bartender, Callie's life changed.

For a moment, when she first looked through the window, she thought it had ended. And, she supposed, in a way it had. The old Callie was gone. Now, she had to begin the long and painful process of learning to live with the knowledge that Gavin would never be a part of her life.

Much more of this and the top of Gavin's head would blow right off. He opened his eyes and stared, half-blind and unfocused, out the front windows toward the beach. A flash of light once again caught his attention, and this time, he made out silhouettes standing on the dunes.

Concern gripped him for a moment, but then Sunny did something spectacular with her tongue and he didn't give a shit if anyone was out there or not. The door was locked so no one could get in. He doubted anyone could see into the dark bar from that distance. And, even if they could, they wouldn't be able to see Sunny.

Although, with his entire body drawn tight and rigid with the effort to not lose control, it wouldn't take a genius to figure out what was happening behind the bar.

He dropped his hand to the top of Sunny's head, pushed his fingers through the soft curls, and grasped a handful.

"Am I hurting you?" she asked as she flipped her silver gaze to his. "Is the schnapps too much?"

He shook his head and rubbed his chest, trying to loosen the tight fist squeezing his heart. Whatever she was doing with her tongue was dangerous. The beautiful woman on her knees, looking up at him with those amazing eyes—one hand wrapped around his dick, the other around his balls—was lethal.

He half-laughed, half-groaned. "No, you're not hurting me. But you are killing me. In a good way."

She licked her lips, and wicked intent replaced her earlier concern. "Good."

"Yeah, not good." He relaxed his grip on her hair and slipped his hand under her chin. "I think it's time you stopped, before it's too late."

Her grin dissolved. "I don't want to stop." Her voice was small, almost pleading. "I want to..." She swallowed and looked uncertain. "I want to finish. Like this."

His heart hit a logjam, then broke loose like a raging flood. Flames licked over his body, and his hands began to tremble. "You shouldn't do that, Sunny. I'm clean but... well..." Thinking about Sunny doing this to someone else was like peeling the skin off his body. It hurt like a mother and would eventually kill him if he dwelled on the subject too long.

She saved him from further jealous torment by moistening her lips, then holding his gaze as she wrapped her mouth around him and slid down at an excruciatingly slow pace.

"Fuuuck," he growled and let his head fall back on his shoulders. The effort not to come in her mouth consumed him. Holding his head upright while simultaneously keeping his orgasm at bay required more strength than he possessed.

"I've never done this with anyone."

Her words snapped him out of his trance, and his head lolled forward so he could look down at her. "What?"

The wicked woman was replaced by a shy, uncertain one. "I mean, I've done... this..." She shifted her gaze away, embarrassed. "But I've never finished a guy. I've always had this hang-up about it and never met anyone I wanted to... taste."

Breathing became a challenge, and his vision swam. Her words affected him as much as her mouth, and he wasn't sure he could keep standing. He wrapped his fingers under the lip of the counter and gripped it so tightly it bit into his flesh.

"I've never had a wild, uninhibited fling. But I've always wanted to. I want to experiment and experience everything." Uncertainty filled her eyes again. "I want that with you. Will you let me?"

Wild, uninhibited fling.

The words cut through the spell she'd woven and stung like lashes across his chest. He didn't want to be a wild fling. He wanted more. How much more, he couldn't say. But the idea of spending a weekend romping around in her bed, then being sent on his way didn't sit well with him.

She must have taken his silence as a go-ahead because she flicked her tongue over the glistening pre-cum, then swirled it around and around and—*holy God*—around until his head was swimming. Every time she hit that magical spot—right *there*—a little more of his control collapsed.

He vaguely remembered he was pissed about something, but for the life of him he couldn't recall what the hell it was.

She slid her flattened tongue down the length of him, then sucked on one of his balls. When she moved to the other, they tightened with the impending explosion, and he had to lock his knees to keep them from buckling. She wrapped her lips around him, taking as much of him into her mouth as possible, and sucked.

His body was no longer his to control. His hips pumped in and out, and her greedy mewling sounds acted as fuel to the fire. He was afraid of being too rough, but he couldn't stop. And then... He threw his head back, ground his teeth together, and detonated.

After several moments of labored breathing and continuing spasms, he thought he might be able to pull himself together. He blinked his eyes, trying to clear the stars, and drew in a long, ragged breath while reaching for Sunny.

She licked her lips like a cat that just finished a satisfying bowl of cream.

He pulled her body flush against his and crushed his mouth to hers. He'd thought he was back under control, but he was wrong. Despite the orgasm that just wreaked havoc with his system, he wanted more. Needed more.

She was a drug he couldn't get enough of. He couldn't get close enough. And dammit, being a weekend fling wouldn't be enough.

He swept his tongue into her mouth, tasting the schnapps and himself. It was an aphrodisiac that once again zapped his control. "More. I need more of you."

Sunny laughed and pulled back to catch her breath. "You promised me sex on the beach."

With shaky fingers and jerky movements, he made a half-assed attempt to tie the drawstring of his pants. He slipped his feet into the borrowed flip-flops, grabbed her hand, and damn near sprinted for the door.

Chapter Seventeen

As they hustled over the dunes and out to the beach, Sunny was tempted to laugh at Gavin's exuberance. But she was right there with him, and the sexual energy thrumming through her propelled her on at his breakneck speed.

While he flipped the blanket open onto the soft sand, she pulled off her shirt and unzipped her jeans. Gavin's harsh intake of breath caused her to pause with her waistband partway down her hips.

"That is so fucking hot," he murmured, staring at the body necklace she'd put on just for him.

Three chains fell from the one that circled her neck. The two outer chains attached to her nipples. The center chain fell to her belly, where it attached to another chain that created a diamond pattern around her naval, then circled her waist.

His eyes filled with appreciation, lust, and searing heat. She kicked off her flip-flops, shoved her jeans the rest of the way down, and stood before him in only her turquoise panties and the necklace. He shed his clothes, then sat Indian style on the blanket. "C'mere." The command was spoken in a sandpaper-rough voice.

She trembled as he traced the diamond pattern with his forefinger. His touch was soft and reverent.

He wrapped his hands around her waist to lock her in place and pressed his lips to the sensitive skin of her inner thighs. He kissed, nipped, licked, and laved a path up her thigh, stopping when he reached the juncture of her legs. He closed his eyes and drew in a deep breath, then blew hot air across her damp panties.

"Please don't tease me. I need you inside me. Now."

Blue eyes studied her through a hooded gaze. "I need to taste you. Now."

"But..." Her argument died a quick death as he slipped his fingers under her panties and pulled them to the side, leaving her exposed.

His tongue flicked across her clit, then stroked the folds of her sex. Her knees weakened, and she stumbled. But Gavin was there, his hands holding her waist tight. He slipped his fingers around the back of her knee and lifted one leg so it draped over his shoulder.

Oh. My. God.

She had the sense she should be embarrassed about acting like a total wanton, but all she found in her emotional toolbox was hot and desperate lust.

The moon glinted off Gavin's dark hair and cast shadows across his face. His expression was one of intense concentration, and watching him love her with his tongue and mouth was an erotic image she'd never forget.

When her trembling became uncontrollable, the corner of his mouth tipped into a grin. He pushed a finger into her, then curled it in a come-here gesture that sent vibrations rumbling through her entire being. All of her senses heightened to a sharp, almost painful extreme.

When Gavin rolled his finger again while clamping down on her clit with his teeth, a lightning bolt struck her nervous system.

Everything went black and bright-white simultaneously. She felt nothing... and everything. "More," she croaked. She must be the greediest lover Gavin ever had, but he didn't seem to mind. She needed to feel him inside her, filling her... making her feel this freaking good again.

"Let yourself go; I've got you."

If she let go any more she'd be scattered all over the beach. As the spasms subsided, she realized he was trying to pull her down.

"Baby, let yourself go. I swear, I won't let you fall."

Her knees buckled and she crumpled into his arms. Gavin caught her and gently laid her on the blanket. Her only contribution was to lie there like a boneless jellyfish, going where the flow of the water took her. He grabbed a condom from his shorts pocket and quickly sheathed himself.

"Climb up here on my lap."

She didn't have the strength to climb anywhere. But as she rolled her head to the side to look at him and tell him so, she became incapable of speech.

He was an irresistible temptation: naked, aroused, and waiting for her. His half-closed eyes roared with heat, and the passion reflected in them made her shiver.

He mistook the shiver of excitement as her being cold. "Come up here, and I'll warm you up."

To the point of meltdown.

With jerky and less than graceful movements, she crawled to her knees, then onto his lap. She hovered over his erection for a moment, then dropped in one fluid movement, impaling herself.

His hands tightened on her waist, and he sucked in a sharp breath as his eyes slammed shut. She stilled, thinking she hurt him. But when he opened his eyes, pain wasn't emanating from them.

He wrapped a hand around the back of her head and grabbed a fist full of hair. His other hand stroked a blazing path over her shoulder and around the side of her neck. He cupped her face in his palm and kissed her temple. "I swear to God, I have never in my life felt anything as good as being inside you."

Bubbles built in her stomach and pushed out to her extremities. She wanted to tell him she'd never felt anything like this, either. But her voice wouldn't work, which was probably for the best. She was vulnerable enough without him knowing how deeply he affected her. So rather than communicating with words, she wrapped her arms around his neck and kissed him like there was no tomorrow.

And where they were concerned... there might not be.

When she pulled back for a breath, his gaze drifted to her necklace. He tugged on the center chain, which tightened the clamps. The pinch caused her to cry out, while the erotic sensation shooting from her nipples down through her stomach and into her sex brought forth a moan of pleasure.

"Do you like that?"

She nodded and rocked her hips.

He did it again, slightly harder. "You had this covered tonight. Did you wear it just for me?"

Yes, she did. As soon as he told her the plan for tonight, she thought of this necklace. Although she'd worn it to work many times, tonight she didn't want anyone to see it but Gavin. Rather than outright confessing, she pressed her lips to his and murmured, "Arrogant man."

His mouth lifted into a smile, and he whispered, "Thank you." He tenderly brushed a few strands of hair away from her eyes and out of her face. "What do you think about sex on the beach?"

"Amazing." She let her eyes drift shut, imagining how glassy and dreamy they must look. She probably looked drunk out of her mind. And, if a person could be drunk on incredible sex, she would be. "You're amazing. I never knew sex could be like this. Missionary position in the back of a car or on a bed is all I've ever known."

He stilled, and she opened her eyes to find a stunned expression on his face. After a moment, he squeezed his eyes shut, wrapped his arms around her waist, and in the blink of an eye, had her flat on her back. "My turn to drive." He grinned. "This probably seems like the same old, same old, but I'll try to keep it interesting."

The humor faded from his expression and everything about him grew serious. His eyes were those of a predator, but his touch was tender as he swept the hair from her face, then rested his elbows on either side of her head.

"Is something wrong?" she asked.

He didn't answer, only swallowed hard before beginning the dance inside her. His strokes were slow and methodical as he retreated, then slowly stroked back in. The depth of his stare and the emotion behind it was bottomless.

She wrapped her legs around his and dug her heels into the backs of his thighs. The change of the angle sent shockwaves through her, and when Gavin slipped a hand under her butt and lifted... *boom*. Flashes of light blinded her, and surges of electrical energy shot through her. She yelled his name and grabbed hold of his shoulders, as the two of them rode the tidal waves.

"I have to be crushing you," Gavin muttered, trying to find his voice and the strength to roll off Sunny. With a deep, shuddering breath, he pushed himself up and off her, then crashed onto his back.

He found his shorts next to his shoulder and retrieved the Ziploc baggie he'd stuck in his pocket. He smiled. Granddad always said, "Never go to the beach without a bag for your trash." He doubted a used condom and wrapper were the kind of trash Granddad had in mind when offering that sage advice.

Doing the best he could with one hand—because for some ridiculous reason, he didn't want to let go of Sunny—he stripped the condom off, shoved it and the wrapper into the bag, then tucked it into his pocket.

A breeze blew off the water, and Sunny shivered.

"Are you cold?"

"A little." Her fingers absently stroked his chest hair. "But I'm okay."

He scooted to the edge of the blanket and took her with him. Making sure no sand hit her in the face, he flipped the free half of the blanket over them, like a cocoon, and curled her tightly against his side.

She sighed and cuddled closer. His last serious girlfriend had been in college and since then, he hadn't spent much time cuddling with lovers. He always felt like cuddling was emotional, whereas sex was strictly physical.

At least, that's what he thought before tonight.

With Sunny, there'd been lots of emotions involved, and just thinking about it caused his chest to tighten and his stomach to bottom out. He drew in a deep breath and blew out a mixture of frustration and fear. When he looked into her eyes, he felt like their souls were fusing, much like their bodies. At least, his soul had melted. Christ, he even considered saying something crazy like *I love you*.

He'd always appreciated great sex. But what he felt for Sunny transcended sex. He admired her strength and determination. He found it remarkable that she remained childlike in her ability to laugh and enjoy life, while also retaining her tenderheartedness, rather than turning cynical and vengeful toward the world.

Her love for Robby and the sacrifices she'd made for him left Gavin in awe. Other than his grandfather, he didn't know anyone who would have sacrificed themselves the way Sunny had.

Guess that said a lot about his current associates.

And hell, he was no better. Since going to work for Holden Enterprises, he'd been concerned with climbing the company ladder and not much else. He contributed financially to his grandfather, paying the taxes and most of the maintenance expenses associated with the farm. But he didn't lend any emotional support.

He rubbed his chest, trying to kill the ache. But guilt was a formidable foe and wouldn't be brushed aside.

Sunny's breathing had grown slower and deeper, and when she gave a soft snore, he grinned. The women with whom he normally associated would be mortified to know they snored. But Sunny would probably make a joke about it and laugh it off.

Her dad sure as hell hit the mark when he dubbed her Sunny. She brought sunshine to Gavin's world when he hadn't even realized how far into the darkness he'd wandered.

She made him smile and breathe easier and want to be a better man. And she'd somehow gotten the idea she could trust him to keep her property safe. He, of course, hadn't made any effort to make her think differently, and the reasoning behind that baffled him.

He'd spent a lot of days on this beach as a kid, fishing with his grandfather, watching the horizon, hoping and praying his parents' boat would miraculously appear. He often wondered if part of the reason he was so driven to succeed had anything to do with them.

Logically, he knew they were never coming back. But there was a little boy inside him who still looked at that horizon and wondered if somehow, someway, they managed to survive. If they did come back, he wanted them to be proud of him. He wanted them to see a successful, wealthy man perched to take over one of the largest hospitality companies in the country.

Given his current circumstances, life should be better than ever. But after being hit with the recent deluge of memories from a simpler time, he had to admit that wasn't the case. Even though he'd changed over the years, Anticue was the same. And he refused to allow it to be changed and tainted as he had been.

He spent the next several hours listening to the waves, enjoying the cool breeze blowing across his skin and warm Sunny curled against him.

When the morning light cracked the horizon, he nudged her awake. "Good morning, sunshine."

She crinkled her nose and rubbed her eyes, then settled back down.

He grinned and squeezed her tight. "Sunny, baby, you need to wake up. We need to get dressed and off this beach before someone sees us."

There was a moment's hesitation, then her eyes popped wide open, and her head shot off his shoulder. "Ohmigod. We're on the beach. Naked."

"Yes, we are. I'd hate for word of this to get back to Ed and Joe. Or"—he shuddered—"Miss Jane."

In an instant, she became a flurry of activity, searching for her clothes. "Robby!" Her eyes were wide and wild. "I didn't tell Robby I wouldn't be home. Has he—"

"He stayed at a friend's house."

She sagged to the ground in relief. "I forgot. Okay, deep breath." She flipped her gaze to his and smiled sheepishly. "I know... I'm almost thirty years old. But I'd kill him if he didn't come home without telling me. I didn't want him worried."

Gavin slipped on his shorts and searched the surrounding beach for his shirt. Oh yeah, it was behind the bar. "We should probably stop at the bar and get my shirt..." He paused and grinned. "His shirt."

Sunny threw a hand over her mouth to squelch her laughter. "If he knew what we did while you were wearing his clothes, he'd burn them."

"He'll never hear it from me. I don't kiss and tell."

As they headed over the dunes, Sunny stopped and brushed the sand off of something shiny. "Oh my goodness." She held it up for him to see. "I don't know much about good jewelry, but this looks real. And expensive."

"Let me see that." Gavin snatched the bracelet from her fingers and snarled. "Son of a bitch."

Sunny's eyes widened, and she took a step back. "Do you recognize that?"

Rage boiled through him as he clenched his fist around the silver-and-onyx bracelet. "It's Callie's. Max gave it to her for her birthday last year."

Sunny's brow wrinkled. "You guys came out here the other night?"

"No." He couldn't believe Callie would lower herself enough to set foot on a beach—she was more of a concrete pool kind of girl—but he knew this was her bracelet. The moonlight catching her bracelet, and probably another five pounds of jewelry, must have been the flash he saw from the bar. "I thought I saw shadows out here last night, but I assumed it was locals enjoying the night." Remembering what they'd been doing at the time, he added, "Then you did something crazy with your tongue, and I didn't care."

Protective possessiveness took over. He grabbed Sunny and pulled her to him as if she were in immediate danger. "I doubt she could see anything from this distance, but even if she could, she wouldn't have been able to see you. I'm sure she was gone by the time we got out here."

The thought of Callie watching him while he'd been making love to Sunny was too disgusting to consider. "By the time I'm finished with her, I promise she'll never spy on us again."

Chapter Eighteen

*T*he insistent knocking on the pool house door had Callie cracking her eyes open and peering at the bedside clock. As she suspected, she'd missed breakfast... which explained the relentless pounding on the door.

She never missed having breakfast with her father, but this morning, she wasn't able to face him. It had been daybreak before she stopped crying and fell asleep. She'd never be able to fake her way through breakfast—heartbreak had a way of showing itself, regardless of the effort put into hiding it—so, she decided to avoid her father altogether.

She should've known he'd come looking for her, making sure she was okay. She rubbed her hands over her face to clear away the sleep and padded to the door. "I'm coming. Please stop pounding."

She opened the door and took a step back, certain that, as soon as he got a good look at her, he'd come sweeping in, asking a million questions, demanding answers.

He didn't disappoint. "My God, Callie, what's wrong?"

"Nothing" would sound stupid, because obviously *something* was wrong. People didn't cry until their eyes were nearly swollen shut for no reason. Sooner or later, she would need to tell him she'd given up her pursuit of Gavin. She just hadn't intended it to be right now.

However, just thinking about it broke her heart all over again. "Oh, Daddy." She threw her arms around his neck and cried like a three-year-old who had fallen and scraped her knee.

He didn't say anything, just hugged her like a protective father and let her cry herself out. Again.

Sure that this time there couldn't be a tear left in her scratchy, swollen eyes, she drew back and flopped into the chair. She took a shuddering breath, then blurted it out. "I went to Anticue last night. I saw Gavin with that bartender. I'm finally ready to let go of the stupid, childish dream I've had of him falling in love with me." Tears started again. Dammit.

Her father's face fell into an expressionless mask. "What do you mean you went to Anticue? Why?"

She hugged a throw pillow tightly to her chest. "We were sitting out by the pool, and I got this wild idea to go to Anticue. I know you wanted him to be friendly with the bartender, but I needed to see how friendly he'd gotten."

She squeezed her eyes shut as the images of Gavin and the blonde rushed at her. She'd seen more than she ever dreamed possible. Daddy didn't need to hear the details, and she didn't want to repeat them, so she opted for the basic version. "The bar was closed, so we watched through the windows. I saw the two of them together—"

"Callie, he's working out negotiations with her. I told you, sometimes Gavin is going to need to do things you might not like."

Callie blinked a few times before settling into a blank stare. He had said Gavin needed to be friendly with the bartender, but Callie didn't realize he expected Gavin to actually have sex with her. "Sleeping with her is part of his job?" Callie's voice was shrill and filled with disbelief.

Her father shoved his hands into his pockets and turned away to look out the door. "If that's what it takes to close the deal."

She stared at her father, too numb and shocked to speak. After a moment, she found her voice and asked, "What if he and I were involved? Would you still approve of something like that?"

His body tensed, and he grew more agitated. "It's only sex, not a marriage proposal. As part of the job, sometimes we have to do things that aren't pretty. But we do them, nevertheless."

Callie felt as if, for the second time in twelve hours, her world was snatched out from under her. Her head spun, but her limbs were too heavy to move. She felt like she was floating in space, with nothing to ground her.

Had her father cheated on her mother over the years, in the name of doing his job?

Did she have a clue who the two most important men in her life really were? Cold desperation seeped into her chest. She didn't want to believe any of this. She wanted to wake up and find she was having a terrible nightmare.

But that wasn't going to happen, and it was time she grew up and faced the facts.

The man standing before her, the man she'd adored all of her life, was a complete stranger. She realized this was the dangerous man she'd heard people whispering about when they didn't think she could hear. A man who would sacrifice her happiness for *the job*.

The man who groomed Gavin to be just like him.

She stared at her father's back and fought off a fresh wave of tears. She needed time away from everyone, and everything, to sort things out. She'd been concerned about trying to pretend nothing was wrong when she saw Gavin at the retirement party tonight. But this was even worse. While this confused and heartbroken, she couldn't possibly pretend to be her father's perfect little princess in front of his employees.

"I don't think I can go to the party tonight."

Her father turned to face her, his expression fierce. "Of course you can. And you will." When she drew back from his anger, he softened his posture and smiled.

Rather than seeing the smile of a wonderful father who loved her more than life itself, she saw the smile of a man who engineered everything and everyone around him.

"I'm sorry I snapped, princess." His smile widened. "How about I take you shopping? We'll buy a necklace and earrings to go with your new dress." He pulled her out of the chair and hugged her tightly. "We'll take your mother with us and get her something, too."

Callie absently nodded her consent and numbly returned the hug. This is the way it had worked her entire life. She'd just been too naïve to notice the mechanics. Anytime her father messed up or did something unpleasant, he made up for it by taking Callie and her mother shopping. And afterwards, everything was fine.

Had he taught Gavin that trick, too?

Callie withdrew from his embrace and gave him the best smile she could muster. She was too emotionally exhausted to argue with him and desperate to be rid of him so she could crawl back into bed and pull the covers over her head. "I'll see you and Mother after lunch."

Callie stared at his retreating back and burst into tears again. Was anything or anyone what they seemed? She'd always believed her mother to be the self-centered, pompous one, her father to be the loyal, friendly one.

Boy had she been wrong. At least about her father.

She considered her feelings toward her mother and where they'd originated. She finally realized it wasn't her mother's actions that had caused those feelings, but rather the opinions her father had expressed over the years.

She loved her mother, but they'd never been close. Had that been part of her father's engineering, too?

She fell into bed with a sob. She needed to talk to Gavin. He knew her father and mother better than anyone. If anyone could help her sort this mess out and make sense of things, it would be him.

But... oh, God! She hugged the pillow to her chest and tried to deaden the tremendous, searing pain. She couldn't call Gavin anymore, could she?

There wasn't anyone left who she could trust or depend on.

Sunny was standing on the stoop, staring at Gavin like a love-struck teenager, who didn't want to be away from her new boyfriend for more than twenty minutes, when Robby pulled into the lot. He whipped into a parking space, slammed his truck door shut, then stormed across the lot.

Sunny took a deep breath, then slumped against the banister and crossed her arms. "I hoped the night away would mellow him out. Apparently not."

"There's more aggression rolling off him now than last night." Gavin's brow furrowed and he flipped his gaze to Sunny's. "Do you want me to stay? I can go to New Bern later today, or even tomorrow."

Sunny shook her head. "No, thanks. I think it's time we have that talk I've been putting off. It'll go better if it's just the two of us." Switching her attention to Robby, who was halfway up the stairs, Sunny said, "Did you have a good time at Chad's?"

He moved around them on the stoop and opened the kitchen door. His mouth twisted into a menacing smile as he said, "It was enlightening."

Normally, he would have followed the statement up with some kind of wiseass comment, like how much he learned from the late night shows on Skinemax. But this Robby wasn't in a teasing mood, and she had no idea what had him so irritated this time.

She hated the tension between them and felt it as a constant burn in her gut. Crossing her arms over her stomach to shelter herself from Robby's anger, she said, "Gavin's getting ready to leave. I'll be right in, and you can tell me about it."

He flipped his gaze to Gavin, then stepped through the doorway and slammed the door shut behind him.

"I'm so sorry he's acting like this. I don't understand what's going on with him. I didn't think he had an unfriendly bone in his body."

A series of emotions crossed Gavin's face as he propped his hand on his hip and leaned against the railing. "Maybe I shouldn't come back here tonight, like we planned."

Frustration and anger fought for the top spot on her emotional scale. "This is why I've never dated. It's too damned complicated."

Gavin ran his thumb across her lower lip. "We just have to give him time to adjust."

We? Adjust? To what?

"What are we doing here, Gavin? I live here. I'm not leaving. You live in Myrtle Beach. Our *business* is finished." Unable to maintain eye contact with his intense blue stare, she turned to look at the water rolling onshore. "What's the point in continuing any of this?"

"Our business isn't finished." When she snapped her gaze to his, a shadow flickered in his eyes and a crease furrowed his brow. "I know you think it is. But I keep telling you, I know Max Holden. He isn't going to accept your refusal without a fight.

"On a personal level… I care about you. Way more than I should at this point in our relationship, if you want the truth." He took a step forward and ran his hands down her arms before linking their fingers. "I think we've connected pretty well."

"Our connection has been great," she muttered, getting hot and bothered just thinking about it.

He tugged on her hands and smiled. "I meant more than the phenomenal sex. I want to spend more time with you, get to know you better." He nodded toward the closed kitchen door. "I'd like to get know Robby, if he'd let me."

A twisted part of her was glad their business remained unfinished because that guaranteed he'd keep coming around. She also liked hearing he cared about her. Whether it was true or not, she didn't know, but at least it made her feel less vulnerable to getting hurt.

When she didn't respond, he said, "I'll stop by and have a beer on my way back from New Bern. If things are better, I'll stay. If not, I'll drink my beer, then keep heading south."

"Okay." She released his fingers and leaned into him for a hug. "I don't know what's going on with him, but I'm going to find out. By tonight, everything will be straightened out."

Gavin dropped a kiss onto her forehead, then headed down the stairs. She watched him until his SUV turned the corner and was out of sight. She didn't want a confrontation with Robby, but she wasn't going to tolerate his rude and bratty behavior any longer.

She took a deep breath, then pushed open the kitchen door. "What the hell is wrong with you?" Well damn, that approach wasn't the way to avoid a confrontation. Maybe she needed a few more deep breaths.

Robby was sitting at the kitchen table, his laptop open in front of him. He didn't move a muscle, other than to flip his cold, steely eyes to her. "How well do you know that guy? And I don't mean in the biblical sense?"

She clenched her teeth together and grabbed a Dum-Dum. "Robby, I've never treated you like a child, because I'm not the parent. But I'm no longer tolerating this shitty, disrespectful attitude you've been throwing at me lately."

He lowered his eyes and sighed. "I'm sorry, sis. I know I've been hard to live with over the past few weeks. I've been stressed over exams and trying to figure out what to do about going to ECU." He met her stare with a hard one of his own. "But this is different." He turned the laptop around to her. "Look at this. Read all about your good buddy, Gavin."

Nausea rose in her throat as she glanced at the computer. "What is it?"

"Sit down," he said, kicking the empty chair out to her with his foot. "Get comfy."

He'd probably spent all night searching the Internet for anything he could find on Gavin. And given his current level of hostility, he didn't plan to show her stories of Gavin helping little old ladies cross the street.

With much trepidation, she sank into the chair and adjusted the screen so she could see. Robby pulled up a picture of Gavin and an older, aristocratic man. The caption read: *Max Holden, CEO of Holden Enterprises, and his protégé, Gavin McLeod, share a moment during the Hadleigh Society's annual meeting*

"Okay."

"Do you know what the Hadleigh Society is?"

She cut her gaze to Robby. "I have no idea. But I have a feeling you're about to tell me."

"It's a bunch of rich guys that get together, smoke cigars, and drink wine. That's all they do. It's not for charity. It's just to smoke and drink… and it costs five thousand *annually* to be a member."

Damn, that sounded ridiculous, but how Gavin spent his money wasn't her business. "Okay, so they smoke expensive cigars and drink fancy wine. What's the problem?"

Robby rolled his eyes at her apparent stupidity, then switched to another article. "Here's the next one."

The next article was a feature on Holden Resorts. "Wow. I knew they built resorts, but… these are *resorts*."

Robby snorted. "Yeah, and if they build that in Anticue, nothing will ever be the same."

No argument there. She certainly wouldn't get to spend any more nights sleeping naked on the beach. And wouldn't it be a real shame to not do that again.

"You're forgetting something," she said. "The island has ordinances in place to keep us safe."

Robby's smile turned feral. "Yeah, some of these other places had them, too. Somehow, Gavin and his boss got around them." Robby flipped to another screen. "Read this one."

By the time she finished reading everything Robby had found, she'd gone through three Dum-Dums, and her stomach was in her throat.

"Do you see the problem now?" Robby said, crossly. "Gavin is a manipulator. Max Holden calls him a negotiator, but it's the same thing. The last article praised Gavin as being the best in the business. He's using you, Sunny."

He paced the small kitchen, his footsteps landing with hard, solid whacks against the linoleum. "He makes millions of dollars every year. Once he becomes CEO, those millions will double. Do you really think he's going to throw all that away to save some shitty little bar like the Blackout?"

Sunny jumped to her feet and barely contained the urge to slap Robby.

He grabbed her and pulled her into a tight hug. "*I* don't think of it that way. I love it as much as you do. But that's the way these Holden people see it. Do you really think someone like Gavin cares about the Blackout? Or you?" He stepped away from her, but kept a firm grip on her shoulders. "He's not going to let this little bar stand in his way of turning Anticue into a resort."

She flopped down into the chair and let her head fall into her hands. Everything Robby said made sense. Why would Gavin risk his career, and millions, over a nothing-special bar or a woman he'd just met?

Sunny felt as if her heart was being slowly extricated from her chest. She liked Gavin and didn't want to believe he'd been using her. But when she put her emotions in a box and buried them in a deep hole, allowing her to think logically, nothing else made sense.

So what did she do now? Confront him?

It's not like he would come right out and say, "Yeah, baby, I'm using you. Can I do it some more?"

Did she tell him to leave and never come back? Or, did she play along and make him think she remained oblivious to his game?

If she played along, at least she'd have a chance at figuring out what he was up to and what his plans for moving forward were. And, okay, it would also give her the chance to have more great sex. She was a woman. Gavin was an amazing man, with an incredible mouth. If he was using her... well, she refused to feel guilty for using him for her own selfish pleasure.

She needed to think this through, and she did her best thinking while pounding copper in her workshop. She pushed her chair back, got to her feet, and gave Robby a quick hug. "I'll be in the workshop if you need me."

Chapter Nineteen

As Gavin pulled onto the lane leading to his grandfather's house, a hum ran through his body. He'd always recognized a subtle, internal shift as he drove the long lane, breathing in fresh, country air, listening to the gravel crunch beneath the tires. He never bothered to analyze the feelings or try to label them, until today. Surprisingly, it was similar to the feelings of contentment he'd found in Anticue… along with a sense of being home.

As he approached the house and outbuildings, his grandfather exited the barn, exactly where he expected to find him. If the sun was up, his grandfather would be outside. The only unknown was if he'd be on a tractor in the field, in the barn working on a piece of equipment, or making repairs to one of the outbuildings.

A broad smile spread across the old man's face as he crossed the yard to greet Gavin. "Hello, son. What a pleasant surprise."

Gavin stretched as he exited the car, then extended his hand in greeting as Granddad reached his side.

Big mistake.

His grandfather's eyes narrowed, and he pushed Gavin's hand aside. "That formal stuff works fine in your business dealings, but I want a hug from my favorite grandson."

"I'm your only grandson."

"Yeah, well, all the more reason for you to give me a hug."

Gavin wrapped his arms around his grandfather and gave him a tight squeeze. As he registered his grandfather's small frame, shock rocketed through him and his breath left in a whoosh. He took a step back and studied the man who'd raised him.

How old was he?

Gavin ran the numbers in his head and came up with eighty, or damned close to it. How had he gotten so wrapped up with his life that he hadn't realized his grandfather was getting old?

He scrubbed a hand down his face. "I hope it's okay I showed up without much notice. As I said in my message, I was down by Wilmington. I wanted to see you while I was that close."

He was intentionally vague as to where he'd been, hoping his grandfather wouldn't ask questions. If he said he'd been in Anticue, his grandfather would be curious and would want to know why. Lying wasn't an option and, well, neither was telling the truth. He couldn't open himself up to the disapproval that would come from divulging that information.

Unfortunately, he'd seen that look too many times over the years, and he didn't want to see it again. Disappointing his grandfather was unacceptable.

"Of course it's all right that you came here," Granddad said, with a pat on Gavin's shoulder. "You don't need permission to come home."

Gavin followed his grandfather across the yard and into the house. The first order of business was a trip to the kitchen, where Gavin was promptly handed a glass of iced tea. "Have you eaten?"

"Yes, sir." A smile crept over his face as he thought of the breakfast he and Sunny shared in bed. His original plan had been to get up and head to his grandfather's early, but he didn't want to leave. When he offered to fix breakfast, she was so excited to eat "real food" he'd been further inspired to feed it to her in bed.

Granddad didn't spend any more time inside than was necessary, so once they'd both been outfitted with a large glass of tea, his grandfather pivoted on the heel of his worn-out leather work boots and headed to the front porch.

Gavin took a seat in the porch swing, which had been his favorite place to spend time as a kid. He couldn't curl up in a ball in the seat like he did at ten. But he still took comfort in the familiar squeak of the chain as he pushed his foot against the porch's wide plank flooring and set the swing in motion.

Listening to the creak of the swing and the *kerthunk, kerthunk, kerthunk* of his grandfather's rocker, Gavin felt so far removed from his life he could easily pretend none of it existed. No hassles. No worries. No deals to be made... or not made.

"What's on your mind, son?"

Startled, Gavin jerked his attention to his grandfather. "Nothing. Why?"

"You didn't come here to visit for the hell of it. It's written all over your face. Something's eatin' at ya." His grandfather smiled a toothy grin and pushed back in his rocker. "Woman trouble?"

Gavin took a drink of his tea and looked at the barn, the outbuildings, and the fields in the distance, remembering how it had all looked to his ten-year-old self. Nothing on the farm had changed, but he saw it all differently now.

Since everything with Sunny on a personal level was great, he wouldn't say he was having *woman trouble*. He didn't even think he could narrow his problems down to one thing. He had the unsettling suspicion his problems ran more along the lines of the sum of the parts, rather than the individual pieces.

Using diversion tactics—commonly known as changing the subject—he said, "Everything's fine. What's going on around here?"

Not the least bit fooled, his grandfather smiled, then allowed the directional change. "There's a new cook down at the diner. She's a spry young thing, not even seventy yet." Granddad rocked in his chair. "I think I'm going to invite her to bingo at the senior center."

Gavin stopped swinging and stared at his grandfather while scanning his memory. "That's the first time you've ever mentioned a lady friend." His grandmother had passed away before Gavin was born, and in all these years it never occurred to him that his grandfather never remarried. Hell's bells, he'd never even dated.

His grandfather had always seemed old, because when you're ten, everyone is old. Looking back on it now, he would have been in his late fifties when Gavin came to live with him. "You never dated when I lived with you. Why?"

"I was too busy raising you to be worried about dating." His grandfather shrugged. "My priorities changed after you came to live with me."

Deep-seated despair and disgust flooded Gavin, and his skin felt like it shrank to three sizes too small. What a selfish bastard he was. In all these years, he'd never recognized the sacrifices his grandfather made. Had he ever even thanked him?

Gavin needed to work. He needed physical labor to help him sort out the feelings of frustration and self-loathing squeezing him. "What were you working on in the barn?"

"Got some rotten boards that need to be replaced. I'm ripping out the old ones, so when I get the new lumber delivered it won't take no time at all to get it nailed in place."

Gavin looked down at his khakis and polo shirt. It was a good thing he still had a closet full of old work clothes here. Filled with purpose, he jumped from the swing and headed toward the door. "I'll get changed." He looked over his shoulder at the old farm truck. "Does the truck still run?"

His grandfather seemed confused at Gavin's sudden burst of energy, but nodded and said, "Sure."

"Good. We'll get a supply list together, then go into town and pick up the replacement boards and nails ourselves." He hadn't planned on spending the day working, but the idea excited him. It would allow him to work off some of his frustration and do something for his grandfather, other than writing a check. He'd also have the added bonus of proving to Sunny and Robby that he could be useful.

As he headed for the door, his grandfather said, "If you decide you want to talk, I'm here."

Gavin backtracked, leaned over, and wrapped his grandfather in a strong hug. "I don't say it nearly enough, but I love you." Forcing the crack out of his voice and the lump in his throat to break loose, he added, "Thank you… for everything."

"Callie, stop fidgeting. Why are you so nervous?"

Callie forced her hand away from the front of her skirt and gave her mom the best fake smile she could muster. "I'm not nervous. I…"

Her mother didn't know about last night's fiasco in Anticue, or this morning's conversation between Callie and her father, and Callie wanted to keep it that way. It wasn't that her mother didn't like Gavin. She'd always welcomed him into their home and treated him like one of the family. But she also always maintained he was too old for Callie.

Every time Callie protested, by reminding her mother that Daddy was twelve years her senior, her mother would nod and give Callie a look that said, "Exactly." Callie never wanted to consider, even for a brief moment, that her parents' marriage might have problems. She'd learned to avoid the discussion by avoiding conversations that involved Gavin.

Now, she was more than a little suspicious about her parents' seemingly perfect marriage. Given the circumstances of her father's acquisition of the company, she questioned if their marriage had been anything more than one of her father's carefully orchestrated plans.

"You what, dear?"

Her mother's concern snapped Callie out of the depressive musings and back to the present. She flipped her gaze to her mother's and studied her soft, blue eyes.

Daddy wasn't who she'd grown up believing him to be. Gavin wasn't the man she'd thought him to be. Could her mother be something different, too? Something more than a self-absorbed woman. "I guess I'm a little nervous about this new dress. It's more revealing than I usually wear."

Pride radiated from her mother's eyes. "Yes, it is. But it's a beautiful dress, and you're gorgeous." The corner of her mother's mouth lifted, and her expression turned conspiratorial. "I bet Jason will agree."

"Jason?" Callie coughed to clear her throat. How did her mother know about him?

Her mother's gaze drifted across the clubhouse to where Jason stood. "He's a nice young man."

"Yes, he is." Callie's voice cracked. She'd made a fool of herself last night, but through it all, he'd been nothing but kind and compassionate. She wasn't in any hurry to rehash last night's events, or trust that any man was as he seemed on the surface. But she did want to thank him again for his help and for being so kind. "I think I'll go say hello."

Overcome by an urge she couldn't stop, Callie wrapped her arms around her mother for a hug. It was hard to tell which of them was most shocked when Callie added, "I love you, Mother."

By seven thirty it was obvious Gavin wouldn't be attending the party, and Callie found herself experiencing an odd mix of emotions over his absence. Out of habit, she constantly watched the door, looking for him. But when it came right down to it, she didn't want to see him.

Max, on the other hand, wasn't handling Gavin's no-show well, and she feared her father was going to have a stroke. Callie, along with everyone else in attendance, had heard her father repeatedly leaving messages on Gavin's cellphone. It was impossible to miss the barked, snarly commands for Gavin to "Call me."

None of his calls were returned, and the longer the night went on, the more furious her father became. She was still upset about their morning conversation and the realization that her father would accept Gavin's infidelity *if necessary* for the cause. But he was her father, and lifelong habits of worrying about someone you loved weren't broken in a matter of hours.

She looped her arm around his and gave him her best little princess smile. "This is a wonderful party. I've never seen Lorraine so happy."

He cut his eyes to her, and though his stare was cold and harsh, his words were soft and kind. "Trying to soften me up so I won't kill Gavin?"

She laughed and squeezed his arm tighter. "He did send flowers and a note." Although, Callie suspected her father was more upset with Gavin's defiance than his disappointing Lorraine through his absence. When her daddy spoke, he expected everyone to listen.

She couldn't help but wonder if some of her father's anger might also spring from an underlying concern that Gavin's loyalties could be shifting. She realized it hadn't been what Gavin said during the phone call with Max yesterday that made her go to Anticue. It was the tone he used while talking about the bartender that led her to believe things between them had moved from professional to personal.

If she picked up on that, her father must have, as well. Gavin's refusal to come to the party tonight served as further confirmation Max might have something to worry about.

A part of her felt it would serve her father right if that happened. He'd sent Gavin to Anticue to seduce the bartender, then use their attraction to make her cooperate.

What would happen if she seduced Gavin and turned the tables on her father?

Gavin swung his SUV into the gravel parking lot of the Blackout and mashed the brakes. "Whoa." What he expected to find at nine-thirty on a Saturday night he didn't know, but apparently it wasn't a full house. Going by the limited number of available parking spaces, the place was packed. Which was good for Sunny's business. Bad for him getting her alone.

The trip to New Bern had been exhausting and enlightening. Who knew working out in a gym, even for hours on end, didn't make up for a lack of physical labor. The longer he'd driven, the tighter his muscles had gotten. He ached from neck to toe and desperately needed a cold beer.

He hoped like hell Sunny had worked things out with Robby, because the thought of driving another hour didn't hold a lot of appeal. Crashing in Sunny's bed, after they took a long, erotic soak in the big-ass tub in her bathroom... that worked for him.

He parked his SUV, levered his stiff body out of the driver's seat, and crossed the parking lot. Dark clouds covered the full moon, leaving the dunes in total darkness, but he still stopped and scanned the area, searching for stalkers.

He couldn't believe Callie had been there last night, spying on him and Sunny. Based on the number of calls from Max and the level of pissed-off radiating through the phone, Gavin figured Max knew about Callie's visit, too. Which meant he also knew Gavin had become intimate with Sunny.

He hadn't intended to tell Max about his and Sunny's relationship, tentative as it was. He figured that would only cause Max to yank Gavin out of the equation, leaving him without access to Max's plans.

But now, since Max was already in the know, Gavin would have to figure out a way to appease him while looking for an alternative solution to the puzzle. Skipping the retirement party probably hadn't been a wise move, but dammit, Gavin was tired of being yanked around like a puppet on a string. He didn't want to be in Myrtle Beach. He wanted to be with Sunny.

As he pushed through the doors, a loud and rowdy cheer rose from the bar. A few guys he hadn't met were sitting near Joe and Ed, and the four of them were laughing and having a great time. Based on the look of things, their fun was at Sunny's expense.

She planted her hands on her hips and glared at the men, a sucker stick hanging from her mouth. He laughed as he pictured her on an Old West movie set: Sunny, the sharp-shooting cowgirl, preparing for a Wild West showdown—eyes narrowed in concentration, hand ready to draw, a piece of straw hanging from the corner of her mouth.

She said something to the men, then swung her gaze to the door. Catching sight of him, her body stiffened and her facial expression froze. Then, as if forcibly relaxing, she took a deep breath and lowered her shoulders as her arms fell to her sides. It even looked like she shook her arms, as if trying to relax her hands and fingers. She smiled as he approached the bar, but her eyes didn't sparkle and the smile was tight.

Shit. Her conversation with Robby must not have gone well. Which meant Gavin's worn-out ass would be hitting the road.

She ran the towel over the bar before dropping the cloth into the soapy bucket. "How was your trip to New Bern?"

There were three empty stools, so he took the middle one, going for as much privacy as one could get in a crowded bar on a Saturday night. "Good. I helped my granddad rip rotted lumber out of the barn. I'll go back next weekend and put up the replacement boards."

A blond eyebrow arched suspiciously.

"I didn't think you'd believe me." He unclipped his phone from his belt, pulled up the photo gallery, and turned the phone so Sunny could see. "That's why I had Granddad take pictures. It took him a while to figure out how to work the camera, but once he got the hang of it, he was unstoppable."

Sunny took the phone from him and flipped through the pictures. Rather than laughing, or at least giving him her trademark million-watt smile, her lips turned downward.

"What's wrong?"

She snapped her gaze to his and handed him back the phone. "Nothing. Those are great pictures. Looks like you were working hard."

He leaned over the bar and quietly admitted, "I'm so tired and sore, I can hardly move."

She reached into the beer cooler and grabbed a bottle of Bud. "Will this help?"

"Tremendously." He waited while she popped the top, then slid the bottle to him. "How did things go with Robby?"

She wrung out the cloth and swiped at the bar. "It's all good now."

Uh-huh. He took a sip of his beer and waited, giving her a chance to come clean. When she stuck with the ridiculous it's-all-good story, he said, "You're a terrible liar."

She smiled sheepishly but didn't deny the lie. "It'll be okay. Do you... um..." She glanced around the bar, looking everywhere but at him. "Want to stay tonight?"

He narrowed his eyes and studied her. What the hell was going on? She was trying to appear relaxed, acting as if everything was fine, but she was as bad at acting as she was at lying.

"What's going on, Sunny?"

She pulled out of her slump and straightened her shoulders. "Nothing. I'm just tired." She grinned and threw off a sexy little vibe. "I didn't get a lot of sleep last night."

His body heated at the reminder, and his cock, which seemed to be the only un-sore part of his body, came alive. "You're closed tomorrow, right?"

"Yes." Her response was a little breathy and a lot sexy.

"So if I kept you up again tonight, you could sleep all day tomorrow?" He lifted his gaze from her lips to her eyes. "At least, stay in bed all day?"

Her lips parted and her eyes liquefied. She glanced toward the kitchen and bit her lip. "Robby said he could stay at his friend's house again tonight."

"That's good. I mean"—he reached across the bar for her hand—"I take it the talk didn't go well. But at least he's trying, if he's willing to stay at a friend's house."

She stared at their linked fingers and took a deep breath. "Yeah.

He's agreed to do whatever I want."

He pulled her hand to his mouth for a kiss. "Tell me what you want."

She snatched her fingers back and shifted from foot to foot. He could tell she wanted to glance at Joe and Ed, probably to see if they were watching. Instead of giving in to the urge, she turned her back to them and leaned against the counter. "I want you at my mercy."

"Kinky." He leaned toward her, angling his head so their mouths were perfectly aligned for a kiss. "You had me wondering before, but now I know. There *is* a dominatrix hiding in there."

Rather than completing the kiss as he'd hoped, she pushed off the bar and took a step back. "Guess you'll find out later."

Gavin drank his beer and watched Sunny work. She laughed and joked and seemed at ease with the other customers as she set up shots and poured beers. But with him, she was stiff and stilted and most definitely not at ease.

It was like she had a split personality disorder. Hot one minute, cold the next, then back to hot. She claimed to be tired, but there was more at work than her lack of sleep.

Oh shit. A terrible thought sent a surge of panic through him.

"Sunny." When she looked up, he made a come-here motion with his head. "When you get a second."

She mixed a couple of drinks, closed out a tab, then made her way back to him. "What's up?"

"Callie hasn't been here, has she?" She seemed shocked by the question, so he added, "I can tell something's wrong, but you won't level with me about it." He rubbed the back of his neck. "I'm at the top of Max's shit list right now because I didn't go back to Myrtle Beach for a function. I didn't think he'd come here personally, but I wouldn't put it past Callie to make a repeat appearance."

"Why did you miss the function?"

"I'm being a brat."

She lifted an eyebrow and her lips twitched. "A brat."

"Yeah. There was a retirement party for Max's secretary tonight. I'd planned to go earlier in the week, but…" He shrugged. "I wanted to go to New Bern, then come back here instead." He looked at the screen on his phone. "I have eight missed calls from Max, but none from Callie." He re-clipped the phone to its holster. "Which had me a little concerned she might have shown up here."

"Does she call you often?"

Does she ever. "Usually. But if she saw us together last night, she might have finally gotten the hint." He sipped his beer and debated how much he should share with Sunny. He finally decided to go with the truth. She might be worried, as she should be, but he didn't want to keep anything from her at this point. "Based on the tone of Max's messages, I'm concerned things are becoming unstable. I got worried for a minute."

Sunny stared out the window, deep in thought. After several minutes of blank staring, she sighed and turned her attention back to him. "You look beat. Why don't you go up to the apartment and relax."

"Are you sure?" He wanted to figure out what had her upset, but he didn't want to continue pushing. He had to trust her and assume she'd share with him when the time was right.

She nodded and pulled a key from her pocket. "Make yourself at home, and I'll be up in a couple of hours."

Chapter Twenty

*S*unny had washed, stocked, and straightened everything she could think of, and the bar had never been cleaner. Unable to put off the inevitable any longer, she locked up, then made her way up the stairs to her apartment at a snail's pace.

She stunk at confrontation. Especially when she wasn't sure on which side of the friggin' argument she stood.

She and Robby agreed she'd keep seeing Gavin. She once asked Gavin if their relationship fell under the keep-enemies-closer rule. Looking back, she was pretty sure he hadn't denied it, only claimed they weren't enemies.

This afternoon she decided to play the same game. It was better to keep him close, so they could keep an eye on him and possibly get him to slip up and give them information. Plus, keeping Gavin around would have the added benefit of more great sex.

At the time she made the decision, it seemed like a great plan.

But when he walked into the bar, looking lickably delicious in worn-out jeans and work boots, she began to question her ability to pull it off. When she looked at his smiling face on his cellphone, her heart splintered and her doubts doubled.

She still couldn't believe the man in the online articles was the same man she'd gotten to know over the past few days.

"Would the real Gavin please come forward?"

Crazy as it sounded, she wondered if Gavin even knew which one of him was the real deal. He seemed offended when she said he didn't look like a farmer, and he was proud of the work he'd done this afternoon at his grandfather's. He hadn't exuded the same sense of pride when he talked about his job, and after everything she'd read, it was no wonder.

The sound of the television and snoring greeted her as she pushed open the kitchen door. Gavin's work boots were in a heap on the floor, and he was stretched out on the sofa. His head listed to the side in an awkward and uncomfortable-looking position, while his arm hung off the edge of the couch with his hand resting on the floor, palming the remote.

She found him so damned adorable tears stung her eyes. A person couldn't help what the heart felt, but it seemed ridiculous to care so much for him after such a short time. It would be impossible to continue sleeping with him and not get more attached. She wasn't even sure she could be in the same room with him, fully clothed, and not get more involved.

What was she going to do? And not just about tonight. What about tomorrow and the day after?

If she woke him and invited him to bed, she feared playing out the part of a sex-starved maniac. But she didn't want to go to bed without him, either. Settling on the safest route, she took the remote from his hand and powered off the television, sat on the floor, and rested her head on the sofa next to his chest.

Her eyes were tired and gritty, and in a matter of seconds, her lids slammed shut. *You wanted a wild, tumultuous fling that would knock your world off its axis... You got it.*

Gavin blinked several times in rapid succession, trying to clear the sleep from his eyes and the fog from his brain. His bed was lumpier than normal. His body felt like it had been put through a blender. This wasn't his ceiling. And something soft was tickling his arm.

Finding the strength to move, he rolled his head to the side and blinked a final time. *Sunny.* He looked around the room and let the pieces fall together.

He'd come up from the bar to wait for her and must have fallen asleep watching television. When she got home, she didn't wake him. Instead, she sat on the floor next to him and fell asleep.

He looked at his watch. *Four-thirty?* Shit, how long had she been like that? And most importantly, why hadn't she left his ass where it was and gone to bed so she could sleep comfortably?

Fighting against the aches and pains—which really pissed him off because they served as a reminder for how lazy and out of shape he was—he pushed to a sitting position, then scooped her up in his arms.

She came awake fighting. The kicking and flailing caught him off-guard, and he nearly dropped her. "Shhh… Shhh… Sunny, you're all right. It's me, Gavin. I've got you." She looked around frantically, then took a deep breath and settled her head on his chest. "You fell asleep by the couch. I'm taking you to bed."

She wrapped her arms around his neck. "Sorry. I was having a nightmare."

"Want to tell me about it?" he asked, gently laying her on the un-made bed.

She unzipped her jeans and shimmied out of them. "In my dream you weren't really who you say…" Her words trailed off, and she momentarily froze. She bit her bottom lip and yanked off first one pant leg, then the other. "It was nothing."

Bullshit. Whatever was bothering her in the bar was now haunting her dreams. Four-thirty in the morning wasn't the time to harass her about it, but tomorrow morning… later this morning, he would get to the bottom of it.

He stepped out of the bedroom and checked Robby's room. "Robby didn't come home. Can I trade in the couch for your bed? I'll set an alarm and move back out there before he comes in."

Her eyelids slid shut, and for a minute, he didn't think she would answer. But then she patted the sheet next to her and said, "Shut my bedroom door. He won't be home until later in the afternoon, and even if he does come home, it's okay. He's expecting you to be here."

He kicked off his jeans, pulled his shirt over his head, and crawled into bed beside her. For the first few minutes, she remained as rigid and unmoving as a piece of concrete. But when he wrapped his arm around her head and rubbed her scalp, she made a soft mewling sound, then relaxed and scooted over against him. She propped her head on his shoulder, and within seconds, she'd gone back to sleep.

For the second morning in a row, Sunny woke to the mesmerizing sight of Gavin lying next to her. She liked having him in her bed, sharing her space. She liked the way his long lashes curled and how his features softened with sleep. The stubble on his face was sexy, and the way he rested with one hand over his heart was sweet.

The major difference between yesterday morning and today was her mood. Yesterday, she'd awakened with a smile on her face, filled with happy on the inside. This morning, she had a headache and was filled with hurt and confusion.

Gavin stretched and rolled onto his side, facing her. "Good morning," he said with a smile and a wink.

She tried to smile but found the task too difficult. She also didn't believe the morning, or the day for that matter, would bring anything good, so she gave a non-committal, "Morning," and left it at that.

While she'd been lying there watching him sleep, she'd been thinking. Using him for mindless sex while she figured out his tactics for acquiring her building sounded great in theory. But it would be impossible for her to pull off. She was terrible at acting, especially when it came to faking her feelings. Gavin had even commented on the way her expressions gave away her thoughts. She'd never make him believe something she didn't believe herself.

Despite her agreement with Robby, she needed to revert to plan B: confront Gavin. However, she couldn't do that while lying in bed with him, so when he reached for her hand, she slipped out of his grasp and climbed from the bed.

He narrowed his eyes and pushed up onto his elbow. "Okay, Sunny, spill it. What's going on?"

She gathered her hair at the nape of her neck and used a Scrunchie to hold it in a ponytail, then pulled on a pair of shorts and a T-shirt—a barrier of protection in case he denied everything and tried to seduce her back into bed.

"Why didn't you tell me you were second-in-command at Holden Enterprises?"

She watched his face for signs of surprise, but he didn't react in any way. He simply held her gaze and shrugged. "What's it matter?"

"You make millions of dollars every year and stand to make even more when you take over."

He had the audacity to look perplexed. "I don't understand what my income has to do with anything."

She waved her hands in frustration. "You told me you'd help protect my property."

"And I will." He rubbed his eyes and sighed. "I'm sorry. I'm not following this conversation at all." He threw the sheet off and climbed out of bed with a moan. "Can we get some coffee and talk about this over breakfast?"

She forced her eyes to stay on his face, rather than granting them permission to take in the hard planes of his chest and stomach, as they desperately wanted to do. "You lied to me."

He swiveled his head in her direction and arched an eyebrow as he pulled on his jeans.

"Well, you didn't exactly lie. You just didn't tell me the whole truth."

His frustration with her was obvious as he pushed his fingers through his hair. Without verbally responding, he shuffled—barefoot and shirtless—to the kitchen.

Sunny's mouth fell open in disbelief. How dare he act like he already owned the damned place. She stormed into the kitchen, intent on giving him a piece of her mind, but he'd already popped the top on the coffee can, and the aroma filling the air mellowed her out.

Coffee was good. And she couldn't deny she enjoyed having him fix it for her. It would be even nicer if he brought it to her in bed like yesterday morning.

Dammit, Sunny, focus.

Annoyed with herself as much as him, she crossed her arms over her stomach and tapped her toe. Those kinds of thoughts were the reason she'd crawled out of bed and gotten dressed. Hell, he didn't need to do anything to seduce her. She did a fine job of getting lusty on her own.

Once the coffee was brewing, he turned and rested a hip against the counter, then crossed his arms over his chest. "Okay, let's start from the beginning... which seems to be sometime after I left yesterday." He glanced to the ceiling, as if he would find the answer tacked up there, then looked back at her. "Does this have anything to do with how angry Robby was when he got home yesterday?"

She diverted her gaze and grabbed a sucker. She didn't want to bring Robby into it, because this was between her and Gavin. But Robby had been the one to find the information. Without his research, she'd still be blindly following Gavin's lead, allowing him to pull the strings and work her however he wanted.

"While Robby was at his friend's house, he searched your name on the Internet. That's how we found out who you really are and what your position is." He looked more intrigued than anything, which threw her off-balance and caused her to lose her stride. "I don't believe you'd risk your career in order to save…" Robby's words came back like a slap across the face. She turned away from Gavin and stared out the window. "There's no way you'd risk all of that to save this bar."

"Sunny, I never said I'd risk anything. I said I'd figure out a way to fix things." He stepped up behind her, then turned her to face him. His eyes were soft and concerned and he seemed so damned sincere she couldn't meet his gaze. "If anything, having me as second-in-command should make you feel better. That gives me more leverage."

Well hell, when he put it that way…

She was so confused and wrapped up emotionally, she didn't know what to think or believe anymore. "I guess the problem is that I don't know which Gavin is the real you. And if I don't know you, how can I trust you?"

He let go of her arms and turned his attention to the hissing coffee pot. "What do you mean, the real me?"

"It's like you're all these different people. The rich guy—although I didn't realize you were *that* rich—who came in here that first night and swept me off my feet." By the time Gavin left for the second time that night, she hadn't given his social status another thought. "When you came back the next morning, you were a business man, but you were still the same Gavin that... ummm..." She smiled against the blush heating her face. "You know."

She reached for the cup of coffee he offered and took a sip. "Then you dressed down in Robby's clothes and talked about being a farm kid. You were laid back and relaxed and seemed to fit in perfectly with the crowd around here. I guess I forgot who you'd been when we first met."

He sipped his coffee and patiently listened to everything she had to say. Although he wasn't verbally responding, his facial expression and body language said a lot. His brow was furrowed, his jaw popped, and his shoulders were tense and battle ready.

"Robby hits me yesterday morning with all these articles of you with Max Holden, looking very much like his protégé... you know, the ruthless guy who won't stop until he gets what he wants. There were pictures of you with socialites and at social events costing thousands of dollars to attend." She flopped down in the kitchen chair. "Then you came into the bar last night wearing those worn-out jeans, a T-shirt, and work boots, and I lost track again. Which Gavin is real?"

A series of emotions crossed his face as he seemed to carefully consider his words. Finally, he said, "I don't know what to say." The light in his eyes dimmed, and he shrugged. "I could stand here all day and give you reassurances, but you won't believe them." He pushed off the counter, dumped his coffee into the sink, then put the cup in the dishwasher. "I guess my actions will have to speak for themselves. I'll go back to Myrtle Beach and work on things from there. I'll keep you posted."

That's it? No argument? No trying to justify anything?

Too numb to move or even think as he turned and walked away from her, Sunny sat glued to her chair. She held her breath, waiting for him to come back for more conversation, but he didn't.

She heard him moving around the bedroom, and several moments later, he returned, dressed, with his overnight bag slung over his shoulder. He opened the door, and, without turning around, said, "I'll let you know what's going on sometime tomorrow."

She wanted him to leave, right? She couldn't trust him, and she couldn't keep seeing him without falling even deeper under his spell.

So, if this was what she wanted, what she believed was best, why did she feel like a piece of her ripped from her chest and walked out the door with him?

Chapter Twenty-One

"God dammit!" Gavin grabbed the file he'd been analyzing from his desk and launched it across his office. He pushed his fingers through his hair, then shoved back from his desk and began pacing the floor.

He'd spent the past four hours going over every scrap of information he could find on the Anticue property, only to find the situation worse than he thought. Online tax records indicated, just as Max claimed, he owned all the property surrounding Sunny's.

For the past several years, he'd been buying up property as it became available. Some of the parcels were in Max's name, some were in Cynthia's, and two, including the old fishing pier, were in Callie's.

He'd probably also used that time to fund several county commissioners' campaigns, ensuring he had *his* people in place to vote for the required ordinance changes. Gavin tried to figure out a way to incorporate the bar into the resort, but Max would never go for it. Sunny's whimsical style and the worn-down structure wouldn't gel with the lavish opulence of a Holden Resort.

He dropped into his chair and let his head fall back. Beating his head against a brick wall for the past four hours had made him angry and frustrated and left him with a pounding headache. The headache, however, was nothing compared to the searing pain in his chest.

No matter how hard he worked to forget, his mind insisted on replaying the conversation with Sunny like a CD stuck on repeat. The problem was, her comments were painful because they were so damned accurate.

For nearly a year, he'd been unhappy with life. He knew it stemmed from job dissatisfaction and his disappointment with some of Max's decisions. But he thought the feelings would pass once he stepped into Max's shoes and could do things his way.

Then, months ago, he started to question if he had what it took to fill Max's shoes. The Anticue situation was a perfect example. He'd never have the heart to ruthlessly pursue the purchase of Sunny's land. And the idea of raping Anticue's pristine beaches made him sick.

Sunny assumed that in order to help her he'd have to give up his career. He hadn't thought about it in those terms until she mentioned it, but now, he wondered if she might be right. Was he willing to make that sacrifice? Was he willing to forfeit not only the career he spent the past twelve years building, but his grandfather's farm, as well?

Granddad couldn't afford to keep the farm without Gavin's financial assistance, and Gavin promised to do everything possible to make sure his grandfather never had to move. Without his job, Gavin wouldn't be able to keep that promise.

Fuck. His head spun like a damned whirlpool, sucking him down into the drowning blackness. Maybe getting out of the office for a while would help him find some perspective and, God help him, a solution to this clusterfuck.

He reached into his pocket and fingered Callie's bracelet. Max was probably on the golf course, so Gavin would have the chance to talk to her privately. Then, after Max returned, Gavin could meet with him.

He wasn't counting on changing Max's mind, but he needed information. The names of the commissioners on Max's payroll would be helpful. He also needed to find out when Max hoped to break ground, so he'd know the timeframe they were dealing with. Actually, at this point, any information he managed to gather would be useful.

He looked at the clock and wondered what Sunny was doing. He'd looked forward to spending a nice, relaxing day doing whatever she wanted. Returning Callie's bracelet, then spending the rest of the afternoon with Max wasn't a good substitution. But it was what needed to be done, so he might as well get on with it.

He pushed to his feet, flipped off his lights, and headed across town.

After two minutes of conversing with Angelina, Gavin confirmed Max was playing golf and Callie was in the pool house. Alone. Thank God, Lady Luck finally decided to toss him a penny. Although he was sure Jen and Tiffany had been with Callie in Anticue, since she never went anywhere without them, he still preferred to have this conversation without her friends eavesdropping from the bedroom.

He knocked on the guesthouse door and waited. The front of the house was floor-to-ceiling glass, so as soon as she stepped through the bedroom doorway, she saw him. Her steps faltered briefly, but she quickly recovered, then walked to the front door with an uncharacteristically confident stride.

"Hi." He didn't really want to know how much she saw the other night, but based on the way her eyes bounced around, looking at anything and everything but him, he figured she'd seen more than enough.

"Can I come in for a minute?"

"Uh…" She shuffled her feet, then took a step back and opened the door wide enough for him to enter. "Sure." Her flawless hosting skills kicked in and overran her discomfort. "Can I get you something to eat or drink?"

Taking a seat on the sofa, he said, "No, thanks. I just came by to return this."

Her mouth dropped open and pink splotches mottled her neck and cheeks as she stared at the jewelry in his outstretched hand. She gulped and took the bracelet, then awkwardly flopped into the chair.

After swallowing a few times, she nervously licked her lips and said, "Thanks. I, uh, won't ask where you found this."

He laughed and stretched his arm across the back of the sofa. "Okay, and I won't ask how much you saw."

She flipped her gaze to his and, much to his surprise, giggled. "That'd be good." Relaxing in the chair, she said, "Gavin—"

At the same time, he said, "Callie—"

They stopped and stared at each other for a few beats. Something in her eyes shifted, a kind of understanding he'd never seen in them before, and in that instant, he knew everything with Callie would be all right.

"Do you know how much I care about you?" he asked.

Her eyes widened, and she flipped at a piece of fringe on the pillow she'd been hugging to her chest. She seemed uncomfortable with the question, so he rushed to explain. "Your dad has always treated me like a member of the family. He invited me to holiday meals, let me spend family vacations with you guys. I'd never gone on a family vacation until I went with your family." He laughed. "Unless you count fishing trips to Anticue as a family vacation."

They weren't lavish, overseas vacations like he'd taken with the Holdens, but thinking about those fishing trips with his grandfather always made him smile. They'd been simple day trips, but he loved their time together and had always looked forward to the next trip.

He snapped back from his reverie to find Callie's nose scrunched up in distaste.

"Yeah, I didn't think so." He leaned forward and rested his elbows on his knees. "Your dad always treated me like a son. You know what that makes you?" She shook her head. "My sister."

"Ewww."

"Exactly. I didn't have any family other than my grandfather. Your family treating me like one of their own meant a lot to me. Because of that, I could never see you in a romantic way. Not because there's anything wrong with you. It's just…" He laughed and curled his lip. "Wrong."

She laughed, a real genuine laugh that caused the dimple in her cheek to pop. "I can see why you feel the way you do… or don't, as the case may be."

"I'm also not the guy you think I am. Not really." Her face crinkled with confusion as he struggled to explain what he was only coming to understand himself. "Going to Anticue and New Bern has made me realize I'm a farm boy at heart. A farm boy who's ended up with a lot of polish on him, in a world where I'm not completely comfortable."

He stared out the window at the main house. "I don't want to live in a house like that. I'd rather have a farm, where I can get away from everyone and everything."

A little place on the beach would work, too.

Callie fiddled with the bracelet. "How did you end up working for Daddy? How did you make it so high up the ladder so quickly?

"I went to work for Holden my senior year of college. Your dad"— he shrugged—"well, Holden Enterprises offered to pay off my student loans if I agreed to work for them for five years."

He never shared the details of his and Max's agreement with anyone. From the way she digested the information, Max hadn't shared it either.

"At the end of that term, I signed another five-year contract. When that one expired, I'd advanced to the position I'm in now. No one figured I'd go anywhere, so I wasn't asked to sign another contract. Technically, I'm no longer bound to Holden. But I owe Max a lot. Some, like Max, would say I owe him everything."

"I'm sorry I went to Anticue to spy on you." She dropped her gaze, and her shoulders slumped. "I'm sorry for a lot of things I've done over the years."

"There's no need to apologize." He started to stand, then hesitated. "Are we good now? You understand where I'm coming from?"

She nodded. "Yeah, I do." She shifted her gaze to the main house and blinked a couple of times, like she was fighting back tears.

"Is there something else wrong?"

After a brief hesitation, she said, "Can I ask you something?"

Prior to today, there would have been no telling what crazy question she might ask. But after this little chat, he didn't have any reservations. "Sure."

"Would you be unfaithful to your wife if it became necessary for your job?"

Huh? Talk about a leftfield question. "Why would it ever be *necessary*, under any circumstances, to be unfaithful?"

"You know, for the job. Like with the bartender?"

Unease rose from the pit of his stomach and banged around in his chest. "What do you mean?"

She shifted in the chair and fiddled with the pillow some more. "Daddy said your…"—she dropped her gaze to the floor—"getting friendly with the bartender is part of the job, and that I shouldn't have been upset. He said if things worked out between us, sometimes you'd have to do things like that. Is that true?"

Gavin's blood pressure shot so high he swayed from side to side and little black spots danced before his eyes. He thought back to the first time Max sent him to Anticue. Callie wanted to go, but Max tried to talk her out of it.

Another ping of awareness hit him between the eyes. The first time he'd called from Anticue, something about the conversation had bugged him. He hadn't been able to put his finger on the problem, but now he understood what it had been.

Max wasn't surprised to learn the owner was a woman. He also seemed to know the owner and the bartender were one and the same. He'd sent Gavin to the Blackout with the intention of him making a connection with Sunny. The son of a bitch had set Gavin up and used him, just like Sunny accused Gavin of doing to her.

And, he supposed, since he'd fallen prey to Max's plan, that's exactly what he'd done.

A loud pounding, followed by the door being flung open so fast it nearly ripped off the hinges, had Gavin and Callie's heads swinging in that direction.

Max stood in the doorway, practically snorting and stomping like a bull. "Where the hell have you been?"

Oh, this was perfect. Max was going to get pissy after the shit he pulled? So not happening. Gavin unfolded himself from the sofa and stalked toward Max. "Let's discuss this in your office."

"That's a damned good idea." Max turned and stormed off toward the french doors.

Gavin leveled Callie with a solid stare. "No, I would never be unfaithful because my job dictated it. That's ridiculous. And I'm not with Sunny for business reasons. Your father is very wrong about that."

For the second time today, a woman studied his face, searching for the truth of his words. And once again, nothing he could say would mean anything. His actions would have to back the truth of his statement.

She looked at Max's retreating back. "I've never seen him this angry."

"I have." Although Gavin doubted Max's anger was little more than the heat of a candle compared to Gavin's raging inferno. "We'll talk more later."

Gavin stepped out onto the patio and drew in a deep breath of humid air. He felt as if his veins had been filled with gasoline and every beat of his heart shortened the fuse a little closer to detonation. It wasn't hard to believe Max had set him up; that was his style. What infuriated Gavin was that he hadn't caught on to Max's plan and had allowed himself to be played.

Anger and frustration swirled until his vision blurred into a red haze. He wanted nothing more than to storm into Max's office and rip him apart. But attacking Max wouldn't get Gavin the information he needed. A verbal altercation would only drive a larger wedge between them, and Max would shut Gavin out of any further involvement in the Anticue plans.

No, Gavin needed to calm his ass down, so he could con the conman.

The instant Callie made Gavin aware that he'd been played, he made a decision. It was too early in their relationship for Gavin to say he'd give up everything for Sunny. But he would give it all up to do the right thing.

It shamed him to admit that, had he been confronted with this situation a week ago, he might not have been as sure of his decision. Today, it was crystal clear. He wanted to be the man Sunny could be proud of. He wanted to talk to his grandfather about his job, openly and honestly, without worry of disappointing him. And he wanted to look in the mirror and like the person staring back at him.

But he couldn't divulge any of that to Max, at least not yet. He had to make Max think that, while he'd had a temporary lapse of judgment over the weekend, he was still squarely in Max's camp.

Gavin blew out a breath and forced the anger to retreat.

Showtime.

Chapter Twenty-Two

"*W*hat the fuck is going on?" Max's voice echoed off the walls and slammed into Gavin with the force of a physical punch.

Gavin had intended to wait for Max to calm down before answering, but the longer the older man stormed around his office, the more concerned Gavin became about Max's health. Gavin had seen Max angry, but Callie was right. He'd never seen Max this furious, for this long. Gavin may be carrying a truckload of pissed-off himself, but that didn't mean he wanted any harm to come to Max.

He took a step forward and in a soft, soothing voice said, "Max, let's sit down and talk."

Max whirled around. His face was bright red, his eyes narrowed slits. "Don't patronize me. I know that let's-be-reasonable tone. Hell, I'm the one who taught it to you."

"You also taught me it's a waste of time to talk to someone who's angry or agitated." Gavin slipped his hands into his pockets and watched Max pace.

While walking from Callie's to Max's office, Gavin had struggled to understand why Max was so mad. His plan had been to get Gavin and Sunny hooked up, and that's what happened. So what was the problem?

Then it hit him. Max was beginning to suspect his plan had worked too well and was concerned it might backfire. That meant Gavin had to be extra careful not to confirm Max's fears.

"I need a drink." Max poured a shot of whiskey, tossed it back, then slammed down the glass. After several seconds, his stance relaxed. "You want one?"

Gavin grabbed a tumbler from the bar and held it out to Max. After pouring a generous portion into Gavin's glass, Max refilled his own. The vein in his forehead still protruded, but in general, his overall attitude had settled slightly, and he seemed less at risk of a stroke.

Rather than sitting in his normal chair, facing Max's desk, which put Max in his normal position of power, Gavin settled into a chair in the less formal, more relaxed sitting area. "What's bothering you the most, Max?"

Max sat in the chair opposite Gavin and fell deep into thought, probably running over the long list of Gavin's infractions, figuring out where to start. Gavin wasn't surprised when Max began with the most recent issue. "Why were you in my daughter's house? You suddenly interested?"

"We were talking."

"About?"

About your warped sense of duty, you bastard. Gavin bit his tongue and said, "Did you tell your parents everything you did or talked about with your friends when you were Callie's age?"

Max's eyes narrowed in warning and his face re-reddened. "I won't tolerate you playing games with my daughter."

Gavin shook his head as his irritation reignited. "I've never played games with Callie. You were the one trying to force something that wasn't ever going to happen. She understands that, and we were having a nice, friendly chat."

Oh, and as a result of that chat, you can expect my resignation, just as soon as I figure out a way to fix the Anticue mess, you son of a bitch.

"What about you and the bar owner?"

Gavin shrugged, feigning nonchalance. "She's a pretty woman. It's nothing serious." His flippant response felt like a betrayal, but he had to be careful. "I've tried everything"—heavy emphasis on *everything*, since, after all, that had been Max's plan—"to make her see the benefits of selling. But she's attached to the property and refuses to entertain any of the offers I've made."

Max ground his teeth together and glared out the window.

"If we can't secure her piece of land, what are the alternative plans?"

"There are no alternative plans." Max's gaze was steely, his voice frosty. "If you can't work things out, I'll take care of it myself."

Max's glacial tone and expression sent a shiver down Gavin's spine. Like the rest of the country, the economy had taken a toll on Holden Enterprises. People weren't vacationing like they used to, and the properties were struggling to turn a profit.

Max wasn't the kind to panic, but he'd sunk a fortune into the Anticue endeavor. He had to be feeling the pinch of having expended the cash, but not yet seeing a return on the investments. He was getting desperate to wrap things up.

Because he'd never wanted to know how Max turned reluctant landowners compliant, Gavin never broached the subject. But for Sunny's sake, and in a way, he supposed, for his own sake, he needed to know details. He smiled, trying to look devious and ratty. "Just curious, Max, how exactly do you take care of things?"

Max leaned back in his chair, crossed his hands over his stomach, and stared at Gavin. Apparently, he was as bad an actor as Sunny, because it was obvious Max wasn't fooled by Gavin's attempt to be oily. "You worry about working out a deal and leave the rest to me."

"How long do I have?"

"Forty-eight hours."

Some habits die harder than others, Callie mused as she sat in her room, listening to her father and Gavin hash things out. Right after moving back from Europe, she'd purchased a listening device off the Internet and installed it in her father's office. It allowed her to listen to all of her father's conversations, but the only ones she cared about were the ones involving Gavin.

Her father had been so angry when he stormed off earlier, she'd almost been afraid to flip it on. But in the end, she hadn't been able to resist.

"What's the rush, Max?" Gavin's irritation with the forty-eight hour deadline was evident in his terse response.

"I've been working on this project for years. I'm not waiting any longer."

There was a brief pause, then Gavin said, "Have you forgotten that I'm taking a vacation?"

"No, I didn't forget." Her father's voice was cold with a dash of nasty. Had he always spoken to Gavin this way and she never noticed? Or had things changed between them? "But the forty-eight hours starts now," her father said. "Not when you return from vacation."

The leather chair squeaked, indicating one of them stood. "You're a real son of a bitch, Max."

Callie gasped and her heart pounded in her throat as she waited for her father's scathing response. He didn't yell, as she expected, only laughed and said, "Don't tell me you're just figuring that out."

There was no reply from Gavin, only the opening and closing of the office door. Leather squeaked again. She reached for the off switch on the intercom, but stopped when she heard Max pick up his desk phone and punch in a number.

"It's Max." Her father's tone was all business. "I have a job for you in Anticue. They have forty-eight hours to come around, but I don't think that's going to happen."

What? Callie's heart jumped to her throat and blocked her airway, causing her to gasp for breath as she waited for him to say more. Something, anything that would convey the call wasn't as menacing as it sounded. But rather than saying anything reassuring, he gave the address for the Blackout and confirmed he'd call back with the final order.

Over the years there had been hundreds of rumors regarding her father's unethical practices, but she never believed any of them. She never *wanted* to believe them. But she couldn't deny that this call had been ominous, with a clear intent.

Since he hadn't used the speakerphone, she couldn't hear the other person. Therefore, she had no way of knowing who he'd called, or the specifics of what her father intended.

Regardless of all she didn't know, she had to call Gavin. Her fingers trembled so badly it took three times to get his number dialed, as she struggled to hold back the tears. "Gavin." She swallowed the painful knot in her throat and sniffed. "He just made a call."

"Who made a call?"

"Daddy. He... I... shit. I have his office bugged—"

"I knew it." He laughed, then immediately sobered. "Are you okay? You sound like you're crying."

"No, I'm not okay. Daddy called someone. He told them he had a job for them in Anticue." She choked on a sob. "I don't know what he meant, specifically, but it sounded bad. I can't believe he'd do something awful. But I also can't deny what I heard."

As the silence on the line stretched on forever, her heart broke under the gravity of the situation. Unable to stand the deafening quiet any longer, she said, "Are you there?"

She heard something that sounded like Gavin hitting the dashboard a couple of times, then he said, "Yeah. I'm here." His voice cracked, and he cleared his throat. "Callie, I need your help. I know he's your father, but will you help me?"

Turning a flat piece of copper into pine needles seemed like a good idea when Sunny dreamt it up last week. But after hours of pounding, with little visible progress, she was beginning to have her doubts. Hell, she was past doubts and now believed it to be her worst idea. Ever.

She tossed the hammer and chisel onto the table, yanked off her gloves, and grabbed her bottle of water. Maybe after a short break she'd be able to, once again, find the brilliance in the plan.

Wiping sweat from her forehead, she sank into her lawn chair and kicked up her feet, exposing as much of her body to the ocean breeze as possible. She swished a big gulp of water around in her mouth before swallowing, then poured the remainder of the bottle over the back of her neck. She closed her eyes and let her body relax, hoping the breeze and pounding surf would calm her, giving her some relief from her out-of-control thoughts.

Since Gavin left, her mind had been a whirling dervish of activity, spinning up thousands of questions, but finding few answers. She'd thought working on this new project would help, but that hadn't been the case.

Several moments into her please-let-me-find-some-peace meditation, she heard the hum of a motor and the crunching of tires on the gravel parking lot. She didn't want to leave the solitude of the trance, but the motor didn't sound like Robby's truck, and common sense dictated she open her eyes to see who'd come to visit.

If she were completely honest with herself, she'd admit to hoping it was Gavin. She still didn't know if she could trust him, but her sweaty palms and rapid heart rate indicated it didn't matter.

A red, low-rider pickup with flames painted on the front idled at the edge of the lot. The dark tinting on the windows kept her from seeing inside the vehicle, so she couldn't make out the driver. She also couldn't tell how many people were inside.

In all the time she lived on the island, she'd never been afraid. People often pulled into the lot to check the hours of the bar or to turn around. But everything about this vehicle, from the red paint and flames, to the dark windows, to the way it sat unmoving, screamed danger. Even though she couldn't see into the vehicle, she had the sense the driver was watching her, sizing her up.

Gavin's words came rushing at her… *He can make your life hell.*

She hoped she was being paranoid, allowing Gavin's ominous warning to overtake logic and freak her out unnecessarily. But in case this wasn't runaway paranoia, she got up from her chair and stepped backward into the workshop.

She didn't want to take her eyes off the truck, but she needed to search the workbench for something that could be used as a weapon. With shaky hands, she grabbed her cellphone and a long piece of pipe she could swing like a baseball bat.

The engine of the vehicle revved and the truck pulled farther into the parking lot. The building blocked her view and kept her from seeing them or what they were doing. The upside was they couldn't see her either. She sprinted toward the stairs and climbed them two at a time, not slowing until she was in the kitchen with the door locked behind her.

She ran to Robby's room, her only view of the parking lot, and yanked up the blinds. The truck was making a slow circle in the gravel. From the corner of her eye, a flash caught her attention.

She whipped her gaze to the road and saw Robby pulling into the lot. Panic for his safety seized her. She fumbled with her phone, trying to open it, so she could call him and warn him to stay in his truck.

The mysterious vehicle's motor revved, and when she looked out the window again, all she saw was the tailgate as the truck disappeared down the road, heading south toward the bridge. She snapped the phone closed and, with shaking knees, made it from Robby's room to hers.

She hadn't believed Gavin's boss would actually inflict physical harm, but maybe she'd been wrong. What kind of man did Gavin work for? And what kind of person was Gavin to condone such behavior?

While working in her shop, she'd begun to consider that Gavin made a few valid points. The money she and Robby would receive from selling the property would pay for Robby's schooling, saving them years of student loan payments. She was concerned about running the bar by herself. If she sold, she could work for someone else and not have the stress of being a business owner.

But she had just as many valid reasons for not selling, and this latest development pissed her off. Selling because she wanted to was one thing. Selling because she'd been bullied?

Hell, no.

She stripped out of her sweaty clothes and jumped into the shower. By the time she finished, she had a firm plan. It was time for Robby to teach her the ins and outs of computer research. However, rather than researching Gavin, she wanted to know everything possible about Max Holden.

Chapter Twenty-Three

*C*allie's call sent shockwaves of rage through Gavin. An hour later, he'd calmed slightly but still felt the sharp sting of reality. Funny how a person's world could change in an instant. Gavin had made the decision to quit his job before Max made that call. But finding out just how far Max would go had cut him to the core.

He was also fully aware his world hadn't been the only one to disintegrate with that call. Callie was devastated, and Gavin was worried about her. He'd called to check on her several times and had even offered to let her stay with him for a few days while she sorted things. But she declined, saying she planned to spend the night with Tiffany.

After Max left for his golf game tomorrow, she'd go back to the house and finish her detective work. She'd already proven herself valuable to Gavin's efforts by slipping into Max's office and retrieving the last number dialed from his phone.

Since Max had given both Gavin and the hired gun forty-eight hours, Gavin felt as if everything—meaning Sunny and Robby—would be okay tonight. First thing in the morning, Gavin would call his friend Marty, a private investigator, and have him track the number. If they could find the person Max called, then maybe they could figure out his plans.

Gavin picked up the bottle of Crown sitting next to his chair and threw back another long swig. He'd started off using a glass, but decided a shot at a time wasn't getting the job done. Tonight, he needed heavy-duty firepower to kill his demons.

After leaving Max, he'd gone to the gym, but quickly lost interest. Rather than calming him, it had the opposite effect. So, in lieu of being healthy, he headed for the liquor cabinet.

Sitting in his perfectly manicured backyard, watching the crimson sky turn dark, had also proved agitating, at first. But the bottle of Crown had mellowed him out, allowing him to contemplate his future.

Although the idea seemed crazy on the surface, he'd always wanted to run a restaurant. He loved to cook and, at one time, considered culinary school. Every time he closed his eyes and allowed himself to imagine that kind of future, he found himself on the beaches of Anticue.

He loved the solitude and relaxed lifestyle the island offered. But that would be lost forever if he didn't figure out a way to stop Max. Taking another swig from the bottle, he assigned his mind the task of figuring out a solution.

"I'm coming. Jeez, knock it off." Sunny scrubbed the sleep out of her eyes and shuffled through the living room toward the kitchen.

Robby exited his bedroom right behind her. "Who's beating down the door?"

"I have no idea, but it better be damned important this early in the morning."

Okay, in all fairness, nine-thirty wasn't exactly early. But to Sunny, who hadn't gotten to sleep until after four, it was obscene.

Once she figured out how to use the various search engines, she'd been unstoppable. She stuck with her plan of finding everything possible on Max Holden, but she also broke the plan and did a fair amount of research on Gavin.

Bottom line: Max was a snake. And while she hadn't been able to find anything concrete about Gavin, she'd come to the conclusion that if he worked for Max Holden, he must be a belly crawler too.

Logically, she knew she was better off without him. Her heart hadn't gotten the memo, though, because as she turned the corner and saw Gavin standing at the door, it took a flying leap toward him.

"What the hell is he doing here?" Robby asked. He planted his hands on his hips and glared at Gavin through the door's upper pane of glass.

Spotting the familiar cups they used for coffee at the Anticue Quick Stop, she said, "I don't know, but he has coffee. I think it's worth finding out." She opened the door and realized the pounding had been so loud because he'd been kicking the door with his foot. He held a large storage box in his arms, with two cups of coffee sitting on top, and a tower of boxes stood next to him.

"Good morning." His tone was soft and his eyes held an intimacy only a lover could pull off. He glanced at Robby and said, "I didn't know if you drank coffee or not, so I only got two. I can go back and get another if you like."

Sunny took one of the cups but didn't step aside so he could enter. "What are you doing here?"

He glanced at the boxes next to him. "We have some research to do." Wicked mischief glimmered in his eyes, and for some stupid reason, hope flared in her chest. "Some of it I need to do, but you and Robby are the only ones who'll be able to spot the names we need to find."

Robby stepped up next to her. "What are we looking for?"

"I want you to look through all the donations that have been made over the past several years and through the lists of Holden's subcontractors to see if you recognize any of the names."

Sunny took a sip of her coffee and stared at the boxes. "Donations for what? Why would we recognize the names?"

"As you know, the current ordinances won't allow for a Holden Resort. But Max has several county commissioners on his payroll that will vote to change the ordinances. Once we know who we're dealing with, we can go from there."

Sunny gasped. She knew most of the county commissioners. In fact, Ed and Joe were both commissioners. "I don't believe you."

Gavin's face was a blank slate. "Believe it."

Sunny crossed one arm over her stomach and took another sip of coffee. "I have a question for you. The way you answer it will determine whether or not you come into this house."

"Okay."

"How can you stand to work for a man like Max Holden?"

Gavin reacted as if she'd physically punched him in the gut. His breath left in a *whoosh*, and he slumped slightly forward. When he opened his eyes, the pain she'd inflicted with the question was a tangible, living, breathing thing. "Max has been good to me. He paid my way through college and has always treated me like a member of the family. He offered me a chance to make something out of my life."

He took a deep breath, then sighed. "I didn't know Max was capable of some of the things I now suspect. That's what I'm going to look for. Proof that the rumors I've heard over the years are true. Or, hopefully, false."

Sunny checked Robby's face, gauging his reaction to see if he trusted Gavin's sincerity. Apparently he did because he pushed past her, grabbed one of the boxes, and hauled it into the house.

Gavin nodded to his cup of coffee. "I'll get the boxes, if you'll carry that."

"Why are you doing this?"

Gavin picked up an additional two boxes and said, "Because it's the right thing to do."

From his position in the floor, propped up against the fridge, with an open notebook on his lap, Robby said, "Tell me again exactly what I'm looking for."

They'd been at this for almost an hour, and none of them had found anything that proved Gavin's theory of Anticue commissioners being in bed with the bad guys. So far, she seemed to be the only one in bed with someone from Max's team.

"Any name that sounds familiar," Gavin said. He put his finger on the page to hold his place. "Max isn't going to leave a flashing neon sign over the names of the people he pays off. They'll be hidden. Well... hidden in plain sight to someone who knows what they're looking for. We have to put the pieces together in order to figure out the puzzle."

"So what are *you* looking for?"

Gavin rubbed the back of his neck and leaned back in the chair. "I'm looking at past situations where the landowners were reluctant to sell." His face contorted and his eyes darkened. "I'm looking for something that might tell me why they had a sudden change of heart."

Maybe they received a visit from some scary dudes in a red truck, Sunny thought.

She chewed her lip and debated telling Gavin about the strange vehicle. She didn't know that the truck was connected to any of this.

She still hoped she'd been overly paranoid but decided it wouldn't hurt to mention the incident.

"Do you know anyone who drives a red, low-rider truck, with flames painted on the front and really dark tinted windows?"

From the corner of her eye, she saw Robby's head snap up. "You think those guys had something to do with this?" When he came upstairs, he asked Sunny about the truck, but she brushed it off by saying people did weird things all the time. Now, he eyed her suspiciously.

Gavin tensed and his blue eyes turned cold and assessing. "What guys?"

"Late yesterday afternoon, a red truck pulled into the parking lot. They sat at the edge of the lot for a few minutes, and even though I couldn't see in, I had the feeling I was being watched."

"Where were you?"

"Sitting outside the shop, taking a break."

"What happened?"

"They just sat there. All of my instincts screamed something wasn't right, so I got up and went into the shop for my cellphone and…" She laughed, a little embarrassed. "I grabbed a pipe that I could swing like a baseball bat."

Gavin didn't laugh. "And then what?"

"While I was doing that, they pulled on up into the parking lot. As soon as they were out of sight behind the building, I took off for the house. I ran up here, locked the doors, and watched them out of Robby's window."

"They were turning around real slow," Robby interjected. "But when I pulled into the lot, they took off. I couldn't tell much about them, but I did see that there were two men in the truck."

"Son of a bitch." Gavin pushed his chair back from the table with so much force it toppled over backward. He ripped open the kitchen door and stalked out, slamming it shut behind him.

Sunny looked at Robby, who sat wide-eyed, staring at her. "I think he's mad."

Robby didn't laugh as she expected. Instead, he stood and followed Gavin outside.

"What's going on?" Robby's strained voice bled over the sound of the phone ringing in Gavin's ear. He turned to Robby and held up his finger in the universal just-a-minute sign.

On the sixth ring, the receptionist finally answered, then transferred him to Marty.

While waiting for Marty to pick up, Gavin dug into his pocket for the piece of paper on which he'd written the number. Because Marty often worked vampire hours, he didn't usually get into the office until late morning. Gavin hadn't expected to catch him this early but was relieved to hear his voice on the other end of the line. "Hey, man, long time."

"Yeah, sorry about that," Gavin said, rubbing the back of his neck. He and Marty had been best friends through high school and into college. Then, like everyone and everything else that mattered, Gavin let Marty drift away. "I need a huge favor. Fast."

"Of course you do." Gavin heard papers shuffling, then Marty said, "I'm ready."

"I have a phone number I need you to track. I think you're going to find it's a cell. I need to know who it belongs to and everything you can find out about them. I'm especially interested in their occupation and the vehicle they drive."

"What's going on?"

He gave Marty the number, then filled him in on all he suspected and the little bit he knew about Max's dealings. He told Marty to look for anything that would give them an advantage or some leverage in getting Max to back off this deal. And, depending on what they found, they'd turn the evidence over to the authorities, if necessary.

By the time Gavin hung up, he felt better and worse. Better, because he knew Marty would find everything there was to find. Worse, because he had a terrible suspicion Marty would find more than Gavin wanted to know.

Gavin didn't hide any of his conversation from Robby, who patiently waited for Gavin to finish the call. He hoped that gained him some points in the younger man's eyes, rather than making him an even bigger threat to Sunny.

When Gavin disconnected, Robby said, "You really are trying to make this okay for us, aren't you?"

Gavin stood and faced him. "Yeah, I am." He put his hands on his hips and stared at the ocean rolling onshore. "I care about your sister, and you. I'm not going to let anything happen to either of you, or this bar."

Robby nodded and, although he didn't exactly smile, the permascowl relaxed. "Sorry for being a prick."

Gavin clasped Robby's shoulder with one hand and offered his other for a knuckle rap. "S'all good. You had every reason not to trust me, but I hope that changes."

Gavin turned the handle on the kitchen door, pushed it open, and had the breath knocked out of him. The crushed expression on Sunny's face indicated she'd found something. Something awful.

Chapter Twenty-Four

"*W*hat's wrong?" Robby and Gavin asked like a couple of choir boys in perfect harmony.

Sunny couldn't answer around the anvil in her throat, so she held up the paperwork and pointed to the name on the list.

Gavin sat in the chair across from her and eased the file out of her hands. Robby squatted next to her and took hold of her shoulder. "Sis, what did you find?"

"Ed." Her voice cracked, and she cleared her throat for another try. "Ed is on Holden's payroll. Literally."

"What?" Robby shot to his feet and backed away as if she'd brandished a dangerous weapon. "Show me."

Gavin rested the file on the table and pulled out the list of subcontractors she'd been studying. Leaning over the table, she pointed to Ed's name.

She thought this whole thing would be a huge waste of time, unable to believe anyone she knew could be bought. But as she started going through the list of subcontractors, unease stirred in her stomach. She'd found a few names that sounded familiar and wrote them down to check out later.

Then she got to a name she didn't have to check out: Edward P. Hardin. It was as familiar as a family name, especially since she'd written a check to him once a month for the past two years, for all of her store purchases.

"Maybe it's a different Edward Hardin," Robby said, sounding desperate to find an explanation other than the logical one in front of them. When she looked up into his eyes, she realized his vision must have been as blurry as hers.

"I don't think so," she said, shaking her head. "Here's a list of four other names that rang a bell. I don't know them, personally, but I think they're from Anticue."

Robby spun the list around and looked at it. "Barbara Hammond? Isn't she the woman who runs the coffee shop in town?"

Sunny wiped a tear away and put the others on lockdown. "That's what I thought, too." She reached into her jar of Dum-Dums sitting on the table and rummaged around, going all the way to the bottom until she found a butterscotch. At Gavin's raised eyebrow, she said, "They're my favorite." She gave a little sniffle. "I deserve my favorite right now."

A small smile played at the corner of his mouth. "I thought peppermint was your favorite."

She froze and cut her eyes to Robby to see if he was paying attention. He wasn't, so she smiled at Gavin, hoping he understood she appreciated the humor. The mood in the room had grown as solemn as if they'd experienced a death in the family. And, in a way, she supposed they had.

Ed had been one of their regular customers since she and Robby opened the bar. He and Joe had been on those same barstools every single night. She couldn't believe he'd be a party to something underhanded. But she also couldn't deny the proof sitting in front of her.

She slumped in her chair and turned to Gavin. "I guess we found what we were looking for. What now?"

A knock on the door caused all three of them to jump, and the conversation ceased.

"Do you know him?" Gavin asked, twisting around to look through the glass.

"Yeah, it's Sam Penner from the health department." Sunny opened the door. "Hi, Sam. It's not time for our inspection already, is it?"

He shuffled his feet and glanced down at the clipboard in his hand. "We… um… got a complaint about…" His face reddened, and try as he might, he couldn't maintain eye contact with Sunny. "I got a complaint about the bar. I need to check it out."

"What?" She wheeled around on Gavin. "Is this the kind of thing you were talking about?"

Gavin dropped his head and nodded. He stepped up next to her and shook hands with Sam. "I'm Gavin McLeod. I'm a friend of Sunny and Robby. Can you tell us what the complaint was?"

Sam shuffled his feet while his eyes bobbled all around. "Someone complained that the liquor bottles were being used for… uh… personal use."

Sunny gasped, and Gavin let out a curse unlike any she'd ever heard. Apparently, the same could be said for Sam, because his eyes popped wide and he took a step back.

After a second of stunned silence, Sunny swiveled her head around to Gavin. She narrowed her eyes and forced her breathing to be calm and her voice even. "How did he know that? There were only two of us in the bar."

"Callie was on the beach, remember?" He gave his head a hard shake and turned away. "I can't believe she'd do this. If she did, that means…" He cursed again, unclipped his cellphone, and headed for the bedroom.

Sunny turned back to Sam. "I did drink out of one of the bottles." Her admission made Sam even more uncomfortable, which meant whoever reported Sunny had given him all the sordid details. She shivered, despite the heat. She didn't want to think about someone watching her go down on Gavin. And, oh God… had they watched them on the beach, too?

"Excuse me?" Sam asked.

Realizing she'd spoken out loud, she snapped her mouth shut. "I have the used bottle here." She pushed the kitchen door all the way open, so he could see into the kitchen. "Robby, grab that bottle of schnapps out of the cabinet."

Robby handed the bottle to Sunny, then busied himself on the laptop. If she was lucky, she'd never hear another word about this. Luck, however, seemed to be in short supply these days, and she knew this was the kind of thing her brother would never let her live down.

She handed Sam the bottle. "I put a new bottle on the shelf. C'mon, I'll show you." She grabbed her keys off the hook by the door and led him downstairs.

"Given the nature of the call and the friend in your apartment, I get the impression this report might have come from a crazy ex-girlfriend."

Sunny laughed. "You're right. She is crazy, but she wasn't even a girlfriend. Can you imagine how psycho she'd be if she had been?"

She unlocked the door and led him across the bar to the liquor shelf. "See," she said, taking the replacement bottle off the shelf. "The label isn't even broken."

Sam inspected the label, then nodded and handed the bottle back to her. "Technically, I should make you replace all the bottles."

Sunny felt her face fall and her blood pressure drop.

She opened her mouth to speak, but Sam held up a hand to ward off her protest. "I know you, and I trust you told me the truth. Considering the source, I'm not going to take this any further."

Relief flooded her, and she threw her arms around his neck in a hug. "Thank you. I swear to you, I would never do anything to create problems for myself." She fought the urge to roll her eyes. She should have said she'd never *intentionally* do anything to create problems for herself, because getting involved with Gavin had created a shitpot full.

Sam glanced down at his clipboard. "Did you get that leak fixed in the kitchen?"

Sunny grimaced. "Robby's worked on it twice, but it still leaks." She pinched her thumb and forefinger together. "Just a tad. It's not even noticeable… Hardly."

Sam shoved his pen back into his pocket. "I'll be back in two months. If it's not fixed by then—"

"It will be. I promise." Sunny followed Sam to the door, then locked up behind them. "Sam?" She waited until he'd turned to face her. "Have you heard anything about a new resort being built here in Anticue?"

He frowned. "That's not possible."

"What if the commissioners decided to change the ordinances?"

"Well, then I guess it could happen." He narrowed his eyes. "You planning something?"

"Hell, no." She shook her head. "I heard a rumor, and I wondered if anyone else had."

"Nope, but I'll keep my ears open." He yelled over his shoulder as he walked away, "Fix that leak."

Gavin was sitting on the stoop, waiting for Callie to call him back, when Sunny returned from the bar. "Everything okay?"

She sat next to him and nodded. "Yeah, only because he knows me. He said, technically, he should make me replace all the bottles on the shelf."

Gavin's heart lurched. Holy shit, there must be a hundred bottles on those shelves. He must have looked as frantic as he felt, because she smiled and rubbed his leg, as if trying to calm a wild animal. "Since I confessed and showed him the old one as well as the unopened new one, he let it go."

He blew out his breath and wrapped his arm around her shoulder. Dropping a kiss on top of her head, he said, "I'm sorry for all this."

He was so pissed off at Callie and Max and the entire situation, he felt as if his skin would roll off his body. He didn't do helpless well, but until he heard back from Marty, he didn't know what the next move should be. Sitting here doing nothing was driving him crazy.

Sunny leaned against his shoulder. "It's not your fault. If you hadn't been the one Max sent, it would have been someone else, right? And that person might not be as understanding or as willing to help as you are."

Maybe, but he kept wondering how different things would be if he hadn't kept his head buried in the sand all these years. He also wondered how many other families had been put through a similar hell.

She scooted away and studied him. "Why go to all this trouble for us?"

He picked at a piece of peeling paint and threw it over the edge of the step. As soon as this mess was straightened out, he would paint these steps for them. "I can't say it doesn't have anything to do with you, because it does. But it's more than that."

He pushed his hands through his hair and looked out at the street. "I've been pretty unhappy for a while. I thought it was because I was bored, sitting in an office, pushing papers around all day. I've grown tired of waiting for Max to retire.

"Every year he says, 'One more year, and I'm finished.' It's not that

I was anxious to be at the helm, but I haven't always agreed with the things Max did. Or where the resorts were located. Like here. I also don't believe bigger is better. Sometimes a small, well-placed resort would be best. If Max retired, I could do things differently. Make the company a little friendlier—"

The vibration of his cellphone stopped him short. *About fucking time.* "Callie, how could you do that? I thought everything was cool between us."

The silence stretched on for so long, he thought she'd hung up. Just as he was about to hit the callback button, she said, "What are you talking about?"

"Calling the health inspector was a page straight out of Max's book. He'll be proud of you. Or did you cook the idea up together?"

"What? I haven't called a health inspector." She laughed a little. "I don't even know how to find a health inspector."

As ridiculous as that sounded, he had to admit she was probably right about that. "Did you tell Max about seeing Sunny and me together?"

"I told him I'd been to Anticue and that you were with her. But I didn't go into any details. God, I couldn't have possibly discussed that with my father." She gasped. "Jen."

"What about her?"

"She kept telling me I needed to call the health inspector and report the bartender for using a bottle. I told her I didn't want to cause any problems, that I just wanted to forget the whole thing. She must have done it to get vengeance for me."

Holy fucking hell in a hand basket. Now he had Callie's friends to contend with too? He rested his head against the spindle of the railing and pressed his lips shut. He wanted to howl; just walk out on the beach and yell at the top of his lungs.

"Have you found out anything about that number?" Callie's soft and hopeful voice sent an ache through his already fractured chest. At some point, every child realizes their parents aren't perfect. Callie had somehow managed to make it to adulthood without the thought even occurring to her.

Gavin felt the weight of Max's betrayal like a tank on his chest and figured Callie must be near to buckling under its weight. "Not yet. A friend is looking into it for me."

"Will you let me know what you find out?"

"Of course. You're not at home, are you?"

"No. I stayed at Jen's last night, and I haven't had the heart to go back there yet."

Gavin couldn't blame her; he didn't want to go back to Max's house either. But he also wished she'd been around this morning to eavesdrop on Max's conversations. "Do you know what time his afternoon golf game is?"

"He's scheduled to have lunch at the club at noon, and he's playing golf afterwards."

Gavin figured the most incriminating files were in Max's office, where they were safe from prying eyes. He could also make sure they were well protected and couldn't fall into the wrong hands.

Gavin had asked Callie to search Max's office for folders labeled "Anticue," but he was regretting involving her. It wasn't that he didn't think her capable of finding the info, but he didn't want her hurt any more.

And then there was the mysterious red truck. It had him concerned, and he didn't want to leave Sunny alone. But he also couldn't sit here any longer, doing nothing. He tilted the phone away from his mouth and whispered to Sunny, "Is Robby going to be here all day?"

When she nodded, he said, "Callie, I'll be back there shortly after twelve. I'll go through Max's office files and see what I can find. I don't want you involved any further than you already are. Okay?"

Silence was the response.

"Callie, tell me you won't go snooping before I get there."

"I won't go snooping."

He pressed his lips together, then gave up the fight and let the burning frustration in his lungs out in a harsh burst of air. "I'm serious." He pinched the bridge of his nose. "Shit. You've never listened to me. Why do I think you'd start now?"

"Okay, fine." The petulant Callie made a return visit. "It was okay for me to go digging in his office for the phone number last night, but I won't go snooping through his files until you get here."

"Thanks, Cal." He reclipped the phone to his belt and turned to face Sunny. "She didn't call the health inspector."

"And you believe her?" The skeptical expression on Sunny's face told him her thoughts on the matter.

"Yeah. As she pointed out, she wouldn't know where to find one."

She blinked a few times, as if trying to digest that logic. "What?"

He laughed and wrapped his arm around her shoulder, pulling her to him for a hug. "Her friend made the call, seeking revenge on Callie's behalf."

She scrunched up her face, and ducked her head. "How many people saw us?"

"I don't know. I didn't ask."

"That is so embarrassing."

"If it makes you feel any better, they weren't on the beach with us." He laughed at her expression and shrugged. "It made me feel better."

He checked his watch, then stood. "Max has a lunch appointment at noon. If I leave now, I can get there shortly after he leaves. It'll give me plenty of time to go through everything in his office."

"What are you looking for?"

He held out his hand and helped her stand. "Anything I can find. I'm still looking for deals where the landowners were reluctant to sell. I'm trying to find anything that explains why they suddenly became agreeable. It might give us an idea of what to expect. And I want to see if I can find the plans for this resort."

"Do we need to keep the boxes you brought?"

He followed her into the kitchen, where Robby was typing on his laptop. "Not if you think you've found everyone."

"I'm pretty sure we have. We found five, and there are nine commissioners. That gives him the majority he needs to get things changed." Her face twisted with the same raw determination he'd seen when he first approached her about selling. "Ed doesn't know what he's in for when he comes into the bar tonight."

Gavin stopped shoving files into the box. "You can't say anything yet."

Matching silver glares from Robby and Sunny hit him. "Why not?"

"Because we can't risk him warning Max that we're on to him. At least not yet."

Sunny propped her hands on her hips. "Fine. Then Ed won't *know* anything." She rummaged through the sucker jar while muttering, "Good thing I can take the top off a bottle and replace it without anyone realizing it was disturbed."

Chapter Twenty-Five

"There you are," Robby said, rounding the front of the building. "I was beginning to think you'd been kidnapped." He smiled, trying to pretend he was teasing, as he climbed the stairs leading to the bar's front deck, but the tense set of his shoulders gave him away.

"I'm sorry you were worried," Sunny said, patting the chair next to her. "I should've let you know I was going for a walk. I feel like I should be out there doing something. But I don't know what that is... or where to go do it."

At this point, she didn't have any choice but to sit and wait and trust Gavin to take care of things. To deal with her frustration, she took a long walk on the beach, then ended up back at the bar, sitting on the front balcony, watching the surf.

Robby turned the chair so it faced the ocean and sat down next to her. "Maybe we should sell the property."

Unclear as to whether Robby had actually spoken or if the wind was whispering crazy thoughts into her ear, Sunny cocked her head to the side and cut her eyes to him. She took in the crease lines in his forehead and the worry lines around his eyes and decided it wasn't the wind. "Why do you say that?"

He shrugged and tugged at a piece of sea oat that had blown onto the table. "This place is a lot of work. It takes both of us to keep it up. How are you going to do that by yourself if I leave in the fall?"

As stressful as this whole situation was, it was also a blessing. The door she'd been looking for had just opened. "First of all, there's no *if*. You want to go away to college and that's what you're going to do. As for the bar..." She looked around at the building and shrugged. "It's not as much work as it used to be. I'll figure it out."

"If we sold, you'd be free to move. You could do anything you wanted." Robby had grown into a fine young man. But there were times, like now, when he looked like a scared little boy.

"I don't want to move. I like it here."

He frowned, and she could almost see the gray matter in his mind squishing around with thought. "You aren't holding out just to be stubborn, are you?" When she bit into her bottom lip, he laughed. "See... I know you too well. Even if you wanted to sell, you wouldn't because you won't give in." He sat up in his chair and leaned toward her, intensity radiating from him. "That's crazy, sis. Let's sell it."

"Okay, I'll admit, at one point, I thought that way. No one was going to bully me into selling. But that's not what's keeping me here. Where would Liza and Johnny go to hide out? Where will the kids go to play pool? Most importantly, where will you call home?"

His face twisted with confusion, and he leaned back in his chair. "Home is where you are."

"We've moved around so much. Don't you want to feel rooted someplace? Someplace you can go when things are tough and you need a good hug."

He gave it some thought, then shrugged. "I'll have that wherever you are." He kicked his feet up on the railing and watched a seagull. "What about Gavin?"

Her heart fluttered at his name, but she tried not to let Robby see any response. "What about him?"

"I guess it turns out he's one of the good guys. Are you two serious?"

"I don't know." She rested her head against the back of the chair and let the sun shine on her face.

It was early in the relationship to be thinking long term, but that hadn't kept her from doing so repeatedly over the past several days. Until today, the idea seemed like a ridiculous fantasy. But now, she wondered if he might feel the same way she did. He was willing to go to a lot of effort and make a lot of sacrifices for her and Robby. Maybe the fantasy wasn't so farfetched, after all.

"He likes you. You like him." Robby made it sound so easy.

She rolled her head to the side and looked at him from the corner of her eye. "If Gavin was in the picture, would you feel better about going away to school?"

He gave her a sheepish, lopsided grin. "Maybe."

"I'll make you a deal." She snared him with a mischievous look. "You go to college, and I'll see what I can do about getting Gavin to stick around for a while."

Robby laughed and pushed himself out of his chair. "I'm going to be spending a lot of nights at Chad's."

Unable to wait any longer, Gavin called Marty while driving back to Myrtle Beach. "Hey, man, I know it's only been a few hours, but what've you got?"

"The phone number belongs to Miguel Ortego."

The discomfort Gavin had felt since hearing about the red truck increased. "That doesn't sound like Max's usual associates." It did, however, sound like the name of someone who would drive a low-rider truck.

"I'm still digging, but this guy is bad news. He has a record ten miles long."

Gavin's grip on the steering wheel tightened, as did the steel rod in his spine. He couldn't ever remember being this uptight, and this conversation sure as hell wasn't helping. "For what?"

"B&E, vandalism, harassment, arson."

Arson? Ice settled in Gavin's chest as he thought about the flames painted on the front of the truck. "Why isn't he in prison?"

"The police have never been able to make anything stick."

"Did you get his license number? Find out what kind of vehicle he drives?"

"I'm still working on it. And before you ask, no, I haven't had a chance to look into the other stuff yet."

"I know," Gavin said, watching the lines in the road flash by. "I'm on my way back to Myrtle Beach to see what I can find in Max's office. I'll call you with anything that might be helpful." He was about to disconnect when a thought hit him. "Can you send me a picture of this guy?" That would at least keep them from fumbling around blind, not knowing who to look for.

"I'll send you everything I have."

"Thanks, man. I owe you." When Marty laughed, Gavin said, "I'm serious. I know I've been an asshole about keeping in touch, but I intend to change that. We need to get together for a beer. Or ten."

Through the silence on the line, Gavin could tell he'd shocked Marty. "We're good. But I'll take you up on the beer."

"Maybe we can meet up at the Blackout. We can catch up and you can meet Sunny."

"I'd like that." Marty wasn't one for showing much emotion, but the soft inflection in his voice told Gavin his response wasn't just obligatory.

Reconnecting with his oldest friend would be one more step toward reconnecting with the person he'd once been, and Gavin was grateful Marty was receptive.

By the time he reached Myrtle Beach, it was almost one. Cynthia was out doing… whatever Cynthia did on a daily basis. Max was at lunch, and Angelina had left for the day.

Gavin let himself in through the kitchen door and went straight to Max's office. Callie was waiting by the french doors.

"Have you been snooping since Max left?"

"No, I told you I wouldn't." She gave him a smarmy smile and batted her eyelashes. "But if you're here, Mother and Daddy would expect me to be here, too."

"Okay," he said. "You win that point." His stomach twisted in a knot as he sank into Max's chair and pulled out the large, bottom desk drawer. He wasn't concerned about getting caught in Max's private files, but he was scared shitless about what he'd find. He knew Max had crossed the moral and ethical lines. He just hoped he didn't find confirmation he'd crossed legal ones, as well.

The Anticue file was in the very front, and it didn't take long to figure out why Max had gone batshit crazy over getting construction under way.

Peering over his shoulder, Callie asked, "What'd you find?"

"Apparently, your dad didn't put together a group of investors as he claims. All of the land purchases have been made with Holden funds." Gavin twisted his head and peered at Callie from the corner of his eye. "By the way, did you know you own the old Anticue fishing pier?"

She took a step back and curled her lip. "Excuse me?"

He laughed. "I'll explain later." He flipped through the file, looking for copies of board meeting minutes. As he suspected, there weren't any.

"He also hasn't had the board of director's blessing in acquiring *any* of the Anticue property."

"He needs the board's approval?"

"Yeah. Even though…" Too late, he realized who he was talking to and what he shouldn't be saying.

"Gavin." Her eyes were imploring, but her voice was strong. "Please tell me everything. I think it's time I find out the truth about my dad and this business."

He tossed the folder onto the desk and swiveled the chair around so he faced her. It wasn't his place to fill her in, but she did have a right to know, and, God knows, Max would never tell Callie the truth. "As CEO, Max has final decision-making power, but the board likes to be kept in the loop. They want details of all new developments. In all stages."

Max had been operating on his own in Anticue, and he'd sunk a fortune of Holden Enterprise funds into the purchase of land and commissioners. If he acquired the property, got the ordinances changed, and built a resort, he'd pull off what no one else had been able to, and he'd be a hero. But if Sunny didn't sell, Max would have to confess his sins to the board, and the hero would become a zero. At least in the eyes of a very pissed off board of directors.

Callie rounded the desk and sat in the chair Gavin normally occupied. Resting her forearms on the cherry wood, she leaned forward and whispered, "Is it true that Mother can fire Daddy?"

Gavin laughed, imagining the scenario in which Callie had learned that information. He'd bet money, in the midst of a heated argument with Max, Cynthia not-so-tactfully reminded him of his place. Gavin nodded slowly and tried to figure out the best way to explain this little landmine.

"The board can fire Max, and your mother has controlling interest.

So yes, technically, Cynthia can fire Max."

"You know Holden Enterprises used to belong to Mother's family."

It wasn't a question, but a statement of fact, and one that caught Gavin off-guard. "Yeah, but I didn't realize you knew that." Very few people knew the reason for, and the details surrounding, the company's name change from Pelletier Resorts to Holden Enterprises.

"No one told me. I overhead Mother and Daddy arguing one day." Callie leaned back in the chair, and her eyes misted over. "I was pretty young, and I didn't understand much of what I heard. As I got older, I started putting the pieces together. I figured out that Mother's grandfather started the company and eventually, her father took over. Her brothers weren't interested in working, only in spending the family fortune, so Grandfather put Daddy in charge." She looked at Gavin expectantly, as if waiting for him to confirm she had everything right so far.

He nodded, so she continued. "Daddy felt like the company should have his name since he was the CEO. The company changed its name the year I was born." She paused again, awaiting further confirmation. "But even though Daddy is the CEO and the company carries his name, Mother owns the majority of stock. Which means, she ultimately has the control. Is that right?"

Well, well, well. Gavin had always known Callie was a whole lot smarter than she let on, but even he hadn't given her enough credit. He rocked back in the chair and smiled. "Pretty much."

"So what now?"

"I need to copy this paperwork, then see what else I can find in these drawers."

Gavin didn't want to take the folder, because he didn't want to tip off Max that he'd been here. But he needed proof that the file and plans existed. Using his cellphone, he took pictures of all the documents and sketches in the Anticue folder. There were no official renderings, but Max had a basic sketch drawn, showing how the resort would be positioned and what would be included.

There wasn't anything legally incriminating that he needed to turn over to the authorities, and if Gavin decided to go to the board, he had enough proof on his phone to get them interested. A little digging on their part would turn up everything they needed. It wasn't like Max could unload all that property in a day.

"Gavin?"

"Hmmm…?" He absently replied to Callie as he replaced the Anticue file and started shuffling through the rest of the folders in the drawer.

"I think it's time I move out on my own."

He paused his search and looked up at her. She was standing by the door with her arms wrapped around her stomach, as if holding herself together. Tears filled her eyes and she looked like a heartbroken child.

He pushed out of the chair and opened his arms. She barreled into him so hard and fast, she nearly knocked him over. "Shhh…" He smoothed her hair and rocked her back and forth. "The past day has been tough, huh?"

She nodded and sobbed. "Yesterday, I didn't think I really knew or could trust anyone. Daddy isn't who I thought he was, and before our talk, I didn't know what to think about you." She looked at him through teary eyes and smiled. "I'm still coming to grips with the whole sister thing, but I do think you're a good person and believe I can trust you."

His heart squeezed, and he tightened his arms around her in response. Trust was a funny thing, and he wondered if she would still feel that way if she knew he *would* turn Max over to the authorities if he followed through on his threats against Sunny. Or, if Gavin found anything in the rest of the file folders incriminating enough to warrant a legal investigation.

"I'm also beginning to think my mother isn't as self-absorbed as Daddy's made her out to be. I haven't been a very loving daughter toward her over the years. I definitely haven't given her a chance to prove she was more than what he said."

Shock brought him to a stop, so he kick started the rocking again. "You think moving out will give you the space you need to figure all this out."

She sniffed and wiped tears off her face. "Exactly." She twisted her mouth and chewed on the inside of her cheek. "The problem is, I don't have a job, nor do I have any money." She released her death grip around his waist and began pacing. "I don't think they'll want to pay for an apartment, since I can live here for free." She shocked him again by adding, "I don't blame them; that would be crazy." She sighed and rubbed her arms. "I need to figure out a way to get some money."

A thought slammed into his head with the force of a freight train, causing him to burst into laughter. God, the answer had been in front of him the entire time. Before he could speak, Callie tilted her head to the side and said, "Do you know how attractive you are when you laugh like that?"

He sobered, then frowned. "What?"

"You're always handsome. But you're usually so serious that you walk around with a major frowny face. When you smile, and especially when you laugh, you're completely transformed. You should do it more often."

Gavin wasn't normally speechless, but Callie had managed to render him that way. For a second, he forgot what he'd been laughing about in the first place. But the thought was too strong and powerful to be forgotten for long, and he smiled with its return. "I think I know of a way for you to get money. Serious money."

It would also solve the Anticue problem and give Gavin exactly what he'd personally been looking for.

"Give me a second to finish going through these files. Then, we need to go someplace we can talk without any chance of Max catching us."

Chapter Twenty-Six

Sunny sighed with relief when Gavin strolled into the bar shortly after eight. She had no idea what time to expect him, and even though he checked in with her periodically throughout the day, she still felt better having him there. It wasn't that she was scared, just... nervous and on edge.

Gavin dropped onto the stool, rested his forearms on the bar, and knocked her breathless with the biggest smile she'd ever seen. "How are you doing?"

She leaned over the counter and returned the smile. "Better, now that you're here. I'm ashamed to admit I've been a little freaked out since you sent me those pictures. That guy is scary."

He took hold of her hand and rubbed his thumb across her wrist. "I didn't mean to scare you. I just wanted you to know what he looked like, in case he showed up."

"I understand, and I'm glad you did. Although, I'd probably shit my pants if he did."

Gavin laughed and squeezed her hand. "I promise not to let anything happen to you."

His confidence didn't relax her completely, but having him with her certainly helped. "What'd you find out?"

His eyes twinkled and his grin broadened. "Can I have a beer first?" He glanced to the end of the bar, then warily at her. "You didn't do anything to Ed, did you?"

She slid the beer to him and shook her head. "He hasn't come in yet. Robby really wanted to rip his barstool cover off and burn it, but I told him he had to wait. I suck at acting, but I'll do the best I can to pretend nothing's wrong."

Gavin winked and sipped on his beer. "I'll keep you distracted."

"Why? So you won't have to answer my question?"

He paused with the beer bottle halfway to his mouth, then set it back down. "No, so you don't think about Ed. I'm working on not being so evasive anymore."

"And yet, you still haven't told me what you found out."

He scooted forward on the stool and lowered his voice. "Max has acted on his own in purchasing the Anticue property. He's been using Holden funds, but he hasn't gotten the board's blessing on any of it. I think he's starting to panic."

"I don't understand. If he owns the company, what's the problem?"

"It's complicated. He's the CEO and the company carries his name, but he doesn't own it outright. He reports to a board of directors, and he *can* be fired."

Sunny felt her eyes widen in surprise. "No shi—"

Her eyes snapped to the opening door and her body tensed, cutting off her train of thought. So much for being more relaxed with Gavin around. When she saw Ed standing in the doorway with Joe behind him, her nervousness was instantly replaced by burning anger. For the first time, she understood the phrase *make your blood boil.*

Seeing Ed's name on Holden's payroll had left her feeling totally betrayed. Not just for herself, but for the entire town, for everyone who'd voted him into office and trusted him to act in their best interest.

"How's my girlie doing tonight?" Ed asked as he headed for his seat.

Gavin's fingertips touched her chin and turned her head to face him. "You're snarling."

"That's because I'm pretty sure I could chew off an arm or a leg right now."

Gavin laughed, then shocked her by leaning over and planting a good, long, wet kiss on her, right in front of everyone. He proceeded to kiss the anger right out of her, which was probably his intent.

When he pulled back, she swayed a bit and said, "Maybe I should snarl more often."

"Naw," he said, shaking his head before he took a sip of his beer. "I like you smiling better." He leaned forward and cocked his head so the back of it was toward Ed and Joe and they couldn't see his mouth moving. "I can't tell you anything right now, not here. Especially not with Ed here. But as of two hours ago, you have nothing to worry about."

"What?" She didn't think Gavin would tease her about something this important, but she still searched his face for a sign he was joking. "Are you sure?"

Gavin smiled and nodded. "I'm absolutely positive."

Overwhelming joy and relief ripped through her, and she squealed. Gavin's wide eyes made her realize she was drawing attention to them, so she threw her hand over her mouth to squelch her reaction and leaned forward until they were almost touching. "Max has agreed to call the whole resort off? Or he's given up on buying my bar?"

Mischievous evil… That was the only way to describe Gavin's lop-sided grin and glimmering eyes. "He hasn't *agreed* to anything. In fact"—he checked his watch—"he's probably getting checkmated right about now."

Excitement pounded through her and she bounced on her toes—until she noticed Ed and Joe watching her, waiting for her to greet them with their beers. She stifled her excitement by taking a deep breath, then grabbed the bottles from the chiller.

The overwhelming anger and resentment toward Ed faded in direct proportion to her lessening worry over losing the bar. In fact, she might be able to pull this everything-is-normal routine off, after all.

Realizing she never answered Ed's question, she said, "I'm doing all right." She glanced at Gavin, and he winked. She even felt a little relief at not having spiked Ed's beer with something nasty.

She and Robby had made a list of potential sabotage techniques, but in the end, they decided to take the high road and not do anything terrible. Besides, she'd promised Sam she would never do anything to jeopardize her bar, and she meant it. Getting a little payback on Ed wasn't worth that risk.

"There you go, gentlemen." She set a beer in front of each man but kept her gaze locked on Joe. It was easier to be nice if she focused her attention on him and pretended Ed didn't exist.

After getting them settled, she rounded the bar and sat on the stool next to Gavin. Whispering, so as to not be overheard, she said, "Okay, I need details. This is killing me. What happened?"

He brushed a stray hair out of her face and gave her his intimate, lover's smile. Her feminine spots answered in their own particular way, something he must have noticed by the way his gaze dipped to her breasts and his eyelids drooped.

With a slow visual caress, his gaze traveled up her collarbone, to her neck, and then settled on her mouth. "How long until you get out of here?"

"Hours. You're stalling."

"I'm distracted. There's a difference." He leaned forward and tried to peek down the high collar of her shirt. "Which necklace are you wearing tonight?"

She pressed her fingers to her throat to feel the chain, then remembered she hadn't put one on. Rather than ruining a potentially seductive moment by sharing that information, she slowly stroked her finger down the center of her breasts, as if following the length of chain.

Heat gathered in his eyes as he watched her fingers, then, without warning, he grabbed her hand and squeezed. "If you don't stop, I'll throw everyone out of here and slap a closed sign on the door."

She leaned over the bar and grabbed a Dum-Dum. "Okay, tell me what's going on. All of it."

His sexy facade slipped away, and the businessman returned. "I went through all the files in Max's office." He was talking so quietly she had to lean forward and strain to hear him over the background noise. "I don't believe he's done anything horrible, like I was beginning to fear. I think he's harassed land owners, spread rumors, stuff like that."

She must have been glaring, because he added, "I know, all that's wrong. But shit, Sunny." He scrubbed a hand over his face. "I was beginning to think I'd been an equally horrid person for turning a blind eye to his actions." He looked at the ceiling and drew in a deep breath. "Which, I guess I am, because I did. But not to the degree I'd feared."

She ran a soothing hand over his knee. "It might not have been the right thing to do, but you're not a horrible person. And you've learned from your mistakes, right?"

He took a deep breath and nodded. "Absolutely."

She leaned in closer and lowered her voice. "Now, what about this property? How did you fix things?"

The wicked gleam returned. "How would you feel about helping me fix up the old fishing pier? I'm thinking of turning the top level into a restaurant and restoring the lower level to its original state."

"What?" Realizing she was once again drawing attention to herself with her squealing, she shut up and hunkered down on her stool. In a harsh whisper, she said, "I think it would be awesome. But how are you going to do that?"

"To keep things from coming to the board's attention, Max put several of the Anticue parcels in his wife's name and several in Callie's. The fishing pier was in Callie's name."

He laughed, and Sunny realized her mouth was hanging open so far her sucker was about to fall out. She snapped her mouth shut and swallowed. "She's going to sell it to you?"

Gavin's smile was downright cocky. "She already did."

Sunny was flabbergasted. Max Holden had been sneaking property into his wife and daughter's name, and now the sneak had been snaked.

The whispering was driving her crazy, not to mention she was about to bounce off the barstool. Since they only opened the kitchen on weekends and Robby hadn't come down from the apartment, the back of the bar was empty. She grabbed Gavin's hand, yanked him off the stool, and dragged him to the kitchen.

"Okay," she said, shutting the door behind them. She stood on tiptoes and peered through the window so she could keep an eye on things. "Start from the beginning and tell me everything."

"How about the abbreviated version for now?"

She cut her eyes to him, judging if this was another avoidance technique.

He must have understood the look, because he said, "I swear, I'll tell you and Robby everything later, when we're alone in your apartment."

She chomped off the last of the sucker, tossed the stick into the trash, and leaned against the wall. "Okay. Spill it."

"Callie wants to move out and be on her own, but in order to do that she needs money. She had no idea the fishing pier was in her name, until I told her. It's a dirty move, but it serves Max right and fixes all our problems. I made her an offer on the pier, which gives her the money she needs to move out. Since I own the largest piece of property and I'm not willing to sell any more than you are, Max is fucked. Even if the commissioners change the ordinances, he doesn't have enough property to accommodate the resort."

"Not here, but it could be built someplace else."

He looked uncertain. "I'm not sure there's anyplace else that could handle something that size. The town takes up one end of the island, and I think the other end is too narrow to make it work."

She glanced out of the window to Ed. "What about the commissioners?"

Gavin shrugged. "That'll be up to the Anticue residents to deal with. I think once they're exposed, they'll lose their seats. The voters will be more cautious from now on and will thoroughly check all candidates to make sure there aren't any hidden agendas."

"If you own the fishing pier…" What did that mean?

She chewed on her lip and contemplated having Gavin as a neighbor. Robby would be happy, because he wouldn't feel like he was leaving her all alone. Her hormones were thrilled at the prospect of a continued relationship with Gavin, but what was the nature of their involvement? Were they in a relationship, or were they simply using each other for great sex?

"You look terrified."

"Yeah." Well, she kind of was, but she didn't want him to know she was mostly scared because she liked the idea of having him around. "I'm…" She averted her gaze and peeked out the window while searching for an answer. "I was thinking about more nights on the beach."

He shifted closer and wrapped his arms around her waist. Pulling her to the side so no one could see them through the window, he nuzzled her neck. "I'm looking forward to a lot of nights on the beach." He paused, then quietly added, "I'm looking forward to a lot of things with you."

She turned in his arms and smiled suggestively. "Wanna start to-night?"

He laughed and kissed her nose. "I'd love to start tonight." His eyes softened, not the liquid heat they normally radiated when he was turned on, but something more. "I wasn't just talking about sex, though. I want to get to know you. As a person. As a woman. I want to walk on the beach and watch the sunset with you. I want to watch you in your workshop and see how you make those incredible pieces. I want more than sex."

She struggled to breathe while assimilating his confession. She'd held back from having relationships because of Robby. But he'd be leaving in three months, and it was time for her to start living life for herself.

Gavin seemed like a great place to start.

She stood on tiptoes and dropped a soft, tender kiss on his lips. "I can't remember ever watching the sunset on this beach. And I'd much rather walk with you than walk alone."

Chapter Twenty-Seven

*T*he vibration of Gavin's cell was a rude interruption to their sweet moment, and he was tempted to ignore it. But he was sure it was Callie, and he couldn't ignore her, not after everything she'd done today. And not after the torturous past several hours she'd no doubt endured with Max.

Unclipping the phone from his belt, he said, "As much as I hate to break this off, I need to take this call."

Sunny stepped back and nodded. "I'll go out there so you have some privacy."

He snatched her hand before she could disappear through the doorway. "I—"

What the hell was he thinking? "Love you" were going to be the next words flying out of his mouth, but his brain kicked in and overrode his tongue.

Did he love Sunny? It seemed a perfectly natural thing to say. And now that he was giving it some serious thought, it felt right, too.

The phone vibrated in his hand again, snapping him back from whatever freakin' dreamland he'd slipped into. He pressed the call button so it didn't go into voicemail, then whispered to Sunny, "I'll be right out."

She disappeared through the door, and he rubbed a hand over his face to wipe away the sweat before putting the phone to his ear. "Yeah."

All he heard at first was static and then Callie's voice came across the line. "Gavin, can you hear me?"

"Yeah. Where are you?"

"On my way to Jason's."

Jason?

"Who's Jason?"

Through the static, he thought Callie said, "A guy from the club."

Wow, she'd only been over Gavin a day, and she was already back on the horse. He knew all along if Max stopped pushing her, or at least stopped supporting her idea of a relationship with him, she'd find someone else.

"There's a lot of static, so I'm having a hard time hearing you. Bear with me if you have to repeat things."

"I'm scared, Gavin." Her voice shook, and it sounded like she was working hard to not break down. "He's furious, and I honestly don't know what he's capable of."

"Jason?" What the hell was she doing with a guy she was scared of?

"No! Daddy."

Gavin squeezed his eyes shut and tried to switch gears.

"I thought Daddy was going to have a heart attack in the restaurant. I've never seen him so furious. He started yelling about hell to pay, and…" A sob broke through the line. "He threatened to disown me if I didn't cancel the contract with you."

Gavin sank against the stainless steel kitchen counter. He'd been afraid Max would try to intimidate Callie into breaking the deal. He even warned her that Max would play the "disown" card. But she'd been firm in her decision to sell him the property.

She said she wanted to be on her own, and having the money from the sale of the fishing pier was the only way she could do it. Maybe Gavin should've given her more time to think it through, to really consider the risks and potential ramifications.

Guilt and grief swamped him. He had to believe Max would eventually forgive her, but he'd make her life miserable, just as he did everyone else who didn't play the game as he dictated. "Callie, if you want to change your mind, I won't hold it against you."

"Hell, no." The static subsided and he jerked the phone away from his ear, shocked by the ferociousness of the response. "I've seen a side of him over the past several days I never thought existed. I need to do this for me. I need to be on my own, out from under his and Mother's control, so I can figure out who I am and what I want."

Pride shoved his guilt aside. Not pride in the way they'd managed things, because the deal had been sneaky and deceitful. But pride for Callie and how she handled all of this. He laughed to himself as he thought back to his and Max's conversation a few days earlier. This probably wasn't what Max had in mind when he said he hoped Callie settled down.

"I'm sorry he's angry with you. I knew he'd be furious, but I really hoped he'd take it out on me, not you."

A half-laugh, half-sob came through the phone. "He only yelled at me, Gavin. I'm terrified of what he'll do to you."

"Don't worry about me. I'll be fine. I have a picture of the guy he called last night. I know who to be on the lookout for."

"Since Daddy would never think to look for me at Jason's, I'm going to stay there until this blows over. I'll have my cellphone. You can call me on that if you need me."

"I'll check on you tomorrow to see how you're doing." He was about to hang up when he remembered there was a new player in the game. "Wait," he said. "Tell me about this Jason."

A giggle blended with a sob. "He's the host from the country club. He's the one who drove me to Anticue the other night."

"Oh, great. Next time I'm at the country club…" His words trailed off as he realized there wouldn't be a *next time*. He'd never enjoyed his time spent there, and now he had no reason to go. "Have a good night, Callie. I'll give you a call tomorrow."

"Gavin?" After a long pause, she said, "I know everything's going to be different now that you don't work for Daddy. But… will we still be friends?"

Gavin swallowed hard to clear his throat of the emotion welling up inside him. He cared for her, tremendously, and nothing would change that. "Of course. I'd never lose touch with you. Besides, I'll need to check this Jason guy out. Make sure he's good enough for you."

Laughter filled the line as she disconnected.

Gavin's exuberance idled down ten notches while in the kitchen, and a sense of doom and gloom oozed into Sunny's gut. As he approached *his* barstool, she said, "Something's wrong. What happened?"

He shook his head no, then flopped down. He dropped his forehead into his hands and stayed like that for so long Sunny was about to jump out of her skin with concern. Finally, he said, "I feel bad for Callie. She's always adored Max, and the past few days have been rough on her." He took a long drink of his beer. "I think… I hope Max will eventually forgive her, but it's going to be a long, long time before she's daddy's little princess again."

He cut his gaze to the end of the bar, then back to her. "Where's Robby?"

She knocked her head back and glanced to the ceiling. "I wasn't sure I could trust him to behave around Ed, so I had him stay upstairs. I told him I'd call if I needed him."

The corner of Gavin's mouth twitched as he turned his cold, scary-as-shit gaze onto Ed. "Max knows everything now. I think it's time to call Robby."

Butterflies jostled for position in her stomach and she began to tremble. She leaned over and spoke softly, in case she misunderstood Gavin's intent. "We can confront Ed now?"

Gavin shrugged and took another sip of beer. "Ed can't tell Max anything he doesn't already know."

Sunny snatched up the phone and dialed Robby's cell. When he answered, she said, "Hey, c'mon down. Gavin said it's clear for you to say and... well, I'm not going to allow you to do whatever you want. But you can say your piece."

Robby must have been running down the stairs while on the phone, because the door to the bar burst open before she replaced the receiver. She expected him to come in with guns blazing, but he seemed more hurt and disappointed than mad, and the look of despair on his face broke her heart.

He glanced at Ed, then shifted his gaze to the floor, as if it hurt too much to look at the man they'd once considered a dear friend. Rather than heading for Ed, he came behind the counter and quietly said, "I'm afraid I won't say things right. You talk. I'll take the barstool cover."

She laughed as she squeezed him in a hug. "You know," she said, in a low voice, "this isn't personal against us. He tried to hurt the whole town. And I'm sure he only did it for the money."

Robby nodded and rubbed his eyes. "I know. But it still feels personal."

She squeezed his hand, then moseyed toward the end of the bar, where Joe and Ed sat with curious expressions on their faces. Because of her and Gavin's kitchen conference and the way Robby burst through door as if his ass were on fire, everyone in the bar knew something was amiss.

Sunny just told Robby this wasn't personal, and she mostly believed that, but there was one part of this equation she did take personally. And while she was grateful for the way things were turning out, she still didn't appreciate being played.

"Hey, Ed." She paused, making sure she had her thoughts together. "When Gavin came in here the first night, did you know who he was?"

Joe looked at Ed with a ton of what's-she-talking-about on his face.

Ed shifted on his stool and swiped a stream of sweat off his beer bottle. He pressed his lips together, shrugged, and shook his head. "No. I'd never seen him before." He flashed his normal toothy grin, which caused her chest to ache, because, dammit, he was family and he betrayed them all. "He's spent enough time around here lately, though, we've all gotten to know him pretty well."

Ignoring the sadness seeping into her chest and the desire to brush all this aside as a big misunderstanding, she said, "Did you suspect he worked for Max Holden that first night?"

Some of the color drained from Ed's face, but he held her gaze unwaveringly. "Who's Max Holden?"

Joe's eyes narrowed and he flipped his gaze from Ed to Gavin, who sat silently, letting Sunny and Robby handle things their way.

Ed readjusted his ball cap and took a drink of his beer before reiterating his position. "I don't know Max Holden."

She leaned onto the bar and stared at him for a moment, trying to regain control of her crumbling emotions. She was still angry and hurt. But now that her bar was no longer in danger and the town was safe from the threat of a resort, she was mostly sad.

"Did you do it for the money? Or did you have other reasons?"

He laughed uncomfortably and glanced at Joe. "I don't know what she's talking about." He turned back to Sunny, and for the first time, she saw an old man behind those eyes. A tired, old man.

Robby came up behind her. "Do you have to give the money back if the ordinances don't get changed?"

"You son of a bitch," Joe said, vibrating with anger. "I can't believe you took the bribe."

Ed's face turned red and his hands trembled as he stared down his old friend. "You're a fool if you didn't. I'm seventy-two years old. My business is barely hanging by a thread. What would happen to me and Jane if one of those big-chain gas stations came in?"

A few of the others in the bar had started to pay attention to Sunny and Ed's exchange, but now everyone stopped what they were doing and moved closer. Ed must have felt like a trapped animal because his eyes grew wild and his voice escalated to a level she'd never heard from him.

"It's just a matter of time before those ordinances get changed, anyway. Why not go ahead and get on with it? The money I got will make sure Jane and I can make it for the rest of our lives. Hell, I'll even get a day off now."

Sunny pushed off the bar and stood up straight. "The resort isn't going in. I'm not selling this piece of property. And as of this afternoon…" She paused and looked at Gavin, unsure if she could tell the rest.

He smiled and nodded.

"Gavin owns the fishing pier, so the resort will never go in. At least, not right here, not as long as Gavin and I are alive."

Robby's head snapped back and forth between Gavin and Sunny at that newsflash, but she was focused on the panic spreading in Ed's eyes. "Don't do this, Sunny." He reached across the bar for her hand, but she snatched it away. "He'll kill you, if that's what it takes. He's crazy and vicious, and he'll do anything to get what he wants."

Sunny shook her head. "Those are just rumors, Ed. Gavin spent all day looking for proof to the contrary, and there's none to be found. Yeah, he may try to intimidate and bully me into selling, but I can handle that." She turned and smiled at Gavin and Robby. "I have tremendous backup, so I'll be fine."

Ed eased back onto the stool. He was genuinely concerned for her safety, and she had to wonder if he'd been bullied into taking the bribe. Ed's shoulders slumped. "I'm not the only one," he said softly.

Robby snorted. "Like that makes it okay."

"How many are there?" Sunny asked, wanting to make sure they accounted for everyone.

Ed played with the moisture on his beer bottle. "Five." He didn't look up, didn't make eye contact with anyone. "I don't know who they are. I only know there's a majority now." He started to turn his head toward Joe, then looked back to the bottle. "I guess you're not one of them."

"Hell, no, I'm not one of them."

Somewhere, throughout the conversation, Sunny's anger at Ed had turned to sympathy. Sympathy for getting himself into this mess and not only losing his friends, but probably his self-respect, as well.

Joe, however, was still firmly in the angry camp. "That son of a bitch approached me, but I'm no sellout. I told him to go to hell. You could've done the same thing."

Ed's shoulders slumped to the point she thought he might collapse onto the bar. "I had to do something to make sure Jane was taken care of." His voice was so soft Sunny barely heard him. He looked at Sunny with pleading eyes. "Can you understand that?"

She looked away, not ready to forgive, but knowing if she looked into those sad eyes any longer, she'd be sucked in. "I understand desperation makes people do crazy things. But there had to have been another way. A way that wouldn't have betrayed the trust of everyone who voted for you. The trust of your friends."

He stared at his bottle, not speaking, just thinking. "I guess I better head home and tell Jane. She needs to hear it from me, rather than someone else."

Sunny grabbed his hand to stop him from standing. "Jane doesn't know you took a bribe?"

He looked at the floor and shook his head. "No, she'd never approve." He sighed like a broken-down, defeated man. "This just might be the end of forty good years."

Chapter Twenty-Eight

Gavin took a long drink of his beer and looked around at the long faces of the few remaining bar patrons. The atmosphere had taken a serious nosedive during Sunny's confrontation with Ed, and it pretty much stayed in the shitter since. He'd walked out nearly forty-five minutes before, ass dragging the pavement, and everyone was still wandering around in a state of shock and disbelief.

"I can't believe he took the bribe," Joe said for the fifteenth time.

"Do you think Miss Jane will really leave him?" Robby's eyes were wide with concern, and his earlier rage seemed to have dissipated.

Joe's anger had also come down a notch or two, but wasn't anywhere near gone. "She won't leave the sorry bastard. She'll make his life hell for a while, and he deserves it. I've known Ed most of my life. Believe me, this isn't the first stupid thing he's done in the past forty years. It's a doozy, but it's not the worst."

Whoa, what the hell had Ed done that was worse than—

Gavin's thoughts were cut short when Joe's black-as-night stare landed squarely on his face. "What's your role in all this?"

Gavin had braced himself for that question and was surprised it took so long for someone to ask. The others in the bar turned toward him, awaiting his explanation. "I used to work for Holden Enterprises—"

Sunny gasped. "Used to? What do you mean used to?"

Oh yeah, he hadn't gotten around to sharing that information with her yet. "After screwing Max over the way I did, I was going to be out of a job, anyway. I figured I'd beat him to the punch and tendered my resignation this afternoon." He kicked back on the barstool like he didn't have a care in the world. "I'm on vacation for the next sixteen weeks, and then I'm out of a job."

Sunny's eyes widened even farther and her jaw nearly came unhinged.

"I told you I had a lot of accumulated vacation time." He shrugged and picked at the label on his beer. "Max'll get my resignation paperwork tomorrow, and then he can decide how he wants to handle the vacation pay. I'll probably get a lump sum compensation check and be done." Which would help with living expenses while he sold his house and began renovations on the fishing pier.

"Do you know who the other paid-off commissioners are?" Joe asked.

Gavin nodded to Sunny, who seemed to be lost in her thoughts. "Sunny thinks she found all five of them."

She wiped her hands on her jeans and nodded. "Robby and I found four other names we recognized on a list of subcontractors." She smiled sadly and grabbed Joe's hand. "I was so relieved when we didn't find your name."

"Sunny," one of the young pool players called. "We're gone. We'll see you Friday." Although the kids probably hadn't understood everything that transpired tonight, they weren't immune to the depressing mood, and Gavin wasn't surprised to see them calling it an early evening.

Sunny waved at the kids. "You guys be careful."

Since Ed left, the other patrons trickled out pretty consistently. With the kids gone, Joe was the only one left. He slid his empty bottle across the bar and said, "I think I'm gonna head out too. Maybe go home and watch a little TV." He started to slide off the stool, then paused and looked at Ed's seat cover. "Whatcha gonna do with that?"

Sunny sagged, deflated. "Robby wanted to pull it off this afternoon and burn it, but I wouldn't let him." She chewed her lip and stared at the seat. "Maybe we'll leave it there for a while." Tears filled her eyes. "I feel kinda bad for him. I know that feeling of being desperate and trapped, but..." She pulled in a breath, then slowly released it. "Dammit, I don't know what to think or feel."

Joe nodded. "I know what you mean." He swiveled his gaze around to Gavin. "I guess since you own the fishing pier, you'll be a permanent fixture around here."

Gavin laughed. "Yeah, I guess so." He looked at Sunny and winked. "What do I need to do to get my own barstool cover?"

She blushed, and before she could answer, Joe said, "Wait until I'm gone to answer that. I don't want to know."

Robby carried a load of glasses out of the kitchen and began restocking the shelves. "It's only nine. I can't believe the place is empty."

Sunny dipped her rag into the bucket of water and swiped at the bar. "It'll take a few days before everyone settles down and things get back to normal."

"Since everyone's gone, I'm going with the guys to Wilmington." Robby paused and looked up. "I mean, if that's okay." He looked at Gavin, then back to Sunny. "He's here with you, so you'll be okay. Right?"

"I'll take good care of her."

Robby made an *ewww* face, and Gavin laughed. "I didn't mean it like *that*. I just meant I'll make sure she's okay." But, if Robby was going to be gone... he'd work on *that,* too.

"Right." Robby grabbed his keys off the back counter and headed for the door. "Is it okay if I come back here tonight? Chad's floor is starting to get uncomfortable."

"Of course it's okay. Gavin'll be here, but you can come home. He'll be…" She let the words trail off and cut her eyes to Gavin.

Robby opened the door and yelled over his shoulder. "I'm locking you guys in to work it out. See you later."

"I'll be what?"

She bit her lip and gave the bar another swipe. "I was going to say you'd be spending a lot of time with us, but… will you?"

Gavin stalked around the end of the bar toward Sunny, who watched him with wide-eyed anticipation, not moving, barely breathing. He dropped his bottle into the recycling can as he passed it, then took her hands in his. "I'll spend as much time here as you'll allow. How about if we go upstairs, get in that kickass tub of yours, and negotiate."

Gavin brushed Sunny's hand away as she reached for the faucet. "You go relax; I'll do this." He turned on the water, held his fingers under the spray, and adjusted the temperature. "I'll call you when it's ready."

She hip-checked him out of the way and grabbed her bottle of bubble bath. She took the cap off and sniffed. It wasn't too girly smelling so hopefully Gavin wouldn't mind. A bath without bubbles—lots of bubbles—just wasn't a bath. She dumped a generous portion into the water and watched the suds form. "You go relax. Your day has been a whole lot rougher than mine. I'm not the one who flushed my entire career…"

Her breath caught in her throat as the enormity of the situation hit her square in the chest. She twisted the top back on the bottle and turned to face him. "I can't believe you bought the fishing pier and quit your job."

His eyes softened as he took the bottle from her hand and set it on the counter. Pulling her to him, he said, "I've had my doubts for months, I just…" He sighed and rested his chin on the top of her head. "I didn't want to look at them too closely, or try to figure out what they were telling me."

He always projected so much confidence she found it hard to believe he could ever have doubts, about anything. She pulled back from the tight embrace and studied his face "Doubts? About yourself?"

A cocky smile indicated that was a ridiculous question, but after a second, the cockiness waned and he turned pensive, maybe even a little sad. "I haven't doubted my ability to run the company. The problem has been my desire to." His hands dropped to her waist, then slipped under the hem of her shirt. "I started to question if that's what I wanted to do for the rest of my life."

His blue gaze melded with hers and in a flash, the heat in the room spiked—not just the sexual heat, but the emotional intensity of the moment, as well. Without saying a word, his eyes and searing touch clearly expressed his intent. The rest-of-his-life plans now included her.

They hadn't discussed the future, but there no questioning what she saw in his face. For once, he was the one broadcasting his thoughts, and she found herself nodding in agreement to his unspoken declaration.

He drew in a shaky breath, then slowly… very slowly lowered his lips to hers. As he deepened the kiss and his hand crept up her ribcage, she stiffened and held her breath.

When she dressed this afternoon, she hadn't had the energy or mental focus to figure out a good necklace/shirt combination. She finally decided clothes were clothes and settled on a plain bra and high-collared shirt, without a necklace. But now, in this erotically charged moment, she wished she had on something sexier than a boring white bra and panties.

Sensing her tension, Gavin pulled back from the kiss. "What's wrong?"

"I'm afraid you're going to be disappointed."

He flinched, then frowned. "What?"

"I'm not wearing a necklace." Recognizing her fears as foolish and anxious to have the awkward moment behind her, she stepped back from his grasp and stripped off her shirt. "In fact, I'm not wearing anything special, just a plain old white bra."

He tilted his head to the side and looked at her with such deep tenderness her insides ached. With a soft, gentle touch, he flipped open the front closure on her bra and smiled appreciatively. "The necklaces are hot. But...," he cupped her breasts in his hands as if he were holding a precious piece of glass, "...you are extraordinary." He tweaked her nipples and dipped his head. "It's not the necklaces that make you beautiful."

She moaned and pushed her fingers through his hair as he kissed a trail across her shoulder and down to her breast. While he lavished one breast with the attention of his tongue and teeth, he massaged the other with his hand.

Through the steam and her own lust-filled haze, she noticed the bubbles encroaching upon the edge of the tub. She tugged on the ends of his hair to get his attention. "If we don't shut off the water, we're going to spend our time cleaning up a mess, rather than making our own wet, sloppy one."

He unlatched from her breast and rolled his eyes upward to meet her gaze. His eyelids were heavy, his eyes dreamy. He looked happy and sated, and if she didn't know better, she'd swear he was drunk.

"I definitely want to get sloppy wet. Inside you," he said, reaching around her to shut off the stream of water.

His words were like a match to the coals, and within seconds, Sunny had her clothes off, not-so-patiently waiting for him to do the same. She'd just about decided to forgo the bath and jump him where he stood when he stripped out of his pants and stepped into the tub.

Gavin in her tub, surrounded by bubbles, proved too much to resist. She took the hand he offered and stepped in with him. She sighed with appreciation as the two of them eased into the warm water together, and bubbles crackled and popped as she relaxed back into the inviting cradle of his body.

Held in his warm embrace with the water sloshing against her in a gentle caress, the troubles of the past several days evaporated like the steam coming off the water. Lost in a relaxing trance, the rough loofa sponge touching her elbow made her jump and sent bubbles dripping over the edge.

"Ooops." He chuckled. "Didn't mean to startle you." He dipped the sponge into the water, then squeezed the suds over her chest and shoulders.

Relaxing deeper into the water, she said, "You're spoiling me."

"Spoiling you makes me happy."

Despite her body's relaxed state and her desire to forget everything except the feel of Gavin's body wrapped around hers, her mind continued to work overtime. She'd only gotten bits and pieces of information, leaving her with more questions than answers. "What are you going to do?"

In a low, sexy drawl, he said, "Do I really need to spell it out, or are you just trying to get me to talk dirty to you?"

Her stomach did a somersault as she twisted to look at him. She was asking about his future plans, like... Would he stay in Myrtle Beach and commute, or would he move to Anticue? What about his grandfather and the farm? What would happen between the two of them now that he owned the property next door?

She didn't excel at taking a back seat and letting life drive itself. She liked having a plan and knowing where she was headed. But looking into the fathomless blue depths of his eyes, she decided the future didn't matter. The only thing that mattered was right now.

She returned to her relaxed position, corralled in the strength of his body, and said, "I want you to talk dirty to me."

He nipped at her ear before scraping his teeth over her neck. In a deep, raspy voice, he proceeded to describe in graphic detail exactly what he planned to do to her.

The pictures he painted with his words lit her up like a torch. She threw her head back onto his shoulder, arched her back, and pressed her breast into his hand. It felt as if all her nerve endings were exposed, and she couldn't wait another minute to have him inside her.

She crawled out of the cradle of his body and onto her knees. "I need you inside me. Now. Hard and fast."

Gavin's voice was a gravelly croak when he said, "Condom," and crawled out of the tub. Soap bubbles slid off his shoulders and elbows and landed on the floor in thick globs. He grabbed a towel, but she wasn't sure why he bothered, since he didn't use it to dry off, only halfway wrapped it around his waist.

His broad shoulders and back glistened with water droplets, and the thought of slowly licking them off his skin, drop by drop, propelled her into motion. Water sluiced off her body and sloshed over the edges of the tub. Bubbles dripped off her, joining the ones that had fallen from Gavin. Out of habit, she grabbed a towel, but it made even less contact with her body than Gavin's had.

She squealed and grabbed the doorframe to catch her balance as she slipped on a puddle of water. With her next step, her foot caught purchase on the bedroom carpet. Then she was practically running across the room toward him.

Already sheathed with the condom, he met her halfway. Either as desperate as she was or understanding her intense need, he picked her up, then backed her toward the closed bedroom door.

By the time he'd taken the first step, she had her legs wrapped around his waist and her arms around his neck. The next step had her back against the door and him ramming into her in a fast, solid stroke.

"Oh, God. Yes." This was exactly what she needed. Hard, fast, animalistic.

His tongue plundered her mouth in a rapacious kiss as he drove into her in a relentless, pounding pace. She gripped his shoulders and dug her heels into the backs of his legs.

In a matter of moments, the fireworks lit off in her stomach, then spread like wildfire throughout her body. She screamed his name, bit his shoulder, and rode out the storm.

"God…" Gavin threw his head back and rammed into her so hard her teeth rattled. "…Damn." He continued to pump into her, mumbling and cursing incoherently as his storm raged on, then peaked.

Once it passed, he dropped his forehead to hers and, in a breathless burst, said, "I think I love you."

Overwhelmed by her own emotions, his declaration was more than she could handle. She didn't know whether to laugh or cry, so she wrapped her arms around his neck, buried her face in his chest, and did both.

Chapter Twenty-Nine

Gavin kicked the sheet off his feet and enjoyed the cool rush of air spreading across his heated skin. He had one arm wrapped around Sunny, the other flung over his head. They'd made love three times in the past hour, and it still wasn't enough.

He wondered if it would always be like this or if the constant, pulsating need would eventually cool. He could see it now: the middle of the day, the pier packed with people, and him sneaking across the yard for an afternoon quickie.

Maybe he could convince Sunny to marry him. Then there wouldn't be a need for anyone to sneak anywhere.

A funny smell invaded his thoughts and had his nose twitching. It smelled like the Georgetown paper mill, but he couldn't imagine the odor from that plant carried this far north. As the odor continued to grow stronger, he jiggled his arm to get Sunny's attention. "Hey, you awake?"

"Mmmm… hmmm…"

"Is there a paper mill in Wilmington?" Damn, the stink was getting stronger by the minute. It smelled like rotten—

"Fuck!" He jerked upright in the bed, snatching Sunny with him.

"What's wrong?" Her eyes were wild as she looked around, trying to figure out what caused his panic. "What's the…" She sniffed and her eyes grew even wider.

"Gas," they yelled at the same time.

Gavin didn't know where the leak was coming from, but the odor was so strong it had to be somewhere in the building. The slightest spark would send the entire building up in an explosion, taking them with it.

He rolled out of bed on one side, while Sunny fell out on the other. He jammed his legs into his pants and grabbed a shirt to take with him, and Sunny did the same. They ran barefoot down the hall, pulling on their shirts as they went.

Sunny jerked to a stop and yelled, "Robby!" She turned to head back toward his room, but Gavin grabbed her hand.

"He's gone," he said, dragging her behind him as he plowed through the kitchen.

He yanked the kitchen door open, and they hit the steps running. He put his hand to the waistband of his pants and said a prayer of thanks when he found his cellphone still attached.

"Sunny!" Robby's panicked voice drifted up to them from around the building. As they hit the bottom step, Robby rounded the corner. When he saw Sunny and Gavin, his breath left in a burst. "Thank God you're okay."

"Run to the far side of the parking lot and get behind Sunny's car," Gavin said while dialing 9-1-1. Neither he nor Sunny had shoes, so picking their way across the gravel driveway was slow going, even with the threat of an explosion propelling them along.

As Gavin gave their address and the reason for the call to the emergency operator, he heard Robby say to Sunny, "I saw that truck. It was going across the bridge to the mainland as I was coming back this way. I tried to call and warn you, but my phone battery was dead." Tears sprang to his eyes, and he turned away. As if his legs wouldn't hold him anymore, he sank to the ground next to his truck.

"Jesus, Sunny…" Robby rested his elbows on his knees and dropped his head into his hands. "I thought you were dead." He grabbed the ends of his hair between his fingers and pulled. "I thought you were both dead."

It seemed to take every ounce of control he had to keep from falling to pieces in front of them, so Gavin walked away to give him some privacy. Gavin also needed a little space to glue his shit back together.

He'd never been as scared as when he realized the rotten egg smell wasn't a paper mill. He could never forgive himself if something happened to Sunny. Of course, he would've been dead, too, which would have totally sucked ass. But if something happened to her, he would've spent all eternity exacting revenge on Max.

Gavin heard the sirens of the fire trucks at the same time the first wave of volunteer firefighters arrived. Within moments, the parking lot and street were filled with men and equipment, and the source of the leak was shut off.

"What the hell, Sunny?" the fire chief asked as he approached, his face a mask of fury. "Someone tried to blow you up. Literally."

"Yeah, Gary," Sunny said, running a hand over her forehead. "We figured that out."

"What was the incendiary device and why didn't it work?" Gavin asked, wanting… no, *needing* answers. Since the building was a crime scene, the fire chief wouldn't let them in until the sheriff's crime scene unit processed everything.

"A match stuck through a lit cigarette placed close to the open gas line." He shook his head like he couldn't believe it. "It looks like a leaky sink saved your ass. There's two drops of water on the cigarette, just enough to keep it from burning down to the match and triggering the explosion."

Hearing the details sent a ball of fury ripping through Gavin.

Trembling with the force of his anger, he stepped away from the noise and confusion, grabbed his phone, and dialed Max's number. The ringing stopped on the fourth ring, but Max didn't speak.

"What's the matter, Max? Afraid a ghost is calling you?"

Max took a deep breath, then said, "After what you and my daughter did, I didn't expect to hear from you again."

Gavin gripped the phone so hard the case cracked. "Really? Is that why you didn't think you'd hear from me? Or was it because you sent someone to kill me and I should be dead by now?"

"I don't know what you're talking about." Max's voice was like cold steel edged with fear.

As fucked up as it was, Gavin found himself *almost* feeling sorry for Max. It was entirely possible that after this all shook out, Max would lose everything he worked for his entire life. And, in the process, end up in prison a broken, lonely man.

"Miguel Ortego. Does the name ring a bell?" He probably shouldn't warn Max, but he couldn't stop himself. "And before you lie to me... I have proof you called him last night. I know his job qualifications, and there's a witness who can place him in Anticue tonight." A slight exaggeration, but Gavin was confident the authorities would find enough evidence to tie Max to this attempted arson. Shit, attempted murder. "I thought you might want to warn Cynthia and Callie, so they aren't caught off-guard when the police show up and haul your ass off to jail, you motherfucking, cocksucking son of a bitch."

He disconnected the call and turned to find Sunny behind him. She wrapped her arms around his waist, rested her cheek on his chest, and melted into him. "I'm so sorry. This is a million times worse than what Ed did, and that wasn't even personal against me. I can't imagine how much this must hurt."

Apparently she'd come to the same conclusion as him. While Max wouldn't mind getting rid of Sunny, his focus had switched from her to Gavin. With Gavin dead, the sale of the fishing pier would be dead, too. Callie would be stuck at home, and Max would have a clear road to proceed with his plans. At this point, Sunny and Robby would be collateral damage.

He wrapped his arms around her and pulled her as close as possible. "I could care less about being betrayed." That wasn't exactly true. It did hurt that Max actually tried to kill him, but his biggest concern was Sunny. "Thank God you're okay."

A shudder wracked his body, and his knees nearly buckled. "I'm calling my friend Marty and having him put twenty-four hour surveillance on you. I don't think there'll be any more incidents, but I'm not taking any chances."

Speaking of taking chances… He needed to call Callie and warn her. He couldn't imagine Max doing anything to harm a hair on her head, but he never would've believed Max capable of something like this, either. He couldn't take the chance of leaving Callie in the dark and unprotected.

Sunny nodded to the street and eased away from him. "I'm going to talk to the arson investigator. I'll be over there if you need me."

He grabbed her hand and pulled her back to him for a kiss. "What I said earlier…" He drew in a shaky breath and continued. "I do love you, Sunny. There's no maybes or I thinks about it… I love you."

She pressed her palm to his cheek and searched his face. With tears glistening in her eyes, she smiled and said, "I'm glad I'm not alone in this love thing. That was a scary place to be for a while."

She looked to the dark pier and her smile grew. "I'm really going to like having you for a neighbor."

"Me too." He kissed the top of her head and grinned. "How do you feel about afternoon quickies?"

Epilogue

Gavin found it hard to believe the remnants of his entire career could be reduced to a shoebox, but as he placed the photo of his grandfather and the paperweight Callie had given him for Christmas into the box, he was forced to accept the depressing truth of his previous existence. With a deep breath, he took one last look around the office to make sure he hadn't missed anything. Nope, sad as it was, he had it all.

He tucked the box under his arm and turned toward the door, only to be stopped short by Callie, leaning against the doorjamb, tears spilling from her eyes, her bottom lip quivering.

"I can't believe you're really leaving," she said. She sucked in a ragged breath and wiped her eyes. "I feel like I'm living in a horrible nightmare and I just can't wake up."

He leaned onto the corner of his desk and smiled. "You've had three months to get used to the idea of my leaving. Don't tell me you thought I'd change my mind."

She shrugged a shoulder and pushed off the doorframe. "No, I knew you wouldn't. But that didn't keep me from living in denial about the whole thing." She stopped a few feet in front of him and bit her lip, probably in an effort to stop the quivering.

The pain and embarrassment she suffered over the past several months had been tremendous, and Gavin couldn't be prouder of the way she handled herself. She surprised him by demonstrating a strength and determination he never would have believed possible.

Having Max's picture—taken while wearing an ugly orange jumpsuit with a matching set of bracelets—plastered on the front page of all the major newspapers had only been the first layer of Callie's humiliation.

As the Holden name gathered more and more layers of shit, she had to face friends and enemies alike, all who now knew her as the daughter of a criminal. The rumors abounded for years, but now there was evidence to support those rumors, and almost everyone in her social circle turned on Callie.

Jen and Tiffany, however, hadn't blamed Callie for the sins of her father, and Gavin was pleasantly surprised by their loyalty. They stood by Callie through it all, usually with a pitcher of margaritas in hand, but that's okay. They were there, and that's all that mattered.

"What am I going to do without you here?" Callie sobbed, losing the battle with her tears. "You've always been here for me, and now I'm going to be all alone."

Gavin reached out and pulled her into a hug. "I will *always* be here for you, Callie. Geography doesn't change that. I've been living in Anticue for the past month and still managed to talk to you just about every day, didn't I?"

She sniffed and nodded. "Yeah, but you won't be here in the office. Your life is in Anticue now, and I'm afraid you'll eventually fade away."

"I'm not going anywhere. Besides, I've signed on to be a consultant for the next six months. I won't be here all the time, but I will be here some."

As far as they could tell, Max hadn't done anything else as horrific as trying to blow someone up. But there was a lot of harassment and bullying in order to convince landowners to see things his way.

Gavin didn't know how Cynthia and Max's marriage would shake out, but as far as Holden Enterprises went, Max was permanently out of picture. Regardless of the legalities, and whether or not he served jail time, he was still out of a job.

Gavin agreed to step in as temporary CEO while Cynthia and the board of directors found a permanent replacement. The new CEO started two weeks ago, and Gavin was more than happy to turn things over and get on with his life in Anticue.

Callie took a deep breath and eased out of Gavin's embrace. "I expected you to be here all day. I was hoping we could have lunch."

He glanced at his watch, then eased off his desk. "Sorry, I can't. I have a meeting with Kevin Mazze, the builder who's going to help me with the renovations on the restaurant, in an hour and a half. Robby's moving to ECU this weekend, and I also promised him and Sunny I'd be home early to help with that."

Callie took a step back and crossed her arms before averting her gaze.

"Hey," he said, touching her chin and turning her face so he could look her in the eyes. "I'm always a phone call away; you know that. And you and Jason are coming to Anticue next weekend, right?"

She smiled and nodded. "We'll be there." Then she crinkled her nose and said, "I don't have to go out onto the beach, though, right?"

He laughed. A few remnants of the old Callie still lingered. "Nope, you don't have to go out onto the beach." He lifted the box and headed toward the door. "But be sure to wear some work clothes..." He turned to catch her shocked expression and added, "If you have any work clothes, that is. If not, wear something old that you don't mind getting paint on. There's a lot of work to be done."

"Wha..." Callie's words died off as she yanked the strap of her purse higher on her shoulder and ran after him. "You're kidding, right?"

Gavin leaned into the push bar to open the stairwell door and winked. "See ya next weekend."

He left Callie standing at the top of the stairs, mouth hanging open, still trying to decide if he'd been teasing or not. As he jogged down the steps, he felt lighter than his mostly empty shoebox. Between getting the fishing pier ready to open and moving his grandfather to Anticue—something his Grandfather insisted on doing so he could be a part of reopening the pier—Gavin had more than a full workload ahead of him. But he'd never enjoyed life more, and the future had never been brighter than the one he and Sunny faced.

You've just finished reading *Last Call (Heat Wave Novel #2)*. If you enjoyed this book, please help others discover it by leaving a review.

If you'd like to stay abreast of contests and new releases, please join my newsletter: www.alannahlynne.com/contact/
or follow me on
Facebook: facebook.com/AuthorAlannahLynne
Twitter: @alannahlynne
Tsu: www.tsu.co/AlannahLynne

Other books in the *Heat Wave* series are:

Saving Me (Heat Wave Novel #1)
Crossing Lines (Heat Wave Novel #3)
Going All In (Heat Wave Novel #4)
A Matter of Time (Heat Wave Novel #5)

Each book in the *Heat Wave* series stands alone and can be read out of order.

Turn the page for an excerpt from *Crossing Lines (Heat Wave Novel #3)*.

Excerpt – CROSSING LINES – Heat Wave Novel #3

Chapter One

Can this day get any worse?

Flipping fate the bird with a taunting question was foolish, but Kevin Mazze couldn't help himself as he glared down at the pixie standing between him and the grand opening of his exclusive subdivision.

Dieci, nove, otto, sette...

Why bother counting backward from ten to try and diffuse his anger? Rather than calming him, he always felt he counted down to an explosion.

Take now, for example. The pulse pounding in his temples suggested if he kept going, his head would explode, splattering fragments all over the pavement.

The up side was it would also make a mess of the petite, blond building inspector threatening to not only ruin his day, but his whole fucking year.

Stopping the countdown before he reached detonation, he scrubbed a hand across his forehead, then slowly and plainly said, "I need the Certificate of Occupancy. Without it, I'm dead in the water." Okay, talking to her as if she were deaf and dumb probably wouldn't gain him any favors—

Annnddd, there it went. The squashing of hope, along with a quick tightening in his stomach as he prepared for another swift kick in the nuts. She slammed her hands to her hips and squared her shoulders, pulling herself up to a truly impressive height of five foot one. If the situation weren't so dire, and she didn't hold his entire career in the palm of her hand, he would laugh. He might even get a little turned on, because her feisty back-at-ya attitude was sexy as hell.

"Is your hearing defective, Mr. Mazze? Or are you just a little slow on the uptake? I know you need a CO. But you don't have enough water pressure to operate the sprinklers." Mirroring his speech pattern, she slowed her cadence so even a first grader would understand. "You're not occupying the building until the problem is solved."

Several things kept his hands fisted at his sides rather than wrapped around her pretty little neck. One, she was a woman. Two, she was right.

She wasn't responsible for the county's negligence in following through with the promised water tower that would provide the pressure necessary for powering the sprinklers. Ultimately, the responsibility for this massive failure lay squarely on his shoulders.

His father insisted on taking the gamble and jumping the gun with this project. Kevin recognized the risk from the beginning, but he'd acquiesced to his father's wishes. Now, while Papà visited family in Italy, reliving his childhood, Kevin was left with a mop and dry bucket, figuring out how to clean up the mess.

"I've been on the phone with Public Works every day for ten days," he said, hoping to appeal to her sense of reasoning since his attempts at charming aggression had gotten him nowhere. "They said the tower would be up and running in another few weeks."

Of course, the bastards promised that six months ago, too, and he still hadn't seen any evidence of progress. But Samantha Wallace was new in town, so maybe she didn't know how badly the county dragged their feet. Relaxing his posture, he gave her a stretched, confident smile and prayed she bought the massive pile of bullshit.

She cocked her head to the side and smiled, indicating a shortage of spending cash. Despite the ominous black clouds rolling in, she still wore her sunglasses, which prevented him from seeing her eyes. Pity, because based on her smile's amperage, he'd bet her eyelashes were fluttering like crazy behind those mirrored lenses. "I may be blond, Mr. Mazze, but I'm not an idiot."

After snapping the words like a whip, emphasizing her unwillingness to back down, she crossed her arms over her chest and glanced away. Her sharp exhale and creased forehead projected her sympathy, the show of regret doing more to diffuse his anger than counting backward from a thousand.

Despite her reputation for being a hardnosed bitch, she wasn't busting his balls to be difficult. Code dictated what she could and couldn't do, and in this case, her hands were tied.

An image of her naked, hands bound, kneeling on his bed, flashed through his mind. He had no explanation for the inappropriate thought, but this obviously wasn't the time or place for his junkyard dog to wake up and fight against his chain.

He shook his head to clear the thought and leaned against the landscaper's bumper. He worked his neck in a circle, finally looking to the heavens for guidance. An answering flash of lightning wasn't reassuring.

"You have any suggestions?" he asked Wade Neumann, the job foreman, who'd been standing off to the side, silently watching the drama unfold.

"No, sir. I've never dealt with anything like this." Wade sighed and his shoulders drooped. "I'm sorry."

"Not your fault, bro. Papà and I took the gamble." A huge, *pricey* gamble that might set Kevin back years.

In a perfectly coordinated display of I'll-show-you, lightning flashed and thunder shook the ground at the exact moment his cell phone erupted with the theme from *Psycho*.

"*Yes,*" Fate cackled. "*I can fuck your day up a little more.*"

Wade's mouth twitched, but as a smart young man concerned with job security, he bit down on his lip and squelched his grin.

Far superior and unconcerned with job security, Samantha Wallace flashed a grin brighter than the lightning. "Nice," she said with a husky little laugh. "I should use that for my ex."

Kevin didn't correct her assumption Lizbeth was an ex. He also didn't answer the call.

"Unless you wait for the water tower,"—she cast him a pointed look—"which won't be up in the next two weeks, the only thing you can do is put in a booster pump." At his muttered curse, she lifted a shoulder and gave a regretful shake of her head. "I know you don't want to take the additional cost on the chin, but I don't see any other option." She threw her hands up animatedly. "Hell, even if I gave you the CO, the fire marshal would swoop in here and shut your ass down before you cut on the first light."

Frustration chomped at the back of his throat, begging to break free with a growl and a massive curse. What the hell was he supposed to do at—he glanced at his watch—four o'clock on a Friday?

"*Shit!* It's four o'clock."

Wade and the building inspector exchanged glances at his outburst. One of her blond eyebrows lifted, and Wade answered with a shrug.

To Wade, he said, "I'm supposed to be in Riverside in two hours." To Samantha, who didn't appear to understand his predicament, he said, "I have a three-and-a-half-hour drive, besides a stop in Anticue to check on the progress of a restaurant. Needless to say, I'm real fucking late." He winced. "Sorry, excuse the coarse language."

He hadn't intended to be funny, but she found something about his apology hilarious. Her braid swung side to side when she tossed her head back and laughed from deep in her chest, making him wonder if her hair was as soft as it looked.

He also found himself oddly curious about the color of her eyes and wanted to demand she take those damned shades off so he could see. Based on her fair skin and nearly white hair, he figured blue.

A sweet baby-blue.

While he stared like a dumbstruck moron, she said, "I'm the last person you need to apologize to for cursing. You know how when someone quits smoking, they'll gravitate to other smokers so they can inhale the secondhand toxic waste? Well, that's me with cussing." She waved off her copious explanation. "Never mind. Have a safe trip."

Caught in the moment of seeing her as a beautiful woman, not the building inspector shitting on his parade, it took a while for him to realize his phone was ringing. Again.

He unclipped it from his belt and wrestled with the urge to toss the thing in the retention pond. Instead, he hit the silence button, then stuck his hand out as a peace offering. "I'm sorry for being an ass. Can we…?" When she placed her palm in his, heat from the contact washed over him, causing him to slip and nearly ask her to dinner. Fortunately, his brain reengaged and overrode the impulse. "Can we meet first thing Monday morning? I have to work this out."

Her soft, sympathetic smile conveyed her thoughts. *You poor, dumb son of a bitch. You just don't get it, do you?* But her mouth said, "Sure. Here or my office?"

"Here. I'll bring breakfast."

As he turned to leave, Wade asked, "Will you be back tomorrow?"

"Yep," he yelled over his shoulder. "I told Marianne I'd keep Spencer so she can have the day to herself."

"Enjoy your night, boss."

Yeah, right. Kevin waved to acknowledge Wade's comment, but didn't turn around. Instead, he pounded the pavement to his truck and recited his new mantra.

Two more weeks. Just two more weeks…

Crossing Lines (Heat Wave Novel #3) – Available now!

www.ingramcontent.com/pod-product-compliance
Lightning Source LLC
Chambersburg PA
CBHW021950170626
46808CB00001B/97